Winter's Divide

Winter's Divide

M. LaVon

Copyright © Winter's Divide
All rights reserved.

Cover image Restyler / Agency / Shutterstock
Book design by LaVon Studios
All Scripture quotations are taken from the King James Version.

ISBN: 9798614047856
Imprint: Independently published

This is a work of fiction. Any resemblance to persons living or dead is purely coincidental.

This book is dedicated to my biggest fan, my mom. Forever heartbroken without you.

Contents

Preface	1
A to Z	2
Tom	10
Awake	14
Fever Pitch	20
From Bad to Worse	28
Liz	47
Fix Her	57
Strength in Numbers	67
The War Around the Corner	86
Like Father, Like Son	93
Like Mom	97
What to Expect	101
Whoville	111
No Precious Gift	119
What's Mine Is Mine	124
Roses or Rifles	129
Twinkies	142
The Edge of Normal	152
For Every Season	159
Lose, Lose	164
Good-byes Bring Hellos	178
Sonia	191
Epilogue (Preview book 2, *Destin's War*)	197
Cami, June 2026	
Liz's Playlist	204
Acknowledgments	205

M. LaVon

Preface

Warning Signs

The lies were so deep it was hard to see past the margins. It was easier to believe someone based solely on desperation. The people in the middle, duped with promises of unlimited jobs and stable wealth. The fine print not obvious, and the long-term impact covered in a cloak of unfulfilled promises. Big business came in as the savior. We kowtowed with reverence to our grand leaders. We fueled our own decimation with naivety, or more the absence of clear understanding of consequence.

We were too busy living our lives and ignoring what was happening around us. This is on us.

There is no one to blame but us.

M. LaVon

A to Z

The end of the world did not happen with one single event or all of a sudden without warning. There were no people running and screaming down flooded highways, no single fiery moment when our perfect society was plunged back into the Stone Age, no alien warships invading our planet. No, it happened a little at a time, slowly creeping in like a coastal fog, obscuring what was once clearly there just enough to leave a hazy memory of what it looked like before it disappeared completely.

Events would happen, there would be a moment of shock, and as quickly as that, we would be over it. Global climate crisis, we adapt. Failing social infrastructure, we adjust. Deteriorating political system, we accept. Masters of making up a new normal.

We should have known there would be a point of no return, yet we let the scales tip just a little more.

Looking back, I can't believe how obvious it was, and how we were so quick to dismiss the possibilities. How quick we went on with our daily lives as if nothing was happening. We didn't slow down for even a second. Everything had a rational explanation, and there was nothing we couldn't live through. How stupid we all were, how stupid I was.

We pretended it was so complex, no one could have had a clear picture of what was to come. One of those five-thousand-piece puzzles that as a single piece is abstract and unrelated, but when each piece finds its place, reveals the picture of our future. Only to realize the picture was on the box, sitting right in front of us the whole time.

The single catalyst that would define the events leading to the apocalypse could have been described as uneventful. It was so uneventful, in fact, that I was sitting in traffic, drinking my morning coffee, when it happened, then I continued to my office and went to my morning meetings. For lunch I ate quinoa, kale, and chicken salad at my desk while reading the news. Worked through my final afternoon call, met the moms' club at yoga before picking up my fourteen-year-old son, Asher, from soccer.

Dinner was a rush as always. My husband, Tom, and our twelve-year-old son, Zavier, picked up takeout and met us at the house. We chatted about the day, passing veggie yakisoba between us.

"Z, how was baseball? Did coach let you... Baby, you look flushed, are you feeling okay?" I glanced at Tom, who looked unconcerned.

"The whole team apparently has a touch of the flu. There were three out, and Luke's mom said he was feeling a bit under the weather but didn't want to miss practice, especially with the tournament coming up next month."

"Well, it won't help any of them if they're all out sick... You remember the last time they all shared the flu? Go, team spirit." I rolled my eyes.

Zavier stopped shoveling noodles long enough to give me a saucy grin and a slight smirk that translated to 'Geez, Mom, I am not a baby.'

Asher and Tom were now giggling across the table talking about something that happened at soccer. I caught a couple of lines about a girl, and my mind went immediately into overload. Had we reached that point already? And in that moment, I regretted not opening wine with dinner.

Off to bed, only to crack open my laptop and work a bit before finally dozing off. Tom, a night owl, was clicking away in his office. An average day.

***

Morning autopilot initiated, pencil skirt, simple blouse with matching cardigan. Long gone were the days of cutting-edge fashion. Tired eyes swept down my mom frame with layers of brutal honesty; my simple blouse fit loosely and landed in all the wrong places, slightly faded, overused cardigan to compensate, and a pencil skirt that was less pencil and more eraser. Last look in the mirror ended in a deep sigh, claw clip in hand, a quick spin, swoosh, hair was up and done. *Messy mom bun—eat your heart out.*

The rumble from below told me the boys were up and ready for school. Asher kicked on the Nespresso for me, trained since three, for a quick double-shot cappuccino, and I grabbed my bag, and we were ready for the mad rush to begin all over again.

I took one look at Zavier and noticed he was covered in angry red spots. "Did anybody think to tell me about the rash?"

Zavier was the first to quip back with the 'duh' response... "Mom, we aren't babies, we're fine." His new one-liner response for anything involving me.

I grabbed Asher by the jersey and checked under the hood—sure enough, rash times two. My eyes shifted to Tom, who was casually looking at his phone. I could tell he had already started his workday and was lost to us in the mountain of emails that had been accumulating overnight. My Supermom cape unraveled from the collar of my mom cardigan, and immediately the schedule flipped open on my calendar. I moved my 8:00 AM meeting to 1:00 PM, and I sent the executive admin a warning email that I might need to push the 9:00 AM back, too, depending on the line at urgent care. And I moved my 10:00 AM to a Skype meeting in case I needed to take the meeting in my car on the way back to the office.

How did I miss the rash onset last night?

I pulled into the parking lot of the urgent care at Winter Memorial Medical Center, which was adjacent to the emergency room, and it was full—they were both full. Urgent care was busting at the seams, spilling over into the hospital parking lot and out onto the arterial and the neighboring Wendy's parking lot.

My boys were calmly sitting in the back seat, oblivious to the parking lot chaos. Both with headphones on, watching the world through the eyes of YouTube. Gone were the days of inquisitive questions about the world. I could feel the slight pull of the mom-strings, missing those moments of little voices asking what was taking so long and why there were so many people. My subconscious mom voice was tempted to reply out loud with an exasperated, impatient, and nervous 'I don't know.' And then I looked through the rearview mirror at their mature faces and saw the glowing reflection of their screens, reminding me they weren't paying attention and didn't care.

I pulled behind a poorly parked minivan that was not within a spot, which would obviously be towed otherwise. It had back window–sticker people: four humans—two adults and two children—and a cat, all inspired by *Star Wars*, light sabers and all. *If I'm towed, at least I would be in good company.*

The automatic doors opened to reveal a cacophony of people. Every chair was full. We waited in line to register. The line behind us built with rapid persistence, almost like we'd brought a wave of scourge with us. Parents holding young ones, people wheeling in old ones, and they kept coming. The boys quickly dropped their phones and looked at me curiously. Not knowing what to do, I shrugged my shoulders. They looked around and then returned to their digital worlds.

As we marched on, I canceled my 10:00 AM, registered, and then canceled my 11:00 AM. The registration staff had very little information regarding timing; in fact, they said very little except for the standard: repeating their dates of birth, insurance information, address, and asking, "Have you traveled outside of the country in the last thirty days?" There was a slight pause when I gave our name, but then they quickly asked us to take a seat and reassured us a provider would be with us soon.

I watched the line outside grow without pause. I canceled my 3:00 PM before we were called back to a room. They put us at the end of the hall, and the boys shared a bed, which was far better than the quickly filling halls. I didn't argue, just gently nodded in appreciation at the triage nurse. It was 5:03 PM before a provider even came by. He took a basic assessment, not even bothering to ask about symptoms, and shuffled out of our room.

Tom arrived shortly after 5:37 PM. From the look on his face, he seemed slightly panicked and concerned. He parked a few blocks down, and the line stretched around the building. He said the people were eerily silent except for general coughing and a few kids running through the crowd. He said the office was mostly empty, people were calling out with flu-like symptoms. The news was much of the same: widespread flu, mostly on the West Coast.

Zavier was the first with a fever of 100.2 and climbing, but coherent enough to talk Asher into a bottle flipping challenge. By 8:24 PM the physician on call came in to check the boys, a medical assistant following behind him, both wearing yellow protective gowns, gloves, and facemasks. *A little late for that, I think.* The doctor took Zavier's temperature and then Asher's, shook his head and walked out, the medical assistant scribbled on a clipboard and was out, too.

I could feel the space between my breath and the world separate, forming a gasp. There was a certain level of disregard in his demeanor, maybe defeat.

I stepped to the door and looked to the world clad in yellow gowns rushing from room to room. Urgency and weary fatigue were building, a storm of latex and plastic coverings beginning to build. Lights blinking, phones ringing, pointing and shifting, running and hustling, ripples of sheets covering the army of beds staged in the corridors.

My feet stepped back behind the curtain, muffling everything beyond the fabric. A little curious voice whispers, "Mom, what's happening? I don't feel so good." My voice catches in my throat. "I know, baby, Mommy is here."

My boys were gathered on the bed like little pups huddled together. Tom had left in search of food and answers, and I was left in the silence of uncertainty. What I had seen as mature little bodies this morning were now those of my baby boys. I saw their faces as I did when they depended on me for everything, chubby cheeks and wide eyes, framed by sweet, soft curls.

A nurse came in and rapidly connected an IV to each. They were brave and unflinching. My voice, ripe with frustration, croaked out, "Is someone going to tell us what is going on?" And with that, the nurse was gone.

As if sensing my panic, Tom came through the curtain with two bags of Cheetos, one bag of Lay's potato chips, a pack of mints, one and a half bottles of orange juice, and a look of pure terror.

He eyeballed the corner of the room like only parents would, and I answered with a silent 'What?' I stepped to the corner of the room. He was sweating and out of breath, not like he had been running, but out of fear. I could see his mouth form words, and I wasn't sure I understood what he was saying. Like when you are saying, 'Ice cream' in parent-speak, half-spelling it out, and the other half whispering. He said it again, and I was still unsure and so I responded with an exasperated, terse whisper, "What!?"

"People are dying," he said again under his breath.

To which I replied with gritted teeth, "What do you mean?"

He looked to our boys, his eyes glistening, as if he could physically see them floating away. I imagined his arms reaching out, fingertip to fingertip, Michelangelo's *Creation*, trying to grab them and pull them back.

Oh God, people are dying. Our boys are dying.

My heart began to pound. I was overwhelmed by a sudden helpless feeling and dashed over to them.

I clung to them, afraid to look away too long, afraid if I did, I would look back and they would be gone.

At around midnight, a doctor came in and asked us to step to the edge of the room, its glass partition hanging uselessly against the wall with the curtain bunched at the entry. There were people lining the walls with blue sheets covering them. Feverish, speckled bodies, coughing and writhing beneath the soft blue ocean. Yellow flashes were darting about, exhausted robots following useless checklists.

I could see the doctor's mouth moving, each word meaningless, clouded by what I knew he was saying but I couldn't hear—or I refused to. He grabbed my husband's shoulder, squeezed, released, and Tom crumpled like a discarded piece of paper. He slid down the wall and folded at the floor. His hands pulled at his hair, tears soaked his face, tiny droplets cascaded to the shiny vinyl below, forming little puddles of preconceived grief. Time slowed, I could see the faces of the staff frozen as they passed by, like I had folded time and captured that instant between two sheets of glass. I stepped back behind the curtain and time continued.

A little mouse voice squeaked out from beneath the shadow of the protective shoulder of his older brother. "Mommy, I am tired."

"I know, sweet pea, just sleep."

I pulled up a chair beside the bed, gently stroking Zavier's hair until he drifted off to sleep.

At some point, I must have fallen asleep against the gurney. I could feel the imprint of the bed rail embedded in my cheek. I checked my phone— 5:16 AM. Overnight someone swapped out the IVs and brought Tom a blanket. Zavier was shivering in his sleep, and Asher was huddled next to him.

I stepped to the curtain, it was closed, and I could feel the energy as people passed. I hesitated to step to view what was behind it. At the edge, I could feel the rush of the air seeping through the bottom. The fabric fluttered against my blouse as I took position against its border. I grabbed the edge, slid it to the side. The curtain clips traveled down the track collecting in one position, stacking together, revealing the stale, heavy air of death.

The yellow flashes had slowed, the hurried nature had wound down to a deliberate, focused pace. The waving blue ocean of writhing bodies had weakened and for some had stopped completely.

I collected some water and ice from the machine outside the nurses' station and returned to the room.

Asher had woken, and looked to me with bloodshot, deep brown eyes. "Mommy, I am scared."

I ran my hand through his curly brown hair, and I could feel the intense heat radiating off his little body and building against my hand. I prepared a cool towel, dabbed his sweet forehead, and encouraged him to drink.

"I am so tired," he said. My breath quickened, as his became ragged and broken. His little hand grabbed mine. "Don't let me go, Mommy. I am afraid I won't wake up." His grip was weak, and his hands were soft.

"You can't leave me, baby. My heart will break into a million pieces…and I don't think I will ever be able to fix it. Can you stay with me?" My composure compromised as I began to lose any ability to hold it together.

"Mommy, can you hold my hand while I sleep?"

My voice was broken in shattered fragments. "I am here. I am with you. I won't let you go."

"Will you tell Z… that he is my best friend… in case I can't?... And tell Daddy…" His voice grew faint and lethargic, and then trailed off.

"And tell Daddy what, baby?"

The bed began to shake and shift as Asher began to seize.

I could feel my soul leave and float up high above my boys, far from my body, separating more and more with every passing second.

Tom jumped from his seat and ran out of the room. The curtain, which had been defending our internal reality from the external chaos, whirled up and drifted down to the side, opening, letting the grief and despair spill in like a tidal wave.

My hands reached across their bodies, calling my soul back down, pouring everything back into them. Holding each little hand folded in mine, clutching little fingers, they are my everything, A to Z.

"You're going to be okay, Mommy is here." Begging them to be okay, for me.

The seizure stopped. Asher's hand went weak, sagged, and pulled down and away. Zavier's squeezed tight, loosened, and then dropped. I searched their little bodies for motion, I grabbed them and shook them, begging them to stay with me. I pulled up Zavier's little fingers and kissed them, calling my boys to wake up. I snuggled Asher, pulling at his limp arms like he was a broken doll, wrapping his arms around me.

"Please, you can't leave me! Remember, Mommy's heart will break. I am yours and you're mine." I plead, "Come on now!" I couldn't breathe, the weight of it all was so heavy. Desperate pleas unanswered. "Please! PLEASE!... Please…" The choking sobs were building, and I couldn't breathe.

The rush of heat built past my cheeks, and a sharp ringing in my ear pierced my desperation. *My boys.* Through a fishbowl, I take one final look at my boys. The fragments of my heart shattered into shards of broken glass, a kaleidoscope of mismatched pieces tumbling around.

A bright warm haze overtook my vision and faded. There was nothing left for me here.

My legs folded and my arms fell limply to my side as I let their little fingers go. As I let 'them' go.

I could feel the cold vinyl floor gaining speed beneath me like I was crashing to the end of the earth. The black collapsed in from my peripheral vision. The shuffle of shoes and muted voices were the last of it all, and blackness overtook me as I chased my A to Z into the darkness.

M. LaVon

Tom

    Her small form lay flush on the floor, one arm slightly under the gurney and the other propped up against its side rails, like she had slipped off and away, reaching. My heart climbed up my rib cage, its little tendrils clawing up each rib, tearing and ripping from the inside, and then perched itself in my throat. My strides expanded, my flat work shoes struggled to hold traction, the polished leather and smooth surface produced little friction, I could feel myself sliding as I rounded the corner. I passed the curtain, and it whirled up, fanning out and rippling as it was tugged back by the snapping fastenings at the tracks. I slid down beside her, one foot forward like coming into second base following a lightning line drive down the third baseline. She was on fire, her skin red and flushed. Not like after two glasses of wine on date night, different. I scooped her up. She would be furious if she knew I'd let her touch the floor of a hospital room. I had the overwhelming urge to dig through her bag and grab the hand sanitizer, but I knew that was wrong.

    How did I miss it? How was she sick, too, and I had no idea?

    The last standby doctor came rushing in. He looked like those doctors you see running an entire hospital in a developing nation, frank, no eye contact, and mechanical. He began shouting orders. He passed right by me as if I was not holding the dying love of my life in my arms. He reached over and began attending to my boys. *Oh God, my boys.*

    How was I so distracted that I lost track of my boys?

    She would have had my ass in a sling if I didn't focus on them first. Her feverish body lay across my lap, draped in my arms, her breath was shallow and ragged. And I couldn't let her go. My eyes locked on the doctor, he was pulling blankets off and peeling off clothes and demanding ice, IVs, and various supplies.

Crumpled, I held her. She took charge. She would NOT have been sitting on the floor holding 'dying me' watching our boys slip away, too. She would have left me on the ground where I lay. She would have remembered that our boys were first.

Asher was at one end, Zavier the other, his little hand dangled down along the sheet, his fingers still. I could feel my heart slide down and pass to my stomach. He was gone.

My life all gone. A collection of sprawled bodies was all that remained. And I'd let it happen.

I could hear the rhythm of CPR, two shifting teams trying to bring my boys back. Alternating like a seesaw, one up, one down, one down, one up. I needed to throw up. I couldn't breathe. My throat was pulsing. My mouth was watering. It was all over, the panic smothered me, it was all over. I couldn't breathe! I was alone. I was going to throw up.

I clenched my teeth together, holding back the urge. I pushed her body down my legs, slid my shoes out from under her, gently set her shoulders down, and silently asked her for forgiveness. Just in time to crawl to the trashcan and dry-heave. She would have never let me down. She would not have puked in a trashcan.

When I was done losing what little manhood I had left, I swooped her back up in my arms, tucked my fingers under her armpits, which were sweltering, and pulled her across the floor like a caveman retreating to his cave. Pulling along my woman. I cowered against the wall watching these strangers fight for me, watching them pray for a miracle. Watching them trying to pull the souls of my boys back down into their bodies.

Hours, maybe just minutes, I huddled in the corner clinging to my nearly dead wife. Holding on with overwhelming insecurity. I nuzzled her hair and whispered everything I saw in her ear. She would fix this.

How could she leave me here? I could feel the anger building and bubbling up. She knew I couldn't do this. *Damn it, damn you, Cat. We had a deal.*

My face was wet, her soft hair pressed to my cheeks clung there. I clutched her close, praying for God to transfer our souls. I peered over her and watched as they backed away from my boys. They were full of tubes, and there was nothing more they could do for them except watch them die.

The activity stopped. The room was silent. *Oh my God, they are all gone.* Anguish screamed out. I was nothing but the monster who had done nothing.

Eli flung open the curtain only to find me huddled on the floor embracing Cat's lifeless body. He signaled to the nurses to help lift her to a waiting gurney. He was going to take her away now. He held my shoulder with one hand as he peeled my hesitant arms from around her body.

It didn't matter now. They could take it all—I had nothing left.

He waved over a staff member to help lift me from the floor, where I left any bit of dignity I had. Step by step, they walked me to the hall, softly released me to a waiting chair. With a wave of his hand, he signaled the staff to leave.

"Everything happened so fast, faster than we ever could have predicted. How could they let this happen? We had time!?" My anger was building in my throat.

Eli's face was tired, his salt-and-pepper hair and aged appearance made him look so wise. With a long pause, he choked out what I already knew: "It is too late... Cate and the kids are not coming out of this, they will be gone in a few days, if not sooner. I am sorry, Tom." His voice cracked, fighting between his professional and his personal sides. Cate was the closest thing he had to family.

"Tom, we have been in contact with the Centers for Disease Control, and they need your help to pull more data. They are looking for patterns. They need to figure out how it picked up speed. With Cate... unable... you are the only one who can access the data."

Nothing we did at this point will matter. "Why are *we* not sick?"

Eli shook his head and looked longingly across the hall. "From what I am seeing, there is a little latency in the spread, so the worst is yet to come. Many children, elderly, and the vulnerable have contracted the virus. So far, most have died."

"Why not me?" A squeak cut out, the tears built again, and they fell past my already-saturated cheeks. *I can't feel the souls of my boys anymore.*

"Most likely there is some antibody some people carry... Some may have not had enough exposure and they will fall ill soon. I want to run some tests on you." He reached over to pat my arm, but instinctively I pulled back.

I was on the edge of hell, one foot stretching over the flames, they were hungry for me. Every inch of me was crying out to jump in and let the demons take me. I didn't care, let the virus come for me, I deserved it.

A monster.

I grit my teeth, my hands clenched. "Don't bother, I can't live without them. So whatever happens, happens." I stood and went back to the room where everything I had ever loved lay lifeless and piled on two gurneys. So quick it all changed. I kissed them and took one last look. And promised we would all be together again.

"Eli, please don't bury them without me. I will come back."

Within thirty minutes, I was in a chopper heading to no place that mattered, to save nothing I cared about.

M. LaVon

Awake

Muffled white light behind heavy eyelids, red eclipse as they flicker open and close...beep...fade to black.

Standing at the edge of consciousness, weak and paralyzed. The desire to live growing in me...beep...

The hum of the mechanical world steady, ever present...beep...

Dry air gently blowing, relentless, unchanging, astringent and plastic...beep...

Twitch of fingertips wrestling against stiff sheets...beep...

The light was back, cascading into crystal gray eyes. An artificial sun reflecting off pockmarked ceiling tiles. The grid spreading across the visual plain, crisscrossing, sporadically interrupted by sprinkler heads, large light shells, facility labels, and trim, leading to the beginning of a soft blue edge that flowed down, a waterfall flowing downward revealing the makings of a hospital room. All shapes bathed in fluorescent hues.

My fingers fumbled across my arm, finding an IV stub and an occlusive transparent cover protecting it from wandering hands. They worked their way up along my shoulder past the collar of my gown to the nasal cannula resting precariously in my nose. Like octopus tentacles my fingers slipped around the clear tube. Wrapped them around its smooth surface, pulled it gently away and let it fall to my chest, releasing a reluctant hiss as the air found its way free.

I pushed my hands down beside me to slowly lift my shoulders, eyes closed, my arm shuddered and shook with resistance. Partially upright, I slumped, half-folded, with my head bent, resting my chin to my chest. My head swam, the wave of lightheadedness washed down my body and out my fingers. I paused. My fingers tingled as the blood returned and I knew I could move again.

I turned slightly, dangling my legs over the edge. I stared straight down at the polished gray vinyl floor, my view framed by small feet in olive-green nonslip socks.

There was no one at my bedside. I was alone. No cards with get well stick figures and rainbows, no flowers left behind from the parade of visitors. No books on the bedside table from the dedicated reader pining for my return. Nothing. Not even a half-eaten cup of Jell-O and bowl of chicken broth. There was no one left for me. I felt weak and listless, without purpose, but I continued.

Lifting my hips, I slid off the bed and onto the floor. The nonslip grip was gaining traction on the slick grayness. Shaky, tingling legs flexed and stiffened with the attempt to establish stability. I squeezed my hands, punishing the stiff sheets, holding tight, working hard for balance. Pushing up, I stood like an infant standing for the first time, wide gait and toes pointed outward, arms outstretched like a starfish.

I bumbled past the foot of the bed and slowly worked my way to the door. I rested against the frame, my shoulder pressed heavy with the burden of a million miles before me.

There were no people rushing about, no other machines beeping, no chatter.

I shuffled down the hall, resting against the wall, drifting below cheap art reproductions with fake wood framing, advertising posters with healthy, smiling faces, and sequential room numbers.

No nurses at the station, no family in the waiting room, no patients in beds.

I must be dead, too.

Purgatory.

No harps, no angels, no pearly gates.

I worked my way over to the family waiting room and slid into a chair closely situated to a fish tank with two playful clown fish and a couple of angel fish. I watched the clown fish chase and tease around the fake coral through the sea grass and out the conch shell. I smirked. Funny little clowns.

They raced back and forth, and I could sense their laughter and giddy play. Like brothers. Like my boys. Like Asher and Zavier.

The hot flush boiled up through my face and to my eyes, the tears welled then fell. Seismic sobs formed as I choked on my breath, grabbed air and released it in chunky spurts. I imagined their little faces looking up at me as the disease consumed them, helpless, hopeless, weak, I had let them die. I grabbed the arm of the chair and squeezed until the skin in my hands turned white. I was going to throw up. Dry-heave, choking sobs. Crumpling to the floor, I remembered Tom's face as the doctor squeezed his shoulder, confirming the boy's death sentence. *Tom.*

Grief became a burden too heavy to bear, the blackness faded out the light again. On the flat, rough carpet, I grabbed my knees, tucked them up, and died a little more. And I let the darkness take me back.

***

I was back in my room, and I woke more panicked than before, unsure of what had happened, unsure of what WAS NOW happening. My arms were searching, grabbing for nothing. I was scattered, and I needed to see my boys, my sobs were mixed with determination. *Bury me with my boys.* I was not there for them, I did not hold them when they drifted off. I clawed at the sheets, pulling them and squeezing them, writhing like a caged animal. Something was squeezing my chest, crushing my ribs, and I couldn't breathe. The pain was overwhelming, consuming me.

I heard a familiar voice in the hall, distant, faint. I slowly sat up. And croaked out a weak 'help.' The voices paused, I croaked again. My throat was dry and my vocal cords unpracticed, unused.

"Eli, help...me... My boys... Let me...die." The wave of grief washed over me, dragged me out to an infinite sea past the barrier, adrift without solid ground in sight. Lost to its vastness. It pushed me down, broken, my body sank, my eyes fixed. The blood washed from my face as my soul faded, I was pale and weak. *I let them die.*

I watched as Eli came slowly into the room, arms out as if to calm me. His eyes on me, as if cornering something wild. "Cate...stay with me, stay with me, Cate..." His soft voice was familiar, and for a brief second, comforting. His white lab coat drifted beneath his outstretched arms and floated open like angel wings. *Oh Eli, please tell me you have come for me.*

My cries weakened and turned into faint whimpers of defeat. Broken, my petite frame shook, gently floating out to sea farther and farther. *Eli...don't bring me back.* I felt relieved when the black returned, I could feel my body float down below the surface, a silence so deep it engulfed every ounce of sadness. Time slowed, and I could imagine the flicker of light, sunshine, and warm summer days. I could hear their faint giggles as they chased each other, like the little clown fish. And I was gone again. *Please don't bring me back.*

***

I could feel the energy in the room shift, something was different, there was sun in the room. I could feel the warm heat seep through the window, the light rays warmed my hand and inspired it to shift and move. The rays passed through my lids, casting a warm pink light to my lenses. Maybe things were different. I slowly willed my eyes to open, and to my disappointment it was the same tiled ceiling. I was still in the hospital. And I was still not dead.

There was someone at the door, maybe a nurse, talking to someone in the hall. She was mumbling quietly, calmly, in a whisper, like she was afraid she would startle me. She looked back and quickly turned her head when she saw me looking at her. The familiar face of Eli came slowly through the doorway. He put his arms out to his sides, palms open, approached slowly, like I was an animal that needed reassurance, taming. "Eli..."—my voice was weak—"what are you doing?"

Eli's face lightened, his soft smile lines built on the corner of his eyes and framed his friendly, upturned lips. With relief his posture transformed, and with a bounce he was at my bedside. Eli had been a constant, steady figure in my life, a welcomed adopted uncle. He had watched out for me longer than I could remember. His southern charm, sweet nature, and scholarly dedication to his profession made him an amazing doctor and friend. "Cate, I am so glad to see you awake." His hand reached for mine, they were warm and welcoming. For a moment, I felt unbroken.

Looking into his eyes, I forced out what were the most painful words, "Eli, what happened to my boys?" I could feel the tears begin to well up again. He squeezed my hand with gentle, reassuring pressure.

"Your boys are alive, they are alive, Cate."

I pulled my hands to my face and gasped and the tears poured out, relentlessly, and without restraint. Eli pulled me close, an angel bringing the greatest solace. His previously open arms collapsed around me, folding over my weakened form, the grief and despair absolved. I pulled away and looked up at this wise old man and he smiled down. "And Tom?" His smile wavered, his happiness faded, and his eyes turned away.

"Eli, what happened?"

He looked back with almost guilt. "The night, you and the boys…slipped away… We thought the virus would take you and the boys… We are still unsure why it didn't. There was so much chaos, we were losing nearly a hundred percent of those who showed symptoms of the virus, and the CDC wanted to pull the data directly from E-nfinite."

Confused I asked Eli, "They requested access to the EMR network? Why? Their system gets data directly from Winter Medical Solutions."

"From what they said, most of their systems were down, and they needed up-to-date trend data, and…" "And Tom designed the systems," I said, completing his sentence.

"But…" Eli said with a pregnant pause full of hesitation. His eyes again shifted to the floor and away from my worrisome glare. "Like I said, during the first few days there was a lot of confusion. I lost contact with Tom after a few days, I haven't heard from him for some time. I called my contact at the CDC. There was an attack at the site, there were a lot of casualties, and several people were taken hostage."

"What do you mean, 'attacked'? By who? Why?"

"They don't know who or why for sure, but there has been a lot of government scrutiny and rumors this virus was manufactured, and several facilities have been attacked."

"Eli, how long have I been out of it?"

Eli hesitated. "About six weeks."

"Oh my God, who has taken care of the boys?"

"A few nurses from the hospital are staying at your grandmother's place in Woodside, and I have been staying there with them, too."

"And the company?"

"We lost several board members, and even more employees, but we are doing our best with who is left."

With a renewed sense of purpose and determination, I pulled myself up. Eli shot me a look of exasperation but he knew not to question when I had set my mind to something.

"Call an emergency meeting at Winter Estate, bring me any of the leadership team. I need our business operations and continuity plan, anyone from legal...and I want whoever has been running the war room for the data centers. And I need someone to take me to my kids..."

Fever Pitch

On the way to Winter Estate, my new chief of staff filled me in on the happenings of the last six weeks. She was young and extremely nervous. I was not sure who appointed her while I was circling the drain, but I was pretty sure she used to be a receptionist from the business department. I didn't have the best reputation for being the easiest CEO to work for, maybe it was my high expectations. *Maybe unrealistic*. When you lost so many people overnight, I guessed I should be happy to even have a company to run, let alone a chief of staff who was willing to work with me.

It was a hard pill to swallow, we had lost close to 38 percent worldwide in a matter of five weeks, and the world economy was at a standstill. The virus originated in Asia as a severe fever with thrombocytopenia syndrome (SFTS). It had started off easy to contain because of how it was transmitted. Then it mutated, shifted behavior, and became as easily transmitted as the flu. Unfortunately, by the time they learned that it had mutated, it had spread so quickly it was impossible to control. The majority of people who contracted the virus died within a few days. First, the most vulnerable: children, the elderly, people with compromised immune systems, and then those who took care of them. Several types of animals were also affected. It was still unclear why some died and others didn't. Eli talked about a potential antibody they had begun to test for and what the CDC had been looking for prior to the attacks.

The demand on resources to attend to the outbreak, and the sheer number of those lost, sent the dominos falling forward, a cascade of uncontrolled events compromising any sense of order. After the first week, martial law was declared. Several essential services were overwhelmed. There was widespread panic, accompanied by looting, protests, and riots. Many people were left without financial resources when digital services began to fail. Stores were hit the hardest, especially stores with gear and food. Many store staff began taking extreme measures to protect their assets. Supply chains quickly began to break down. Many people just stopped showing up to work because they were either dead or figuring out how to survive.

Hospitals who had staff enough to still operate were overwhelmed by the virus, then by emergent injuries, and then by looters.

Many religious groups declared that 'the end' had come, and the news called it the 'apocalypse.' There was speculation that this was an act of war, but that was soon discredited after there were no countries left unaffected.

A domestic militia group began to claim it was a bioweapon used by the US government as part of a conspiracy to regain global dominance and decrease the world population to a manageable number. They claimed the government knew and could have shut the borders and prevented the spread. The group had taken many research and health-monitoring facilities. They had also taken control of several military facilities in an attempt to 'take back our country from our power-hungry government and the corporations that control it.' They had fortified and stockpiled resources across the country. They were actively recruiting those with antibodies to join the initiative.

Somehow, they had figured out how to identify the antibody and somehow they had the data to target their recruits. They had been successfully feeding off of panic, grief, anger, despair, and desperation. From the sound of it, every doomsday prepper, domestic militant group, and conspiracy theorist had come together and built an army.

***

We pulled into the driveway of my grandmother's Woodside estate, a former equestrian manor with a Spanish-inspired villa, surrounded by meandering adobe walls; lush, temperate foliage; and a small orchard. There were several small cottages on the property for what would have been the groundskeepers, staff, and horse trainers. We never had horses to train. Occasionally, a traveling guest, college student, or charity used a cottage, but for much of the time the buildings were unoccupied. There were also a large barn and horse stable, pool, and pond.

My grandmother was an avid gardener with a number of hobby greenhouses, mostly for fruits and vegetables. The estate was equipped with solar panels, wind turbines, and an onsite well and water-recycling system.

M. LaVon

The estate was a showcase for sustainable living and had been featured in several magazines. It was truly a testament to my grandmother's 'I will do it myself' independent, tenacious personality.

After she passed and I took charge of the estate, I didn't visit the property much—I preferred my simple suburban life. The estate still had its fair share of visitors, including several community organizations who used the estate for large fundraising events; a group of volunteer gardeners maintained her gardens, providing valuable food to a few social organizations she had supported; and I had a few groundskeepers maintain the property; they sublet the land to local farmers who used the fields for grazing and the barn for livestock.

We continued down a long, lingering driveway flanked by ornamental plum trees and expansive green lawns. I traced the fence line with my finger pressed against the windows, following the flowing lines back in time to where I began. The Suburban pulled around the center fountain, the water trickling down the sculpted rock, splashing to the rock bed below, and the truck stopped short of the front walk.

There were large tents on the lawn and people everywhere. I shot a quick look at my newly appointed chief of staff in training. Reading the shock and confusion on my face, her voice bumbled, and she stuttered out, "They had no place to go, things are really unsafe out there, and there is so much here."

"Just a few nurses…" I muttered, repeating Eli's words from our earlier conversation.

I opened the door, swung my legs out, and took an unsteady step onto the waiting stone driveway below. The magnitude of what was happening was clear on the faces of those standing about, lost looks of despair and grief, tired and unsure, each a little broken. Some strangers and some familiar. *How am I going to fix this?*

Two faces appeared at the door, and in a split second they were out and bounding down the stairs and into my arms. I could feel the warmth of their bodies, and without warning the tears cascaded in a welcome release of elated joy. My arms were full, and the day they were born flashed before me, their little bodies wiggling and rooting, and unending love bubbled up. Not so little anymore, their arms were outstretched, too, encircling me in return, and strong. Their faces were wet with relief, tears streaming, loving whispers exchanged.

***

I stood at the threshold of the towering solid oak doors, arched, hand-crafted with wrought-iron brackets and fixtures. The warm wood is welcoming and familiar, far from the sterile landscape of the hospital. I took a step away from the chaos and turmoil behind me, my grandmother's hand seeming to lead me back home and into the safe space she had built just for me. My practical flats tapped rhythmically against the terra-cotta tiles as I walked through the foyer. My boys followed one step behind me as if sensing my fragility. No amount of yoga or dance aerobics could have prepared me for my six-weeks-almost-dead-coma.

I knew where I needed to go—her library. Before my grandmother met my grandfather, she had attended Barnard College in New York. She was a liberal arts major with a passion for English literature, and she focused her studies on social science—although I think she missed her calling in environmental science. She was brilliant in anything she did, and she was my best friend.

Her library was a jewelry box of literature, and here, her prized possessions lived. Classic wood paneling lined the walls, ornate carvings depicted scenes from some of the greatest stories, and my hands again led me by the fingers around the room. Fingertips stroked the carved pieces, swirling up and around the curved features. The polished varnish was soft and smooth, cool and warm. The smell was of aged books and dust, the scents that filled my childhood with beautiful dreams and imaginary places. I made my way to the corner just past her desk, where my own private library was waiting, small bookshelves built just for me, little furniture and large, fluffy pillows. I could feel the soft stuffing against my stomach as I lay across the bulging pile, my child-size feet kicking behind me in shiny patent leather. Squealing as the adventures unfolded, my grandmother's eyes on me, glowing with pride and admiration.

I slid into her chair, maybe searching for courage, begging for guidance, wishing for direction, or maybe just needing comfort.

My grandmother, Cecilia Cade-Winter, was a force, a strong, brilliant leader. After my grandfather's death, she took his company, Winter Medical Solutions, and built it into an empire. She drove the evolution of the business from simple paper records to the premier electronic medical records solution with the launch of E-nfinite. The E-nfinite network connected Winter-owned secure data centers across the United States and worked with partners across the globe. Her mission was simple: The more connected the services, the more people she could help. She would say, "Cate, it is not complicated, the principle is simple: We are in the business of helping people help others, and the better the system, the more people we can help. When you go to school, don't come back with ideas on how we can make more money. Come back and tell me how we can do the most good."

When I came home, I brought her Tom—*Tom*. The lump in my throat bubbled up as I pictured Tom broken, leaving. His boys were everything to him, more to him than I ever was. The wave of grief washed over me again, and I was lost in Tom's arms. He came from a complicated past, but he was simple; he wanted for little and required the same. He was a very quiet man, for the most part passive and laidback. I did all the communicating, managed everything, and just told him what he needed to do, and he did it without complaint. What he lacked in leadership, he made up for in technical genius.

Tom and I met at Stanford—he was a tech major and needed help with a few non-tech classes. I was part of the student success team providing study plans. His challenge was mostly emotional intelligence; his EQ was slightly stunted. However, he was easy—I just told him what he needed to do, and he followed my instructions to the letter. I think at one point we became codependent; he was very comfortable, and I was, still am, very controlling.

What was not in the plan was Asher in my senior year. I was terrified. My hyper type-A personality could not digest how I could have gotten pregnant out of order. Tom was over the moon; I don't think he had ever smiled as much in his life as he did when I was pregnant. He couldn't get enough of talking to my pregnant belly, Asher's little body rippling across my stomach every time he heard Tom's voice, best friends even in-utero.

We moved back home right after graduation. I picked out a house for us in the suburbs not far from the office. Grandma Cici quickly put Tom in charge of designing our cloud infrastructure and data centers. I took my position as the executive vice president of Winter Medical Solutions and welcomed Asher a few months later. Tom mostly worked from home and took the primary parental role, including the late nights. Two years later, we welcomed Zavier, and again Tom was super dad.

I could imagine the deep sadness Tom felt seeing his boys slip further and further away. I imagined his helplessness, yet I could not help him.

A switch flipped and fear set in. *Tom, please don't be gone.*

My thoughts were broken by Asher's voice, sounding more developed than it had before. "Mom, there are people here to see you. I sent them to the sitting room."

"Thank you, I just need one more minute." I faked a slight smile and Asher stepped back through the doorway.

I laid my hands flat against the desk, the cool wood finish warmed to my touch. I felt my Cici's hands against mine, telling me it would be okay, reminding me of what we needed to do. *Do the most good.*

I dragged my hands along the desk, clenched the arms of the chair, then lifted up with confidence and restored direction.

***

People filled the room. What was supposed to be a business meeting for Winter Medical Solutions was now a community town hall. I shot my chief of staff, Liz, a puzzled look. She scampered toward me and whispered in my ear a quick 'sorry.' Even her voice was shaking—she was literally shaking with every part of her being. *Do I really have that bad of a reputation?*

I whispered back in exasperation, "You are supposed to tell me about this stuff before I come in the room."

Eli sensed my dismay and came to the rescue.

I took one step out of the room, and Eli and Liz followed.

Trying to steady myself, I closed my eyes slightly and held my hand to my forehead. "Can someone please enlighten me?" I whispered in my irritated mom voice.

More people shuffled by, squeezing into the already packed room, the energy building like a presidential press briefing. I glanced at the front door and saw that more were coming in from across the driveway.

I pulled them into the adjacent lounge.

Eli explained that those left on the board had tried to keep things up and running so the hospitals would have access to the system. They had pulled together any surviving essential staff. Many had suffered significant losses; many had lost children and spouses. Some were in unsafe areas closer to San Francisco, and there were a lot of violent riots and ongoing looting. Eli had suggested Winter Estate, and so they came.

Eli also brought several people from the hospital, and they brought a few people, a few guys from a startup in Palo Alto, a handful of college kids, and the orphans whose families had died at the hospital and were now left with no one, including two infants and a newborn. In total, about two hundred people now inhabited Winter Estate.

Overwhelmed, I felt flush and lightheaded. I ran my hand across my head. Liz grabbed me a cup of water without asking and without hesitation. *Maybe she will work out after all.*

As if channeling CiCi, Eli whispered, "Cate, they need your help."

I dropped my head to my chest and could feel my heart pounding beneath my rib cage. With a weary sigh, I responded, "I know—let's get to work."

"Liz, pull out anyone on the board, leadership team, and reps for essential functions for Winter Medical Solutions and put them in the conference room. Eli, I need someone to brief me about the true state of things and what this community needs. I need to know who is available to help lead this mess, and I want to know every resource we have available. And I need it tonight. And Eli, get those people out of my sitting room. Have anyone nonessential come back at eight AM tomorrow and I will have more answers."

My head was spinning with exhaustion, and my mind was trying to wrap itself around the magnitude of the situation.

I joined the team from WMS in the dining room. There were only four out of twelve board members left, three senior leaders and four second-line managers, only one person from Legal, and two from the business continuity team. I have sixteen people, including Liz and I, to run a company of eight thousand—make that five thousand and dropping.

We went down the tactical checklist to ensure business continuity.

All nonessential functions were postponed indefinitely, and any resources we had available were transferred to essentials, including our network infrastructure, data centers, help desk, data and physical security, etc. We froze updates and code changes and prioritized security patches. We went through each functional business area and recapped vulnerabilities and risks. I delegated the acting vice president to pull up managers and ensure we had people leading the functional areas. We nominated Winter Estate as our temporary headquarters.

The leadership and the essential managers were dismissed, leaving me with the last four board members and those from the legal department. I hated these meetings; this was where the bad news really came out.

Even with all the wheels turning in all the right directions, without funds we couldn't run a business. The world economy was at a standstill. Many of our assets had been frozen when the world banks slowed their operations. We talked long-term, worst-case scenarios. We had a year before we would have to board the windows. Even with that year, we might need to scale down operations and run the essential functions only in the long term. Until things broke down completely.

M. LaVon

From Bad to Worse

Eli brought in a handful of people: one engineer, one doctor, two nurses, a random tech guy, a gardener, a groundskeeper, and someone named Kevin who apparently liked guns. I shook my head at the fact that ninety percent of those clamoring to lead this ramshackle bunch were men.

Liz led the meeting with a summary of the state of things. She pulled up several news sources, and each repeated the same, much of which we already knew.

There are a lot of people dead, and the wave is still working its way through the East Coast... There is widespread looting, rioting, and violence... The majority of the United States is under martial law. The National Guard is the acting law enforcement agency; however, they are taxed, so other groups are taking the law into their own hands... Most regional services, such as sanitation and waste management, are suspended. Anticipate impacts to utilities, including water, power, communications, and internet services... Food and basic supplies continue to be limited... Emergency services have been centralized... There are several 'acts of domestic terrorism' brewing across the United States... People are encouraged to stay indoors for their safety. They can visit the National Guard checkpoints for emergency services and access to additional resources, such as water and food... There are widespread outages to financial institutions, making nondigital currency hard to come by... Many companies have told their employees to stay home until they can ensure they are safe and can be paid...

"Ms. Winter, from my research, we are pretty much on our own for a while. They are anticipating it will take a significant period of time before things are sorted out."

Without invitation, Kevin was the first to jump in. He was loud and domineering, and he started off with aggressive banter about how we needed to defend against the menacing horde, take up arms, and build an army. I took one look at Eli. He looked back and then down at the floor with a smirk. He knew how this was going to go down. I gave Kevin about a twenty-second head start before I interjected. If there was one thing I was good at, it was putting the players in their right positions. "One sec, Kev... Kevin, right? Let me get everyone out on the field before we started running the plays, okay? Liz, break it down for me. What resources do we have to manage on our own?" My imaginary Pandora playlist began to roll: Eminem, something angry; my favorite tactical jam is inappropriate and loud. Not missing a beat, Liz hopped in the driver's seat. Surprising me, she was amazingly confident. Her demeanor changed, and she was a rock star.

"You got it, chief. We have approximately two hundred souls currently within the estate. The majority are adults, with eight children, including your two boys. I have reached out to each able-bodied adult, and we are completing life skills profiles and will bring them to the town hall in the morning. I have set up a resource meeting for us to review them, and we can assign jobs from there. Your community leadership team includes the following: Health team: Doctor Elijah S. Jackson Jr., smartest guy on the planet. He paid me to say that." She snickered.

I was relieved by the humor. "I bet he did," I said with a wink to Eli.

Liz continued, "Doctor Sarah Franklin, family practice; Jack Williams, registered nurse, emergency; Melony Johnson, nurse practitioner, general practice. They are all rotating times at the hospital, so we needed a few leads. Your sustainability team includes Rodrigo Sanchez, electrical engineer; John Ellison, agriculture; Jayesh Patel, ground and maintenance; Jared Mill, IT infrastructure and a WMS leader; Kevin Smith, security."

Pacing the room, I knew we were missing key elements. "Give me the gaps."

"From what I can see, I am guessing we need someone to lead resource procurement, waste/sanitation management, water systems, livestock management, veterinary, housing, communications—"

Impatient, I pushed forward. "Okay, I get it. Lots of gaps, next problem. What about tangibles?"

"From what I can see, we're pretty screwed..." a new voice interjected from the doorway and caught me off guard.

His tall figure was propped against the doorframe, nonchalantly looking down, playing with something in his hands, his keys maybe. He casually glanced up like he had been there for a while and was just waiting for the right time to make his presence known. He was dressed like a Northwesterner, maybe Seattle, with a red and black flannel shirt, jeans, and work boots. His face had well-defined features and a shadow of stubble, crowned by a purposefully messy brown wave of hair, tossed to the side. Handsome in a rugged kind of way. For a split second, I felt flush and it took me a moment to regroup. "And you are…?"

"Adam Hutchenson, but Hutch works, too." I looked to Eli, and he seemed just as taken off guard by the interruption, his facial expression and the shrug of his shoulder telling me he had no idea who the newcomer was.

"From the looks of it, there is only enough food and supplies to cover about one week. And we don't have enough basic necessities for everyone. Not to mention the infrastructure issues, like sanitation. All of these things need to be addressed or we will have even bigger issues. Starvation, disease, for starters."

"I am sorry, Adam…Hutch… I just woke up from a coma, and I'm still trying to get caught up. I appreciate your candor, but what is your…"

Before I can finish asking my mildly condescending questions, Liz chimed in. "Sorry, Ms. Winter, Adam is my older brother. He is part of the 'employees and then some' group I mentioned earlier. He has managed large-scale construction and um…logistics."

I folded my arms across my chest and looked over to Hutch. "Sounds like *Hutch* wants to be in charge of logistics." *Beggars can't be choosers.*

There was some general conversation across the table, about the need for medical supplies, agriculture equipment, and construction materials. Everyone was weighing in from their area of expertise. Kevin and Hutch were in a heated debate over priorities. Liz vigorously took notes, capturing key points we needed to cover at tomorrow's resources meeting. I continued to pace around the outskirts of the table, each step a rhythmic motion that built a list of must-dos that moved me to the next thought. The conversation hummed down to a mumble. My mind slipped through the window and hovered beneath the stars, my steps beginning to slow as my energy fizzled out. *Tom. I need to find Tom.*

I pulled myself back. "Liz, can you work with Hutch? I want a full brief in the morning before the town hall. Please…"

My head went light, and I moved toward the table, my hands trembling, and I attempted to steady myself against it. My eyes closed as the wave passed, and my breath quickened. I could hear my heartbeat drumming behind my ears and the whooshing of the blood as it flowed back down. The warm flash of white light filled the space behind my lids and my knees buckled. My hands reached out wildly, searching for a chair to catch me. The audible gasps of those at table were followed by the clamor of bodies. I could feel gravity pulling me, and without warning I was in Hutch's arms. He swooped me up, my arms heavy, weighed down by lead bricks. His arms were flexed around me, cradling me, my face nuzzled against his shoulder. I could feel his stubble resting against my forehead. I was too weak to resist. Hurriedly, he rushed me out of the room and laid me on the couch in the library. A helpless damsel.

And with that, I fucking hate him.

***

The sun broke through the tall floor-to-ceiling window, building geometric-shaped patterns that shifted and morphed across the floor. The warm spring air wafted in, lifting and fluttering the edge of the curtain. The soft sheets engulfed me, and the fluff of the summer down comforter snuggled up under my chin. My rested eyes peered along the line where the blanket and the sheet met. I rolled over, half expecting to see Tom's sleeping, shirtless, and half-naked body, taking up his half of the bed, but his side was cold and empty. And this was not our bed. Then it all came back to me. Before heartache came to take me away again, Liz reminded me it was not about me.

"Ms. Winter, I am sorry to wake you. It is six thirty, and per your request, we have prepared your brief. We are all set for your review at seven." Liz gave a half smile and appeared even more nervous than before, like she had never awakened an executive facing the end of the world at six thirty in the morning before. *What happened to the confidence from yesterday?*

I made it to the edge of the bed, and I raised my hand, signaling we were a go for seven.

I groggily lifted myself up. My legs hung off the edge, my petite feet grazing the floor below. My grandmother's room was always someplace warm and consoling. I would climb into her bed and subsequently into her arms, and she would read me her favorite stories and an occasional trashy novel. We would giggle and gasp all the way to the end. *What would you think about all this, Cici?*

To my delight, Asher came in, bringing me a double cappuccino, followed by Zavier with fresh fruit and toast, and my laptop. The smell of the warm coffee brought my focus to the present. I swung my legs back up in the bed, and my boys piled in. Zavier gave me the rundown on what the news was saying this morning, and Asher had a list of questions. Most were answered with "I don't know," except "Is school canceled?" to which I answer, "Probably for a while," and under his breath he mutters, "Yes!" and displays a satisfied grin. The idea of sending the boys far from my sight was not something I thought I could handle anyway.

I needed them with me. I felt like something was broken inside and they were the only glue holding it together.

Asher searched for the clock and reminded me I had fifteen minutes before my day started. When did he become so grown-up and responsible? I leaned over and pulled him close to me. Zavier sensed the opportunity and piled in. I breathed them in deeply, holding on to this moment. I could feel the tears bead along my lashes, and before they fell, I took one last breath and loosened my grip, controlled, calculated, and under my own terms.

I slid off the bed, headed to the master bath for a quick Mom-is-late-for-work shower, and then rifled through the closet to find something to wear. I grabbed one of Cici's trademark maxi-skirts and a draping blouse, gripped tightly to the last little bit of cappuccino left in the cup, and headed downstairs.

***

The hourlong resource meeting had left me depleted, a whirlwind of undoing. How could we have gone from a flourishing society to a dismal, downward spiral in just six weeks? How had I been nominated to lead an entire community while I was unconscious? *I guess she who is not conscious gets the short end.*

Everyone had stood and exited, and I alone was left in the lead chair, head down, elbow on the armrest and forehead resting in my hand. The magnitude of the situation was weighing me down, the weight of the world across my shoulders.

"Ms. Winter..." a small voice echoed across the vast room.

"If you are going to help me through this, Liz...Cate, call me Cate."

My Cici had called me Cate—Cate with a 'C.' She said that name had power and strength. Be the leading character. Never settle for anything less than a leading role. Tom called me Cat, or when he really wanted to get under my skin, Miss Kitty. I hated both equally. To him it was endearing and funny; to me it was degrading and annoying, but I let him.

***

Winter Estate—Welcome Address, March 16, 2025

My name is Catelyn Winter, and I am the owner and CEO of Winter Medical Solutions. Some of you are employed by WMS, while others are new to our family. Winter Estate was the home of my grandmother, Cecilia Cade-Winter. I grew up here with her. When she passed, I took over managing the estate. I want to first welcome you. My grandmother would have welcomed you with open arms, and she would have been happy you have found solace and refuge here.

I have spent the last twenty-four hours getting up to speed on what is happening inside and outside the estate, across the country, and globally.

As many of you unfortunately know, the impact of the virus is staggering. We are dealing with a loss not comparable to anything we have ever seen in our lifetime and we hope never to see again. Many of you are dealing with grief that cannot be adequately expressed in words. I know many of you have experienced deep and personal loss, and for that I am truly sorry. I also know we are actively facing many challenges and will face extreme conditions going forward.

I don't know how this happened, and I am not sure what is next. However, I do know the next steps for us will determine how and what we will make of our future. These next steps are full of uncertainty, and we don't know where they will ultimately lead us. But the right thing to do is to move forward.

For the time being, you are welcome to stay here, but the expectation is that we work as a community. Everyone here has an important role to play, and if we are going to make this work, we will need to do it together. You are also welcome to leave at any time.

Each of you has been assigned to a team. Each team will be responsible for a critical function. These functions are not glamourous but essential. There are team leads assigned to each function, and that team lead will report to me, for now, until we establish a council. We will meet regularly as a community to discuss relevant topics. Liz will coordinate those meetings, and if there is an issue you need to have addressed, work directly with her.

Our top priorities are to ensure there are enough places for people to stay, food to eat, safety and security, and health. If something falls outside those categories, we will address it at a later time.

I appreciate your patience and understanding as we work through critical logistics.

And now, questions...

***

We waded through questions and concerns. There was so much we could not answer, and so many issues without solutions. Most concern were in regard to uncertainty, but this was meant to be a short-term arrangement between friends and colleagues.

***

The short-term solution quickly turned into weeks that became months. We soon grew to nearly five hundred, but only nineteen were children.

Only nineteen children out of five hundred adults, who were mostly of childbearing age. Only nineteen had survived—and not all of them were children born to the group members. That did not even describe the scale of loss beyond the children. The sorrow coupled with survivors' guilt was a black hole, a vacuum collapsing in upon itself. With the darkness of night, after the lights dimmed down, the symphony of shallow cries hummed across the encampment, floating high above, echoing its sad chorus. The energy turned into dark matter, weeping out into space and sucking up the starlight.

Those first few weeks eased us into our independence, while the National Guard checkpoints provided extra food and supplies. The American Red Cross and other charity organizations provided for basic needs.

With their help, we were able to amass a large number of oversized canvas tents and temporary shelters, which we set up in the arena next to the stables. The stables became the city center, where people would congregate, share supplies, access resources, and meet before the daily activities.

There was something about the trailers, the tiny houses, tents, and makeshift homes, something that drew people in like a county fair. Maybe it was the openness and closeness of it all. The nights would be buzzing like bees in a jar, the activity warm and welcoming, almost irresistible. The common sadness bonded people like no other experience, like an endless support group, an infinite sharing circle. The evening hours were the time for connecting as a lively collective, making the looming dark hours alone almost bearable.

The vibrant glow from a system of Christmas lights encompassed the alley like walkways. The zigzag of yellow and the occasional multicolored strands washed down, illuminating a maze of mismatched streets lined with cooking stoves, camping chairs, and makeshift gathering places. The smell of slow-cooked meals wafted up from communal pots. The sound of laughter and connection filled the air, and the few children ran wildly through the foot-worn streets. Adults looked on, giddy at the sights and sounds of squealing and little feet pattering past. Other faces cast downward toward table games, competitive, smirking voices challenging each other, building to a crescendo of excitement for the win.

My feet wandered through on the soft ground, soaking in the smells of Winter, our little city, basking in its glow of the warm light, engrossed in the energy of the moment.

Meandering past the edge of the city light and out into the open, where the sunset clashed with an endless sea of stars, my walks led me out into the fields, where we had turned grazing land into large-scale farming and agriculture fields. I followed the evenly placed parallel crops, the leafy sustenance working its way out of soil, reaching and stretching to touch the sun. I admired each meticulously lined row as I passed, my fingers dragging across the leaves of whatever was growing, feeling the cool, smooth surface. Leaves filled with hope and beginning, the row guiding me toward the diminishing haze of dusk that was brushing the horizon. The last of the light folded over, squeezing out the final bit of color before it was consumed by the compressing blackness of another world far from the tragedy of what brought us here.

***

I still was not sure what was the exact moment 'our people' stopped connecting with the outside world. People stopped charging their phones, and soon their phones just stopped working, and they stopped caring about the service. The WMS employees worked from the villa, and the healthcare workers took a shuttle to the hospital. Those who had jobs outside the estate slowly stopped going altogether. The outside became a burden, a place filled with violence, fear, and sadness.

News traveled via the morning gathering at the stable prior to work assignments or through the streets of our little shantytown. The news was never good, and so many just stopped listening.

The civil unrest had spread. There were ongoing domestic uprisings between antigovernment militants and the military. The propaganda from the militants suggested that civil war was coming, and they meant it.

The National Guard systematically closed the checkpoints and pulled out, redeployed to defend joint military facilities and government-sponsored agencies. It was not long before the militants started attacking the few supply chains that had begun to recover after the virus, taking what little supplies that had been feeding the surrounding communities. They then started attacking infrastructure, including communication and power utilities, crippling the survivors and increasing their dependence on the militants.

Businesses that survived the first wave began to wither, including WMS. We managed to keep the data center operational to support what hospitals still had infrastructure to manage the electronic medical records, but those facilities also began to close, unable to operate without supplies, staff, and basic utilities. Many of the four thousand WMS staff members who survived stopped coming into the offices, and then they just stopped reporting in altogether. We scaled down to mostly nothing, and WMS essentially went dormant, except for about two hundred employees who moved to Winter Estates, bringing any family members they had left. It was only a matter of time before the data centers closed, as well.

As supplies, support, and infrastructure systematically failed, people became desperate, and war became unavoidable.

***

Winter Estate, Community Address, June 26, 2025

The Free Nationalists have declared civil war against the United States government. This group is responsible for the various attacks against joint military bases, research facilities, and government organizations.

Radio PSA, June 26: We, the Free Nationalists, believe the government is responsible for the epidemic and subsequent decline of society. The government perpetrated this in an attempt to control the growing civil uprising against their policies, which feed the rich and increase the dependency on US-provided resources. They could have prevented the spread of the virus by closing our borders, but they prioritized our global interests over the welfare of our citizens. They deliberately covered up the threat to deceive us and to provide a false sense of security.

Our great nation has suffered at the hands of bureaucracy for too long. Politicians, with their hands in the deep pockets of big business, profited while we carried them on our shoulders. We believe it is time to rewrite history. We ask all independent citizens to join us to take back our country. Consider this a declaration of war... (repeat transmission)

From what we gather, there is active fighting in many of the Southern states and small skirmishes everywhere. It is hard to differentiate between who is fighting. There are a growing number of independent communities like ours who have built pseudo-governments and are peaceful communities just trying to survive. There are also extremist militant groups who are terrorizing any group in their path. These militias are violent and unforgiving. The Free Nationalists deny any association with these groups and condemn their activity, but from what we have gathered, many of these independent groups support the Free Nationalists.

The subsidies from the National Guard and charitable organizations have dwindled and will soon cease. They have closed the checkpoint in Palo Alto, and many of the guards have been redeployed to address civil defense. The charitable organizations, without the support of the Guard, have no choice but to close their operations. However, with the resourcefulness of the Logistics team led by Hutch, we have built a significant stockpile of goods and supplies, including articles for defense.

The council has met, and we believe it is now prudent to set up extra patrols and additional security measures around Winter Estates.

On a brighter note, we would like to announce that we have successfully negotiated a cooperative partnership between three of our neighboring estates. This will increase our grazing and farming land to over sixty acres, improve access to water for irrigation, and allow us to expand our carrying capacity. Let's congratulate our Sustainability team for all their hard work. *(applause)*

In less than four months, we have built a community from a collection of shattered pieces. We have built a thriving ecosystem. We have turned soft soil into fruitful sustenance. You have poured your energy into connecting, rebuilding families—not just surviving, but living. From this, I know that what *will come will be overcome. Please share your questions and concerns, and the council will be sure they are addressed.*

***

I nodded to Liz as I collected my notes. The rumble of the crowd grew as they prepared to leave and began to speculate at what was happening outside our walls.

"Maybe they're right, princess." A gruff, booming voice broke across the congregation and echoed from the back of the barn, carrying each syllable and mixing it with an audible gasp building from the crowd. Everyone stopped and turned to face the back of the room, and then back to me, and then to the back of the room again.

With a confused expression, I searched for the source of the comment, and my voice cracked out a weak "Excuse me?"

"You heard me. You are one of those corporate bitches, no better than the politicians." A dark figure appeared in the center of the aisle. He seemed familiar, and I thought he might be part of Kevin's security team. They weren't the most-friendly bunch—typically ex-military, rough around the edges and willing to shoot anything that moved across the property line. They were extremely effective for protection; however, they scared the shit out of me most days.

"I am sorry, I am unsure what you are trying to say," I stuttered out. My face flushed with embarrassment, and I could feel the nervousness build. I worked hard to suppress any outward weakness and amp up my confidence.

"A princess treating us like serfs, having us serve you. We are out here living in tents eating bread, while you eat cake off of gold-trimmed plates while you live up in your castle." He was large, over six feet, my small frame was nothing to him. I could feel my nervousness turn to anger, my fear turning into a boiling rage. *How dare he?!? I welcomed him into MY home, fed him from MY table, and sheltered him from what was happening outside MY fences.* My lips began to quiver. My fists clenched, and my boardroom bitch hat magically appeared.

"Umm... You just poked the bear. I suggest you move on, sir. Pack up your tent and plan to brave the wilderness on your own." Hutch assumed his usual position, nonchalantly leaning against the door frame. Tall, mysterious, striking, and a complete pain in my ass. He had been holding back, watching intently as the spectacle unfolded. *I don't even know why he opened his mouth. He needs to mind his own business. I don't need his help.*

Through clenched teeth, I said, "Thanks, Hutch, but that will be all..." He smirked a little, as his hands went up in a gesture of compliance. He spun out of the door frame and retreated into the shadows of the back of the room.

I glanced to the floor, collected my thoughts, and took in one of those long breaths meant to hold back everything inappropriate I wanted to say. "Sir, while I appreciate your astute observations and uneducated comparisons, let me help you understand something, perhaps the definition of a serf. I did not bring you here, I do not make you work for me, and I do not hold you hostage. You are not 'bonded' to servitude. You are free to collect your entitled arrogance and find another 'kingdom' to grace with your presence. This community has been kind enough to *allow* you to serve it. However, sir, I am not as kind... Let me clear something up, I am far from a princess. If anything, I am a queen. And the people who sit around this proverbial table are equal in measure, and you... well, you will never compare. Please feel free to exit the gate with the nothing you came in with, and see how you fare as fodder for someone else's army. I hear they will take every idiot who applies."

Before the man could say anything else he would regret, Kevin stepped into the light along with his fellow henchmen. "Doug, it is time to go," he said and kindly removed the man from view. Liz attempted to gather me from the ring and pull me back to my corner, but I was transfixed, stapled to the ground. *Is that how I am thought of? High in my castle, looking down at the people 'below' me?*

I put my arm out to calm Liz and let her know I was not done.

"Before we conclude for the evening...I want to be sure we are all on the same page. This *is* a communal operation, this *is* a voluntary operation, and your free will dictates your presence here. There will be tough times, but the only way we will survive is by working together. If anyone is unhappy here, then file your grievance with the council or find your way to the gate."

I made my way back to the estate, passing through our city's streets, hearing the soft whispers from tent openings... "We are with you, Cate." The magic and wonder of what we had created had been eclipsed by the reality of what lay ahead. The strength within the walls I was so naïve to think were solid were like anything else—shakable. The walk was cold and dark, the glow of dusk lost to the blackness. The vibrant energy once radiating under the Christmas lights was now tainted by my perceived privilege.

My feet hit the stoop of my 'castle'/infirmary/school/library/townhall/WMS corporate headquarters/council offices, and I saw that the lights were all but out. I could see Liz's small figure standing in the doorway, trying her best to imitate Hutch. She was just missing the unrelenting arrogance. I giggled and rushed to jump into her arms, my artificial Southern accent squealing, "My hero! Thank you for rescuing me from that bad man. I don't know if I would ever have survived without you there to defend my honor!"

We poured through the doorway, dropping to the ground in a heap of uncontrolled hilarity.

She sat up twinkly-eyed, like she was about to share a secret. "Shall we?" Without hesitation, we jumped up and ran down the hall, flinging the door under the stairs open, and like two schoolgirls, bounded to the cellar.

It was a pleasant surprise. My grandmother had left a mega vault of California wines hidden beneath the house. Liz had been the proud explorer who had discovered the buried treasure, and so as her reward, she got to revel in the bounty with me. The cellar had become a secret garden, a place away from the realities of life at Winter Estates. I had grown to value Liz as a number two, a friend, and my closest confidant. She was the little sister I'd never had. She was close to fifteen years my junior, but her maturity made up for it.

As I came to learn, Liz had worked for my former chief of staff, who treated her horribly. The twinge of guilt crept up as I thought about how easy it was to be oblivious to those around me. Apparently, the saying 'shit rolls downhill' had been an actual experience for Liz. Looking back, I could see how someone could be threatened by her. She was brilliant, clever, and a force to be reckoned with. She was totally my girl crush, and she made me a better person. I had no idea she had been the person who had made my number two a success. It was like pulling back the curtain and seeing the Wizard of Oz for the first time—mind blown.

It wasn't until I was on my third glass of wine that I started crying, a total girl cry. Liz was so good about cutting me off at two, but she must have figured that after the night's events I needed to have a little extra. At three, I got all Tom sad. I could feel him like a second heart beating in me. Tom was my best friend, my balance.

I slid off my stool mid-cry, knowing it was time to fumble my way to bed. The stools were made out of old barrels, aged oak stained with wine and branded with various vintages. They were flanked by a tasting table, also made out of aged wine barrels.

I stumbled on the tile floor, and in slow motion I made it to the ground with my hands slightly outstretched, then found comfort in the floor and went full starfish. Liz choked on her wine as she watched me pretend to swim across the terra-cotta tiles, and we busted out laughing. She came to help me up and tripped over my foot, landing on the floor beside me. With that, we were beside ourselves with drunk girl laughter.

"Umm... You ladies okay?" Shit, we were caught.

"Shhhhh... Liz, we got to be quiet. We are going to wake the whole kingdom!" We both erupted into loud cackles once more.

"Come on, Cate, let me help you up..." Ugh, it was Hutch.

"How are you always lurking in doorways and dark corners like some sort of lurk-er? Let me tell you..." I stumbled to my feet, my grace and class muted by the slight (significant) intoxication. "I DON'T NEED YOU. I can do it myself!" My drunk slur grew more pronounced with every syllable. The heat reached my face, and I added anger to the mix. "Let me tell you something, *Hutch*. I don't like you—you are arrogant and...stupid! And you are *not* my hero! Tom is my hero." My drunken tirade seemed perfectly rational...and then perfectly ridiculous...and with that I was crying again. Liz was now back up and absolutely speechless as the massive train wreck I have become seeped out. I was now sobbing, folded over the perfect wine-barrel stools.

"Liz, I will get her to her room," Hutch said without smiling. Liz's head hung low as she slunk out, leaving me behind to face the music by myself.

Relentless sobs burst forth, previously walled away behind carefully laid bricks. *I miss him, I miss him so much.*

Hutch brought me back to the floor, then cradled me across his lap, stroking my hair gently, pulling damp clumps away from the mess of tears. The cool tiles were pressed against my hips and it felt nice. He shushed me, like I had done to my boys when they were babies: *Ssshhhhh* pause *shhhhh* pause *shshhhhh* pause. Add slight rocking. His hand was pressed against my cheek, cool against my flushed skin. "He will come back to you, Cate. We will find him. I promise." I slowly drifted away, comforted by his promise. "Oh, Cate, you are such a hot mess." The blackness made it way past my lids.

I woke in my bed, horribly hung over, and with a fuzzy recollection of the night before. *Oh God, he carried me...again.*

***

After a few weeks, we lost all contact with the National Guard. The power and communication services were out for days at a time. We had some renewables onsite, but with the growth and additional coops, we needed more energy. We also needed to fortify the stockpiles to ensure we could make it through the winter.

Supplies and support outside our walls were scarce, and desperation was at an all-time high. There were reports of local raids and several skirmishes between local communities over resources. We had increased our security after the declaration of war; however, with the extra land, our security resources were stretched. Kevin, loyal by every sense of the word, guarded Winter Estates with every fiber of his being, and demanded the same of his team. I wasn't sure I ever saw him sleep; he just paced about every night.

The council decided to send a party out to scout and bring back more supplies, with a stretch goal of fuel and power cells. A security detail and logistics team were dispatched, Hutch in the lead. The plan was to be out for a day, back in twenty-four hours.

The team piled into the trucks like big game hunters on safari, guns slung across shoulders, eyes focused and serious. The people lined the driveway waving at the wayward explorers. Children chased the truck to the gates, then turning back and running full-force back to the comfort of Winter Estates.

The sun rose and set the following day without their return.

And again, for a second day, and then a third.

On the fourth night, they came—not our scavenger team, but the others.

***

They slipped through the grazing field, past the cows, and into the city without warning. They went past the barn filled with supplies and right up to the tents. Not a raid, but a murderous pillage. I could hear the screams and the gunfire coming from the stables. I sounded the main alarm we used for urgent meetings, then ran to the boys' room and sent them to the cellar. I pleaded with them not to come out until they heard me call 'A–Z.' I ran to Liz's room, but she was gone. I ran and grabbed the pistol from my room that Kevin insisted I always keep with me but I could never remember. My heart was racing, and I was breathless. I passed the threshold of the mighty wooden doors, ran down the steps, across the driveway, directly to the stables. Our security team converged on the glowing wreckage like a swarm of protective bees. They came from all corners of Winter Estates, rapidly chasing off whoever was left.

As quickly as it had happened, it was over. I stood at the edge of the city in shock. I had been brought back to reality by the screams and whimpers. Eli and the medical team transformed themselves into an emergency medical unit, laying out sheets and triaging the wounded, shouting orders, calling for help. They sent the more seriously injured to the makeshift infirmary within the main house. Small trails of blood striped across the ground where people were dragged for help, tents were ripped, cooking pots flipped over.

An adopted mother was wailing, clawing at the ground, her husband folded around her, as she folded herself around the body of a toddler. Her screams pierced my soul, the limp little arms and chubby fingers finding their way out of the cradling arms and dangling listless. She rocked back and forth, mouth agape, lips no longer holding back the anguish, crushed beyond repair. I waved to Eli to get his attention to help the child. He gently shook his head: *No, she is beyond help.* My tears built and were held at the edge of my eyelids. I gritted my teeth and covered my mouth. My breath was broken. I breathed in only to have the air come out choppy and then squeaked my breath back in again.

How did this happen?

A young man ran up, out of breath and panicked. "Ms. Winter, you need to come with me." I followed him to the edge of the stables. Resting against the outer door was Kevin. He had been shot in the shoulder and upper thigh.

I dashed over and knelt beside him. "Go get Eli!" I shouted at the boy. "Kevin, we are going to get you taken care of."

He winced and swallowed. "Liz."

"Liz? I have not seen her." I was gripping at the fabric, bunching up what I could to stop the bleeding. Eli came bounding around the corner with two members of the medical team.

"No, they took Liz." A warm tingle bubbled up through my throat, and my stomach began to churn.

"What do you mean, they took Liz?"

"I had invited her out for a walk—we have been kind of talking a lot lately…" I was confused, and I was not sure how to take what he'd just said.

"What?!... Who the fuck, *Kevin*, takes a walk in the middle of the night in the dark around here?!" I could feel the anger boiling over.

Eli looked up with a stern eye. "Cate, let's keep our cool."

I stood up, pacing, my gun still in the waistband of my yoga pants. And I was considering using it. *How irresponsible! Who does he think he is? How did he let her get 'taken'?*

Kevin stammered out, "She didn't want you to know because she knew you are not my biggest fan."

The anger transformed into panic. *What are we going to do? Oh my God, they took Liz.*

"Who were they?" I snarled at Kevin. I was pacing. My feet wanted to run, run away, run to find Liz, just run.

"We've got to move him, Cate. Thankfully the shots didn't hit anything major, but I need to get him in." Eli spoke with an adamant expression. He was losing his patience with me.

"Cate, it was Doug."

"Who the hell is Doug?" But even as I said it, I knew what he was going to say.

***

Winter Estate, Community Address, July 22, 2025

Today is a day of deep mourning. We lost eleven souls, including that of a child. There are a number of patients still in the infirmary in the care of our medical team. We have one still missing. We are all shaken up by this, especially with the news that one of our own led the raid in retaliation. Please take the time to grieve and find comfort in each other.

We have reevaluated our weak points and have asked for additional security team volunteers. On behalf of the council, I want to thank those who are working so hard to protect us.

I had no desire to inspire.

***

The sound of trucks rumbling down the driveway broke the silence of the somber afternoon. The trucks pulled in honking, the passengers full of triumphant smiles. A fuel truck was at the rear, and piles of supplies were strapped down to the truck bed.

The smiles quickly dissipated as the faces took in the newly dug graves in the ornamental garden. Almost in slow motion, the members of the caravan climbed down from the trucks. Those with loved ones in the camp ran straight for the stables. Others looked to Hutch to explain.

I stood on the stoop, my arms crossed, my mood frigid. Hutch approached the stairs with a look of concern.

"We thought you all were dead," I said with limited inflection.

"Nice to see I was missed... Yah, well, we ran into a few complications and had to take a couple of detours..." He ran his hands through his brown waves. "What happened here?"

"Doug," I said with disdain. "He stormed the castle and killed eleven people, including a child. There are several others in the infirmary—including Kevin."

Hutch shifted nervously from one foot to the other. "Where's Liz?"

My face softened, and I took one step down. Sensing something, he backed away, put his hands up, palms toward me, warning me not to say what he thought I was going to say.

"Hutch..."

"*Cate*, where's Liz?" he said firmly as he took another step back.

"Hutch, listen...they took her."

He looked away, then back and gave an awkward, unconvinced smirk. "No." He backed up more, hands above his head. He grabbed his hair, locking the brown waves in his tight grip. "No!" he cried.

I could see the vein in his neck pulse. His usual arrogance and confidence were shattered, gone. His rage was palpable. "How *the hell* did they take her, Cate? You were supposed to keep her safe! Or were you too worried about yourself?" His teeth gnashed and his lips pursed, the blame spewing out of him like a firehose.

In a low and calm voice, I continued. "Hutch, she was out with—"

Before I could finish, he cut in. "Out with who?" He would kill Kevin, and instantly I regretted saying she was out with anyone. I wanted to take it back more than anything.

"She is a grown woman…" I tried to placate him. People had started to gather, circling around, preparing to watch the volcanos erupt and destroy each other. I took a step down.

"Don't tell me what she *is*… You don't even know her. She worked for you for years, but she was invisible to you, like everyone is… How could you let this happen?!" He took a step in toward me.

My patience and kindness began to melt away. "How could *I* let this happen? *You* were the one who left for days. You could have been dead. *You* let this happen." I took the final step down and off the stoop.

He took the last step in, so close now I could feel his chest rise and fall against me.

"What? Did you need someone to catch your ass *again*? All I have done is pick you up off the floor and hold you up since I met you….and then you discard my sister like trash!"

I could feel the heat coursing off his body. He smelled strangely sweet, like vanilla. His eyes were staring down at me, and I could see the extreme pain and desperation there, mixed with sadness and anger. I wondered if he could see that I'd just lost my only friend and I felt like my insides were being ripped out, too.

He stopped, his eyes full, the blinding weight of anguish held back by a thin, transparent layer. His breathing was rapid and ragged. We held the gaze, nose to nose.

I wanted so bad to fix this.

"Fuck you, Cate." He spoke in no more than a whisper. He closed his eyes, turned his face away, and walked off.

Liz

I was beaten so badly on Day 1 I didn't remember much except the fullness of my face and the coldness of the ground. Day 2 was the first day I learned what it was like to be sold to a camp full of men. I also learned how to cry quietly and not make a sound.

I wasn't alone—there were others with me. Not from Winter. I could hear them scream, but the more they screamed and pleaded, the more they were raped, and the more they fought the more they were beaten. The men weren't as savage when you were quiet. Yes, I learned several lessons on Day 2.

The cold dirt was welcome against my swollen jaw. I rolled to face the flapping blue tarp—a blue ocean crashing against a ragged shore. The cries for help weakened and faded as I clasped my hands over my ears.

Simon & Garfunkel filled my mind, my inner voice hummed along to "The Sounds of Silence".

The familiar rustle of the makeshift tent door broke through the morose chorus morphing it into the cover by Disturbed and I knew it was my turn. A crescendo of darkness crashed against me as I cranked up the volume of my internal playlist.

My body peeled away from the ocean view, shoulders pressed flat against the dirt floor. I fought to keep my eyes to the side. Hard, rough fingers wrapped around my swollen jaw, tearing me back to reality. A palm pressed against my throat, not hard enough to kill me, but I wished it was. *A welcomed, silent, painless death, just squeeze me away to sleep.* This one was not as aggressive as the others, and I appreciated his ravage-free approach. He bit at my neck to where I could feel the teeth touch through. I squeezed my eyes, clamping away the pain.

And then he flipped me over. My internal playlist hit repeat.

My face pressed against the dirt, cool and compact. My tears dried and caked black with soil. The smell of earthy decay filled my nostrils. I gritted my teeth as he wrapped my hair around his fingers, pulling me up away from the surface, and with his other hand he swooped around the front of my hips, bringing me closer to his body. I was small against him. He manhandled me like I was a disposable doll. Relentless, unyielding.

For a split second, I caught the eye of my cellmate. She was maybe fifteen years old, her eyes wide and open, her body sprawled and spent. Not even fully developed, not even a woman yet. She did not flinch or quiver, cry or scream. Her body was cold and lifeless.

He released my hair and dropped me to my hands, still cradling my hips tight against him. I folded, putting my face back against the familiar soil, relieved.

He grabbed both of my hips and began again.

I want to be that fifteen-year-old, just let me sleep forever and set me free.

***

Day 4, I was given a new cellmate. She was quieter, and she cowered in the corner mostly. She was probably the same age as me. She was more voluptuous than me, and they seemed to like that. I didn't mind not being the favorite.

We shared a bucket of water. I decided I would call her Sonia. She must have been captured before or may never have been free, because she didn't have to learn as many lessons as I did. And she looked tired.

My visitor from yesterday came back, and we replayed the same scene.

Between the others, I lay staring at the blue ocean, watching the waves ripple across the tarp, crashing against the pallets that held it down.

I thought of Winter. I was glad Kevin was dead—he wouldn't want me now, tattered and torn to pieces.

When I thought of my brother, I cried silently, letting the tears wash the dirt from my face. Flowing down, tiny rivers collected in my matted hair, returning the dirt to the ground from which it had come. Cate wouldn't have been this weak—she would have murdered the first person who touched her. She would have been strong enough to kill herself, not weak like me.

By Day 5, Sonia and I had developed a secret language, I thought. We got crackers today. I thought I saw Sonia smile with delight—at least that was what her eyes said. We heard new recruits brought into a tent nearby. They cried a lot. I wished they would shut up. But then I didn't, because when they screamed and cried, they raped them more, and when they fought, they beat them. And then they didn't come to our tent.

Except for my daily visitor. Same routine.

On Day 6, the new one had started to like Sonia, and he had a lot of anger. I laid across the tent, eyes fixed on Sonia. I tried to tell her to focus on me. *Focus on me. Focus on me.* Her large brown eyes held my gaze, streaming with tears as he ripped into her. He held her down, choking her, but her hands didn't even move to stop it. *Focus on me, go quietly...sleep.* I found myself a little jealous. Then he moved his hands from her throat and worked his arms around her thighs. Her gaze held tight to me, not moving. I was pretty sure she was dead—then she blinked.

Her visitor glanced over to me. "You like to watch?"

Fuck...

I was grateful when he stacked us together and was done choking her. I laid against her chest. She was warm and kind. I wondered if she had any kids. Where did she come from? How did she get here? We could have been cubicle mates at the office.

He took turns between us. When he was done, he left me there, and she cradled me until I fell asleep.

On Day 7, they came for us and dragged us to the center of the camp with two others. They hosed us off and gave us soap. The water against my badly bruised and open skin burned like acid. I could barely touch myself without wincing. We all cried quietly. The sun was blinding but felt good. The sour, stale air of the tents was washed away by the summer breeze. As we scrubbed, they stood around and watched, smiling and smirking.

They gave us more crackers, and we shared an apple between the four of us as we stood naked in a circle. The sweet, juicy flesh was the best thing I had ever tasted. I rolled each piece around in my mouth, savoring every last bit. We all outwardly grinned with each bite. We ate that apple down to the grainy core, leaving no juicy part behind. Our eyes shifted to each other in communal solidarity. We wished each other luck, or at least I think that was

M. LaVon

what was said. The two I didn't know—I will call them Sally and Janet—were calmly escorted back to their tent followed by their visitors.

A few others circled Sonia, one openly reaching between her legs, then with the other hand, he smacked her for looking at him. So, she looked to me and I looked back. One began to unbuckle his pants, not even waiting to return to the blue haze of the tent. I was not sure what happened next.

Mr. Routine grabbed my arm and took me to his trailer.

It smelled of stale cigarettes and dust. There were a lot of papers everywhere, the place was in general disarray. He cleared the counter, pushed me up against the cold Formica, and forcefully lifted me upward. This time he didn't bite me, but ran his lips across my chest. He pulled my still-damp hair downward, wrenching my neck sideways, allowing me to see out the window. The full leaves fluttered in the summer breeze, creating shade on the sun-scorched ground.

I was out there sitting under the trees, feeling the cool breeze, watching the leaves cast shapes of all sizes, dancing little shadow puppets on my skin.

As the sun set, I was discarded in the blue tent. I crawled against Sonia, wrapping myself in her arms, feeling her warm skin against mine. She was shivering. I ran my hands gently across her stomach and then her leg until she fell asleep.

On Day 8, no one came for me. They came for Sonia, but now they take her out for the big show, making her dance like an entertainer, taking her back to the tent, lining up for their turn with the talent. I held her eyes until they were done. Then when they left, I moved to her side of the tent and cradled her, holding her tight against me.

On Day 9, no one came for me. So I held Sonia until they took her away. And I held her when she returned. Today, they gave us cookies and a piece of fruit. It was like a party, silent in all its celebration. We shared hand gestures and smiles, giddy with the sugar.

On Day 10, Sally and Janet defended themselves. We held their gaze as they slit their throats in the middle of the camp. We don't know what happened to their bodies. I was sure they were still warm when they dragged them back to the tent and fucked them.

On Day 11, he had someone else bring me to his trailer. Passing through the center of camp, I could see the spilled blood from yesterday's sacrifice still clumped in the dirt. For a moment I was glad I was not being lined up to have my throat slit…but then I changed my mind.

He was angry. I was not sure if it was about Sally and Janet, but then I knew better. We were nothing to him, he must be angry about something else. He didn't even wait until the space was cleared before he bent me over the table, slamming my face against the hard surface. I did not resist. He pulled my head back up by the hair and smashed it back down again. The light behind my eyes flickered and flashed as I watched the papers flutter and fall, the force of my body coming down and blowing them free. Gentleness was out of reach. He didn't take me back to the tent after, not back to Sonia's arms.

Instead he cycled through a myriad of angry tirades and left me cowering in the corner of the trailer. There was warm brown carpet below me, the curly, soft texture foreign and irritating. I searched for the coolness of the wall to lay my swollen face against.

On Day 12, when he woke up, he was different, calmer. He gave me a cup of warm coffee, black. I sat in the side chair and sipped it quietly while he watched me. I averted my eyes to avoid punishment and let him watch me without interruption. He approached me, then touched me softly, tracing his fingers along my body, over my breast, along my stomach, to my thighs, making his way in me. It seemed strange, as if he was looking for a different form of satisfaction. He worked his way close to me, gently pressing against me, holding me close. He was breathing so heavy, his breath hot and smelling of coffee and cigarettes. He wouldn't let me go, he wouldn't stop, his hand worked against me, his body pressed to my body, and his free hand reached around cupping my cheeks. I felt sick.

In a gruff voice, he said, "Look at me." I hesitated. He grabbed me hard and repeated his command. I did as I was told. He looked deep in my eyes. I trembled under his control. The tears fell without warning, and my breath quickened. Once he knew he had every bit I had left in his hand, he took it for himself, faster and faster, until I shuddered. There was no world to depart to, no distance to draw, he held me there, forcing me to be present with him. It was disgusting and selfish. I wanted to slit his throat. My breath caught, my eyes fell away, and he was satisfied. He tossed me to the ground.

Ashamed, embarrassed, I knelt on the floor. To further humiliate me, he threw a T-shirt at me, marking me. And then he sent me back to the deep blue ocean.

This time below the waves, Sonia wrapped herself around me as I cried without sound. Her touch was welcoming, calming, soaking in what I could control, the freedom to be cared for.

On Day 22, I got to wear a shirt. And we began to get food more often. He came and took me for a couple of days and then returned me to Sonia. She had a steady stream of visitors who were now familiar, and they had even brought her a couple of trashy outfits to wear. We got to bathe from the drum sometimes, as long as we stayed quiet. There were no more new recruits in this part of the camp, no more screaming and crying and so we stayed silent.

I thought we might be somewhere in a park, maybe Skyline Ridge.

I was pretty sure we had been captured by some kind of army and Mr. Routine was one of their leaders. They addressed him as 'sir,' and he didn't have to share me. He was gone for a few days at a time, but then he would bring me to stay with him at night. He allowed me to sleep in the bed with blankets. But mostly I liked to stare out his windows, watching the trucks move in and out, seeing the trees. Longing for Sonia, waiting for my time to return to the ocean.

On Day 32, something happened. Many of the troops had left, and there was a lot of activity beyond the glass of the trailer. Mr. Routine was in a mood. It would be a long twenty-four hours.

There were a number of maps on his table of San Francisco and surrounding waterways. There were also maps of the former Alameda Naval Air Station and Travis.

He was stomping around the trailer, like he was looking for something or he needed something. I knew better than to get in his way, so I found my corner. He stepped out of the trailer and began talking sternly, with what I would only assume was an inferior. In short order, his report brought what looked like a satellite phone.

He dialed and connected. "Yes, patch me through to Colonel Tom Destin, we have…" He walked away from the trailer and the rest of the conversation became muffled and distorted.

I sat in my corner waiting.

He returned even more fired up than he was when he left. He sifted through his papers, deep in thought. Rested his head in his hand and stared down, lost in the map. He looked over at me, peering from beneath his top eyelids with a sinister glare. He stood with determined attention and stomped quickly over to me. I flinched slightly, waiting for it. I had learned that his moods could come with violent waves, always followed by a subservient mindfuck. I would rather have the violent wave. *Please, choke me out and let me sleep.*

He reached down and grabbed me by the wrist, flinging me upward, slamming my arm above my head, forcing my back to the trailer wall. He grabbed me between the legs, asserting that I was his property, working me. He took the hand from above my head and shoved it down his pants, peeling them away then holding my hand against him and forcing me to look hard into his eyes. I wanted to do nothing more than rip it off. There was so much deep anger in his eyes, it was like looking into the dark parts of hell. I could see he wanted to kill me, rip me to shreds like a paper doll. I was sure he read the same in my eyes.

He slammed up against me, then pulled my back from the wall. He whipped me around, his hand on the back of my head, pressing my face hard to the panels. He bent me slightly, reaching around still holding his property in his other hand, working quickly to take anything I had left as my own. He spread me open and ripped me in half, working to shatter me while satisfying himself. And he did. As if falling into the dark abyss, my soul quaked, my breath caught, and the jerking, silent sobs quivered out. When he sensed his victory, he shifted, brought his hands to my hips, forcing himself into me harder—until the full weight and force of his evil engulfed me, until I wanted nothing more than to die. Just when I could feel my knees buckle and the pain brought the bile up to the back of my throat, his grip loosened, and he let me fall to the ground. Red blood smeared across his front like a sick ribbon of honor. His lips curled into a smirk as if he had won, and he discarded me to the floor in a quivering, sobbing mess. Trash.

***

He had one of his lackeys take me back to Sonia, tears still soaking my face, my body trembling. It hurt to walk, and my legs shuddered with each step. I was so glad to be back beneath our blue ocean. She was huddled in her usual spot. I quickly took my place beside her, snuggled close. I needed her, like I needed air to breathe. *I need her.* My arms wrapped around, spooning her. I stroked her stomach down to her leg. Her skin was cold and firm. My internal playlist clicked and shuffled letting *A Great Big World* play "Say Something" loud enough for her to hear it. *Focus on me, focus on me, sleep now.*

M. LaVon

***

On Day 33, they left us beneath the blue ocean.

Day 34 was August 24. There was no sound outside except for the rattle and rap of the blue tarp snapping against the pallets. I kissed Sonia one last time and left her forever sleeping beneath the waves.

Camp was empty—no men, no trucks, no trailers. Just makeshift tents, discarded women, cans, bottles, and paper.

I grabbed a couple of discarded bottles and filled them from our bathing drum. I stumbled down the access road to the 35 and headed north. The late summer sun was beautiful and hot—not sweltering, maybe 80 degrees, better than the stale air of the tent. Better than the cigarettes in the trailer. Better than any of it. The rocks on the side of the road were sharp and ragged, but the concrete was blistering.

There was no one on the road, and it was quiet, no screaming, no grunting, no rustling of the blue tarp. Just me, Lynyrd Skynyrd, and the only chorus I can remember from "Free Bird."

***

A short driveway jutted off from the 35, lined with a few houses. I stepped off the ragged roadside and followed the soft grass down to a little blue house. The door was ajar. When I peered inside and called out, I jumped at the sound of my own voice. It was not a cry or a scream, but a word. An unsteady and unfamiliar "hello?"

There was no response. It was a cute little house, with pictures of a family on the wall, smiling little faces, school yearbook poses. The couch had a small handmade afghan, and I imagined the rhythmic sequence and the thoughtful planning of its conception. Much of the house had been ransacked, drawers opened, stuff sifted through. I wondered if my captors had visited here. Maybe this was where they got the cookies. It looked like someone's grandparent's house.

I snuck to the kitchen; it smelled sour, like spoiled food. The cupboards were open, as was the fridge. Most of it was picked clean, overturned containers on the floor, ripped-open packages piled around the bottom of the shelves. I spotted a few jars of dried goods untouched on the counter, shaped like different-sized chickens all in a row. I carefully removed their heads, revealing the secrets inside: a couple of packets of crackers, cookies, dry noodles, flour, and sugar. I also found two packets of ketchup, one can of sardines, an unmarked can (which was sure to be a surprise), and a can of chicken broth. I turned on the faucet, which spat and sputtered, then flowed. I filled my water bottles, collected my finds, and went in search of something to hold it all.

There, by the couch, a nice-sized knitting bag held needles and yarn. I rolled up the little afghan; it was soft, warm, and smelled of lavender. I contemplated leaving the two shiny metal needles and ball of yarn behind, but maybe I would want to learn to knit, maybe even an afghan of my own. There was a candle and lighter on the mantel, and I took that, as well.

As I stepped toward the door, I saw a pair of fuzzy house slippers at the threshold. I slid my tiny feet into the pink, velvety soft shells. They were a couple of sizes too big, but I loved them just the same. As I left, I called out, "Thank you." My voice was a stranger, a person I didn't know anymore, so I put it away.

I walked back to the 35 and continued north, snacking on crackers and cookies along the way. I made it about halfway to Woodside before night fell. I found a small shed in which to spend the night. It had a nice corner, and the cool, earthy ground was comforting. I thought of Sonia and how excited she would have been for the surprise in a can. I pulled out my treasures and realized that a can is no good without a can opener. I looked around the shed, but there were no tools to help. I took one last pass at what I had. The shiny knitting needle sparkled in the candlelight. I grabbed it and pierced the top of the can several times. Peaches. Sonia would have loved peaches. I first slurped the syrupy juice, then slid out the soft meat. The succulent fruit was smooth and sweet; it reminded me of the sweet taste of the apple we had all shared.

After dinner, I curled up in the dirt, resting my face in the soil. I pulled the blanket around me, imagining Sonia's arms instead.

The next morning, I enjoyed the sardines and chicken broth. The best morning ever.

I could barely contain my excitement when I started walking again on the 35, turning down Old La Honda Road, a spring in my step. I was almost home.

***

Winter Estates. I stood between the massive stone pillars flanking the gate. It was like entering a magical kingdom. The gates opened without command, and I walked through. The guards just stared openmouthed, and no one stopped me. I walked down the driveway surrounded by the beautiful ornamentals. I could see people in the fields tending to livestock and the crops. The summer breeze wafted by with the sweet smell of the orchard. I stopped at the fence and pulled an apple from the tree, then took a huge bite all for myself, rolling the meaty fiber in my mouth. My lips pursed with the sweet and sour taste. A smile of satisfaction adorned my face without restraint.

People had stopped working, watching me from the fields.

I walked to the center of the roundabout, admiring the fountain, its water sputtering and splashing to the rocks below. Cate was at the doorway, framed in handsome hardwood. She was elegant, stunning, sweet. I was happy to see her, but I couldn't seem to find the right words. I just kept moving forward, hoping she could read how I felt.

Adam came running from around the corner with a huge smile, calling out, "Liz!" but he slowed once he got close. His expression turned, and his gait shortened with each stride, his pace slowing. "Liz?"

Cate stepped out from the door and slowly looked to Adam, then she walked down the stairs, gently grabbed him by the shoulder. "Hutch, why don't you get Eli? He will be so happy Liz is home, and he will want to get her settled." He turned from me, paused, faced Cate. Then he darted away. *Adam, I am home. Adam, "Fix You", by Coldplay.*

Fix Her

Hutch came running in, bursting through the infirmary doors. His face was pale, and his expression was full of concern. I could see the tears building. He was choking on his words and out of breath. I put my hands out to calm and steady him. "Hutch, slow down, friend. Tell me what's going on."

"Liz... Liz is back." The tears dropped, as his heart poured out, softening his distinct masculine features. I watched as his heart began to self-destruct in the pain only a brother could know, responsibility mixed with rage and misery.

"Hutch, take me to her." We walked quickly out the door of the estate.

People had lined the driveway, including Kevin, who was finally mobile with the assistance of a cane. The crowd was speechless. Some were quietly sobbing.

I stopped and then understood. My God.

Liz's small form was standing in front of the fountain, emaciated and beaten beyond recognition. Her hair was matted and disheveled. Her face was swollen, caked with dirt. I was confident she had an orbital fracture and a broken nose. *God knows what else.* Human teeth marks covered her neck, leading down to a filthy, oversized T-shirt that was stained with blood. She was mostly naked except for a pair of fuzzy house shoes. The dried blood along her thighs almost dropped me to my knees. The remainder of her exposed skin was painted in a rainbow of brutality—purple, yellow, green, black, and blue, bruises in various stages of healing. Her childlike innocence had been beaten out of her, stripped away, leaving a hard-as-stone figure, her soul compressed for safekeeping. She was Eve holding her half-eaten apple, standing in the shadow of the man.

"Liz, sweetheart, why don't we get you settled?" I put out my hand to coax her forward.

"Cate, can you help me get Liz settled?" Cate nodded, her eyes red, chin quivering, holding strong.

***

Before we could wash her, I needed to examine her, with the painstaking process of collecting samples for testing. I did the necessary work, then packaged up the samples and sent them off to the hospital with the medical team.

In my entire career, I had never seen someone who had been so brutally abused and survived. She had many broken bones in her wrists, face, and a few ribs. There were too many bruises to count, along with bite marks, scars from cigarette burns, and evidence of other unspeakable atrocities.

She did not flinch or make a sound as I examined her. Cate stood by her side holding her hand, but Liz's eyes were transfixed, lost in the distance, like she wasn't even there. There was nothing they hadn't done to this child, but she did not say a word. She was lucid and aware, and her mental condition didn't appear to be associated with head trauma or impairment, it was more like a choice. Sometimes she made gestures or signals, but there were no real words, only intense expressions.

After the exam, Cate helped me get her into a bath, and they experienced a quiet moment between friends. Liz slid slowly into bath, wincing, and then the tears flowed, a strangely quiet cry without sound, just resting on the wisps of her breath as she exhaled. The water was poured over her head, washing away someone else's sins. Cate, without speaking, pointed out scars and abrasions to me, and my eyes searched for signs of infection, sources of concern. I couldn't help but weep on the inside. The devil had gotten to this precious baby girl. *I rebuke you in the name of Jesus.*

As a black man from the South, I had seen my share of battered bodies. My Father, Elijah Jackson Sr., had been beaten to death when I was just six.

My father had worked two jobs, had said he wanted "to raise me up right…" because "there is no excuse not to be somebody." He knew my grandmama wouldn't tolerate me not having a decent education. He was saving up to send me to "the best black university his money could buy," and he had every expectation that I would someday change the world.

He had been walking to his evening job when he was killed. A car full of white folk pulled up, and they all jumped out. They beat him so badly there was almost nothing left.

The other workers at his evening job called my grandmama and said he hadn't shown up for work. She sent out my uncle to go fetch him. He found him lying on the side of the road, cars had been passing by for some time. By the time my uncle found him, he was unconscious. My uncle took him to the hospital, but there was nothing they could do for him—or nothing they *would* do for him, for sure no extreme measures were taken for a black man. The police said they talked to the men involved; they said my father was "threatening and up to no good," and "they were just defending themselves." There was no further investigation. Just being black was crime enough in the South.

By the time we got to the hospital, he was barely breathing, his chest cavity filling with fluid and his internal organs mush. His face was bloated and bloody. His lips were uneven, bulging and without symmetrical definition. His eyes were hidden behind massive hematomas—long, thin lines squeezed shut, his gentle and kind eyes now forever locked away. I grabbed his hand, mine still so small beneath his massive strong fingers. His hand did not fold or grip my own, like it had every day on the way to school.

Mrs. Eloise Jackson, my grandmama, put her stoic arm around me and gently pulled me away from him. She had seen her fair share of heartache when my father was still pretty young with the untimely death of my grandfather, Elias S. Jackson. She never talked about it, she just said another black man had been worked to death without anyone blinking an eye.

My grandmama was a strong black woman. A true Southern Baptist from Georgia, she would drag me to church every Sunday. There were three things she dedicated her life to: the library, her family, and the Lord, in that order. She was lost in a sea of white society. Her Ph.D. in biology was not enough for a black woman to break the glass ceiling. No one wanted a woman, let alone a black woman, to show them up, so instead she became the town librarian, and she spent her days in a place where she could research when, how, and whatever she wanted, anytime. Her appetite for knowledge was furious, and it consumed anything in her path—mostly science and math.

Every day after school, I would go to the library until she was done re-shelving the books. She would set aside massive volumes full of complex concepts for me to read. The smell of dusty bound pages was the making of my childhood memories, signaling my deep immersion into the unknown. Like an explorer, I would examine the world through each volume. My eyes would trace every word, traversing past the shape of each letter, turning those letters into projected images and those images into larger ideas, until they were cemented in my head.

My father's words became my motivation: 'No excuse not to be somebody.' He died so I could be somebody, and I never forgot that.

I graduated high school at sixteen, with a full scholarship to Howard. I was a medical doctor by the age of twenty-four, and I had my second Ph.D. in genomics by twenty-six.

Mrs. Eloise was a brilliant teacher, strong in both will and spirit. She was my mentor, the model of everything I wanted to be. She was led by conviction and faith, and she said God had called me to be a doctor, so no other black man got less than any other man. To her, we were all equal in the eyes of God.

I could hear her: *Pray for this precious baby, pray for her soul, pray for her healing.*

Almighty God, have mercy on her, lift her soul up before you and let the rays of heaven fill the cracks, making her whole. Deliver her out of the darkness and into the light. Amen.

***

Cate came rushing out to the cottage I shared with the rotating medical team. The screen door pulled open and slapped back as the springs pulled it closed. It was 6 AM, and she was milliseconds away from tears. Her face was moist with sweat, and she was out of breath. "Liz is gone! I checked her room, and she is gone. I checked the entire house and she is—" Her voice had begun to crack and squeak amid her exasperated explanation. I was reminded of little Cate and her driving need to care for everyone. She got the perfect mix of compassion and motivation from her own grandmother.

I brought my arm around her to reassure her. "Cate, take a deep breath, honey. We will find her. I am sure she is around here somewhere."

I had known Cate since she was born. I worked for her grandparents and joined the WMS board before her grandfather passed. Gerald Winter and I had been colleagues, and when I met Cici, we became the best of friends. The Winters were the closest thing I had to family, and Cate was the closest thing I ever had to my own child. Cici was a number of years older than me, but her love for literature and the arts fueled endless conversations. She was my person. I had never met someone who loved a library more than my own grandmother, until I met Cici. The library was the very reason she had bought Winter Estates, and you could say it was what had saved all these people now.

Cici had introduced me to my husband, Christopher Darling, a local writer and professor at Berkeley. It was because of her that I was able to experience the greatest love of my life—and I would be in her debt until the day we met in heaven.

Christopher gave me a reason to really live—before we met, I had been lost in the world of medicine. My time was divided between the hospital, the research lab, and the WMS Board. One day Cici insisted I attend a fundraiser that she was hosting at the estate for the county library system and to fund local community literacy programs. The event was attended by local authors, publishers, scholars, educators, and community members.

I can remember the moment she introduced us. She pulled me close and giggled like a school girl, saying, "I want to introduce you to the most perfect human being, with the most incredible talent, who is as handsome as anyone the *Lord* created personally." She said all of this with her playful Southern accent, as if she were living out a scene in one of her trashy novels. I couldn't help giggling back. She sure did have a flair for the dramatic.

But she wasn't wrong, and when I actually met him, he was stunning. I loved him from that moment on.

Christopher was everything I was not: colorful, fun, artistic, romantic. He loved me without condition, and he supported me with every fiber of his being. He was an amazing cook and the reason I could never maintain my waistline.

Christopher died the year after we lost Cici. I was away at a conference on the East Coast. Cate was the one who called me, the one who picked me up from the airport, and the one who subsequently picked up the pieces of my broken heart when I could not hold it together. He had been in a car accident—it was quick and he didn't suffer. He would have been disappointed by the manner of his demise. He would have said there wasn't enough tragedy, drama, or romance to it. I knew that if he would have written it, it would have been the most spectacular of deaths. In my heart, though, tragedy or drama was not lacking in his passing. Cate and the kids were all I had left.

***

In the corner of our little city, a small figure curled beneath the blue haze of a small tent. It was Liz. She was asleep, clutching her little knitting bag and covered by the small afghan she had carried with her back home. With a sigh of relief, Cate grabbed my hand, looked at me, and then turned back to the house. I stayed and kept a watchful eye on Liz. She slept for almost a day and a half, only to wake for brief moments, and then she went back to her blue tent without a word.

Asher and Zavier came to visit and brought her food. Their jovial, brotherly banter seemed to amuse Liz, who would smile at their jokes. It only encouraged their lively antics, and their visits always ended in loud waves of laughter. Liz would smile so big, the tears would stream, and her eyes would glint in what appeared to be joyous appreciation. Interestingly enough, the boys never missed a beat, reading the nonverbal, subtle cues.

For the first few days, Liz did not leave the tent much. I monitored her healing process, and medically, she was doing well. What surprised me the most was the happiness she projected, she was smiling always, sweet and calm. I could only assume freedom was enough for her.

She didn't move back to the main house. Cate, like a concerned big sister, was constantly hovering over her, and she had someone watching out for her twenty-four hours a day. Cate had always been someone who preferred to control the situation, and I knew this situation felt outside of her control.

After Liz was taken, Cate had begun to spend more time with the security team. She became obsessed with learning self-defense, and she insisted the boys learn, as well. There was something that shifted in her, like an awakening at how dangerous the world now really was. When I would return late from the hospital, I would see her walking the perimeter, her pistol traded in for a more powerful rifle, her board room demeanor transformed into that of military general. I knew the night Liz was taken that Cate was not going to let that happen again. Her eyes were fierce and desperate—and angry. Her soul had hardened just a little more. She reminded me of my grandmother; she had lost so much, there were no tears left.

When she was not building an army or running Winter's day-to-day operations, she was consumed with finding out what had happened to Tom.

The week of the attack on Winter brought interesting information and several new faces to the estate. Hutch and his team had been pinned down by a small band of people who were defending a portion of Redwood city. There was a bit of a stronghold around a fuel depot, and they held out for a day before they began to negotiate terms. Eventually, it came down to simply granting sanctuary in exchange for the fuel.

Many of our newly inherited community members told horrific stories of what was happening in the surrounding areas, others shared heart-wrenching stories of loss, and still others helped piece together the threads of how everything was breaking down. A young man named Maliq provided a detailed account to the council.

I worked on the docks in Bay View, close to San Francisco, repairing boats. When the virus hit, first it was quiet, people putting out the dead, banding together to pull things together. There were pockets of violence, but there was still an underpinning of chaotic order. The National Guard instituted curfews, there were meal rations, and there was still power and communications.

Then things started to shift, and the small pockets of violence started to build into larger-scale looting and rioting, and there were clashes between the Guard and the newly formed gangs over resources and freedom. But then things changed, and there was a new presence.

Many of us had stuck to the docks, afraid we would lose our jobs if we left, but most of us just didn't have anywhere else to go or anything to go back to. One day a group of guys came by and offered us jobs in a "new" army; they needed people with marine skills. They promised protection, food, and shelter, and they claimed to have information that incriminated the government. They talked about raiding an illegal research facility, and they had access to unlimited data and would have full resource control thanks to an amazing hacker whom they had captured and who now worked for them.

Shortly after that, there were targeted power outages, communication systems failures, and coordinated cyberattacks. When war was declared by land, it was also declared digitally. The Guard pulled out of the city. Once the resources were gone and the people were desperate, they joined the army in droves. Some of us didn't know who to believe. I was in the navy until I was injured, so I wasn't about to wage a war against my own people. We banded together just to stay alive.

Maliq's story caught Cate's attention. She had always believed Tom was alive and being held against his will, serving the Free Nationalists. She was determined to somehow bring him home.

Tom had been a very gifted computer technologist, and when I say gifted, I mean genius. He had designed the entire infrastructure for the WMS cloud services and designed E-nfinite, the electronic medical records system owned by WMS. This system had replaced our previous solutions that had limited integration and connectivity. E-nfinite was the number-one solution that joined every major medical service in the United States and internationally, enabling medical services to be agile and respond and treat patients faster, not to mention the benefits it provided to research and diagnostics.

Tom was one of the first to notice a spike in reported occurrences of a new virus in Asia. He had several triggers built into the system, especially for infectious diseases. We worked with the CDC to share these trends, and they worked to contain the disease. For months it worked. Some governments in Asia worked against the recommendations, however, saying they were impacting their economy and trade policies. Of course, it did. But some countries began not to report at all and discontinued WMS services in their nations.

Many countries who traded with Asia banned imports that might contain potential sources of the contagion. Travel in and out of Asia grew more limited. Many neighboring countries closed their borders; others had quarantine areas. The governments began to play down the impact, even so far as censoring the reporting. Some even reported that the disease had been eradicated, going to extreme measures to hide the truth.

The reality was that the virus had ravaged the poorest populations. Close, compact living made the spread of the virus easy, even though the spread was mostly through contact with a person or animal who had already contracted the virus. The sharing of food and water supplies and common utility and sanitation worked to further the spread even more, leaving many countries with a severely crippled working class.

Then, without warning, the disease jumped borders—and the water. Tom issued one final report to the CDC, saying something had changed and the virus was spreading faster and farther, the same day his was family ripped apart. It was clear the virus had mutated; it had become as easy to get as the flu.

We began researching the spread and method of contraction, but by then we were too late to do anything about it. And Tom was gone.

***

Liz continued to improve. The bruises began to fade, and the scars were not so apparent. She met me in the infirmary for a checkup, clean and put together, a far cry from her first day back. Her small hands still clutched her knitting bag. She shuffled in wearing her favorite fuzzy slippers. But more striking was her smile, ear to ear like the Cheshire cat. *What a precious child.*

I gestured for her to sit, and she complied happily. I swallowed around the lump in my throat. The infirmary looked less like a hospital and more like a living room. Maybe the familiarity of the homey space made it harder to separate my professional persona from that of a trusted friend. It made everything personal. It made everything harder and more emotional.

She watched me, reading every breath, every fidget, every shift in my seat, every stammer. Her gaze was intense. One hand came loose from the knitting bag, and she reached across, placing her palm over my knuckles, consoling me. With a gentle nod, she encouraged me to go on. Sensing my hesitation, she gave a little smile.

She knew that what I had to say was eating me up inside. As quick as I opened my mouth, her hand returned to her knitting bag.

"Liz, I am very happy with your progress. I don't see any visible signs of infection. Remarkably, your panels for contracted diseases were negative, except for a bit of staph that we are treating with the antibiotics I gave you. I would like to keep you on a few different antibiotics just as a prevention until your open wounds heal a little more, especially in more sensitive areas. I have requested probiotics from the logistics team, and they are working on that. I still have concerns with your nutrition and your weight, but Cate has assured me you will be first in line for meals for a while." She gave a little smirk.

"I would like you to continue to wear the supportive brace for your wrist for another couple of weeks. The fractures around your eye and nose will take time to heal, and you have a few broken teeth I would still like to keep an eye on…" I paused. The cat had my tongue again.

"Liz, there is something else I want to talk to you about."

She smiled, and I took a long breath.

"Liz, you are...pregnant."

She nodded as if she had known for some time.

***

Council Report, Medical Briefing: Dr. Elijah S. Jackson Jr.

It has been almost eight months since the virus spread to California. Since then we have lost many more people to violence, disease, starvation, injury, and suicide. We are expecting another wave of deaths attributed to people with preexisting conditions not having access to proper medical care and treatment, coupled with the growing shortage of pharmaceuticals; also, the population of people who have undiagnosed progressive conditions will start to die off.

The most concerning area is pediatrics. We lost many children to the virus. Now babies born without antibodies who are exposed typically die shortly after birth. We now know children who are born to two parents with antibodies have a greater likelihood of survival. However, children who have antibodies are not completely immune to the virus, they sometimes develop symptoms and need urgent medical intervention, like we saw with Asher and Zavier. We are trying to isolate the difference between total and partial immunity.

Conception rates have significantly decreased. Environmental conditions have made conception difficult. There also seems to be a correlation to exposure to the virus affecting conception, even for those who did not show symptoms.

We are in the midst of an existential generational crisis. It is critical we work to determine how the virus mutated, catalogue the virus's characteristics, and even more importantly, find a cure.

The research team has been working day and night at the lab of the Winter Medical Center. We request continued support for security and resources.

Strength in Numbers

My sleep is broken, lost somewhere, gone to me. My mind has become a relentless engine, spinning its gears, the motion stealing energy with every turn. The darkness is heartless and cold, the place where I am left to think too much—surrounded by quiet, smothered by the weight of the future, and blanketed by anxiousness.

I know our time is limited, that they will come for us, something will come for us. An enemy without definition or moral purpose will break down our walls, letting the harsh reality spill in. I can feel the building tsunami just offshore. At any moment it will crash past the banks of our utopia, flooding in, collapsing everything we have built and washing it out to sea in tattered pieces. My mind is pulled back to the present.

The shift of air pushed down the hallway and through the bottom of the closed frame. Small shadowed feet appeared and flickered in the space beneath, distorting the faint light from the hall. Then came the gentle squeak of the hinges, metal on dry metal. The motion of the warm wood changed the pressure of the room as it swung slowly open. Alert and aware, I watched. She crept closer to the edge of the bed, slow, steady, almost floating. *She is a ghost.* She approached and stood at the edge of the bed, watching, waiting for an invitation, almost childlike.

She was not like I remember. She was small and fragile, yet stronger than I ever gave her credit for, stronger than I would ever be. My breath caught, and the anguish of not protecting her washed over me. I wanted to beg her forgiveness, I wanted to fix her, I wanted us to go back to two giggling girls in the cellar drinking my grandmother's wine.

I raised the quilted blanket, inviting her in. Her thin legs divided the two sides of the sheets, sliding between each with silent grace. Her presence altered the temperature, warming the space, bringing a familiar comfort with it. She held my gaze, the cavernous centers of her eyes drawing me in, forcing me to face the heartbreak of it all. I could feel each humid exhale brush against my cheeks. Her skin was washed in the soft blue of the moonlight, which accentuated every feature that had been malformed and distorted by villainous hands. The tears broke free from the cinder-block wall that held them back. *I am sorry, I should have protected you, if I had just listened and kept the gun with me, I would have gotten to you.* Her once-delicate fingers, now aged by cigarette burns and brutality, wiped away my apology, absolving me.

She shifted close and worked her way in past the crook of my arm. I didn't hesitate to bring her closer. She nuzzled in against my chest, her head just below my chin, letting me surround her. Her hands worked their way around me in solidarity, gently stroking her fingers along my hip and back. *She is home… And when they come again, I will be ready.*

The morning light broke through the window, warming my face. The much-needed sleep held me down just a little longer, its grip tight, and I submitted. For a split second I forgot where I was.

Then I turned to find the bed cold. I was alone once more.

***

It didn't take long before word spread of the sanctuary of Winter Estates. I was not sure if this was what my grandmother had in mind when she had bought the estate, but I didn't think she would be displeased. What a few months ago had been a simple tent city, had now blossomed into a booming ecosystem of sorts.

New people showed up daily looking to join the community. Desperate faces pleaded for help, people with empty bellies, deprived of sleep, frightened, and not willing to take sides in a victory-less war. I could imagine that this must have been how it felt on Ellis Island: stacks of people lining up with everything they owned in a suitcase or less. We granted priority to people with children and those with critical skills; they were housed within the estate grounds. Everyone else was housed at one of the co-ops surrounding Winter.

We had expanded our collaborative to a number of adjacent properties, including an equestrian racing facility we now used for farming. We had agreements with each co-op for space for livestock, farming, water, solar-

and wind-powered farms, or housing for our growing community. In return, they received food, security, and access to other resources.

Our sustainability team had built an impressive power grid from salvaged solar cells and wind turbines brought back from San Jose. A couple of guys from the logistics team had worked construction with Hutch and knew of a few commercial suppliers. Luckily the commercial suppliers had abandoned their property, and so it was as Hutch like to say: 'easy negotiations.' From his expression, I did not want to know what 'difficult negotiations' were like.

Hutch had stopped coming to the estate except for community meetings, council briefings, and accessing logistics. He had moved from the estate to a co-op with his team the week after Liz came back. We all had a tough time coming to terms with what had happened to her, especially Hutch. I knew I had played a role in adding to his guilt, and I broke what little connection we had had in the process. To compensate, I let him be; he ran his operation and I ran mine.

I was pretty sure he was running a postapocalyptic black market of sorts, and I couldn't vouch for it being 'legal,' but he did get us what we needed, and I decided I would rather just not know. He managed all our imports and exports: We had begun to trade and establish relationships with other communities. Many of the others were not as well established as we were, and they had opted to co-op or sign over full control to the Winter council to access our resources.

Winter was looking more like a town as each day passed, as people had begun to build more solid structures on the property. Looking out from my bedroom window every morning was like watching the time lapse of expansion, with little bungalows and tiny cottages popping up from the ground like a secondary crop. The stables, a center since our first few days, even now had a little market where we traded with each other.

With the progressive deconstruction of the outside world, an environmental microcosm was forced to emerge within our borders. The craving for safety and security, basic necessities, and normalcy was our motivation. Normalcy—such a strange concept in our current situation. It was a contributing factor that desensitized us into thinking that no matter what happened, we would live through it, blinding us from recognizing our vulnerabilities.

When I saw someone putting up a small picket fence in front of their makeshift home, I stopped to watch—the short span was only about five feet. It struck me as very odd: There were no property lines here, there was no purpose for the fence, but the look on the builder's face was sheer contentment, almost pride. When I went by later, a small makeshift bench with a handmade pillow had been placed by the fence line. We humans were so quick to return to the way things were, to ignore what was in our present, to try to rebalance the scales of reality.

I was not blind anymore, and I could no longer pretend that what was happening around us was no more than an inconsequential event that would pass as quickly as it came. I would not be fooled into believing that what 'this' was, was normal.

We spent so much time getting back to normal that we began to find comfort in our obliviousness. But our vulnerabilities were what haunted every waking moment, and it was what would be our ultimate demise if we did not prepare to face the inevitable. There were too many of us, and there was too much at stake for us not to be prepared. We *would* be prepared.

***

Winter Council Meeting, Resource allocation and logistics, September 19, 2025

Team leads, please report the current activity and status to the council:

Hutch (Adam Hutchenson) for logistics: With the new arrivals, we have been able to increase scavenging activity for building supplies, food, basic resources, and fulfillment requests. We were also able to expand the search area with the help of the security team. We have noted, however, several encroaching militants and unaffiliated gangs within our search area. Some appear to be watching and monitoring our activity. Others remain defensive. Wherever possible, we attempt negotiations. Negotiations have given us access to a few supply lines, including communication with areas where the communication has been mostly severed. The people in these areas are truly suffering. There are a couple of contacts who have shared information about troop movement. This information matches what we have been hearing from the refugees seeking assistance from Winter. We have provided the detailed intel to the security team.

Rodrigo Sanchez for sustainability: We have grown our farming in two of the co-op locations, and we have installed several high tunnel greenhouses to increase the yield of the fall crops and get a jump on spring. The weather has been increasingly unpredictable. We are also experimenting with high protein crops, such as soybean, quinoa, and mixed beans. These crops also fare well in long-term storage and they should provide a more dependable food source when we are between seasons. We have also been able to successfully dehydrate and/or dry vegetables and herbs and preserve some meat. The logistics team has been able to collect a significant stockpile of nonperishables, as well. However, with the current unpredictability of the climate and the instability of the region, we advise retaining this stockpile as backup. Our biggest challenge is diverting enough water for the crops, for livestock, and for daily use of the colony. The rainfall has been less than expected. We have diverted some water from Bear Creek, but it, too, is low. We got lucky this year, but if we run into a drought scenario next year, we may need to get more creative in our efforts.

    Kevin Smith for security: Unfortunately, I don't have a glowing review of success to offer for security. We continue to have several encroachment issues, with gangs seeking supplies and resources. We have had nine attacks in the last few weeks, resulting in the loss of two security team members and a number of colonists who were staying within the outer co-ops. There have been several thefts of livestock in the grazing land and one case of someone sucking energy from the outer grid. We still have a number of weak spots around the perimeter of the co-ops, which have proven to be a challenge, especially along the access to Interstate 280. We had a nice buffer zone before, with the co-ops taking the brunt, but now there is no buffer since they are now a part of Winter. Most concerning is the troop activity in San Francisco and Oakland. From what we are gathering from the few news stations still reporting, from radio, and what we are hearing from the logistics team contacts, the Guard has been pushed completely out of California. The Guard has lost most of the northwest as well. Texas, Montana, and Utah have all declared themselves free states and have kept the Free Nationalists and the US military out. There is heavy fighting in the South and along the East Coast. Bottom line, we are surrounded by the Free Nationalists, and while so far they have left us pretty much alone, I am not sure if that will always be the case. It might be prudent to reach some sort of agreement with them at some point.

    In the near term, we have built a hefty defensive force. We have inadvertently benefited from the fall of the West Coast. There were a number of former military service members, mostly navy, who were unwilling to take the side of the Free Nationalists, and who were willing to contribute to defending Winter and the people in it. Our makeshift academy has also provided valuable skills to anyone willing to serve as security. Our logistics team has also been successful at procuring a small arsenal. We are far from *having our own army, but at least we can somewhat defend ourselves if it comes down to it.*

Sarah Franklin for the medical team: I am standing in for Eli. We continue to work to analyze the virus and its associated antibodies in the hopes of creating a vaccine. Eli is currently in the research lab hard at work. We also continue our service to the community with rotations at the hospital. The need for high security is still a top priority for the facility and for those of us left. We are fortunate that many of the gangs and militants leave us alone. Since there are limited resources to treat the sick and injured, it pays to be a must-have ally. We do on occasion run into scenarios with looters and attempted theft. Many of the harder-to-come-by medications are no longer available, as are the specialty services, including transplants. It is just a matter of time before mass-manufactured drugs begin to become less available, as well. We have consolidated what we could from neighboring pharmacies within the hospital to protect what is left. There are a number of pharmacists working to manufacture medicines like penicillin and other essentials. We have begun to see the second wave, as Eli predicted, of those who need interventive care. Without emergency services like 911 and first responders, people with serious, but treatable, injuries or illnesses now tend to die. They just don't get to us in time. And we are unable to respond onsite, due to both resource availability and our safety.

Finally, most disappointing is the nonexistent birth survival rate. Many of the fetuses in utero during the first outbreak presented as stillborn or died shortly after birth, even if the mother survived. And for those lucky to conceive after, the baby does not survive long after birth, even when they have been quarantined from exposure. We are still unsure why this is happening. We are advocating birth prevention as much as possible within the colony to prevent any unnecessary risk to the mothers.

Jared Mill for tech and communication: Most notably for us, we have witnessed several waves of cyberattacks across most major news outlets and communication systems. Most of the attacks have been reverse attacks, in that they are forcing information versus taking information. This has allowed the Free Nationalists to promote their agenda without interruption. Many of the news outlets have gone dark or reverted back to shortwave radio. There are several people using the dark web to share troop movements, area reports, and conspiracy theories. Much of the web has collapsed within itself. Several social media platforms were the first to fall, with the waves of bots streaming nonstop propaganda.

Surprisingly, with the number of medical services shutting down, we continue to see a fair amount of traffic on the system. I am glad to see we are able to provide something to those facilities needing services. However, it is definitely not expected.

We have attempted to use the Winter network to build something reliable, but the security permissions keep pushing us out. There appears to be some kind of safeguard that is preventing us from rerouting data or connecting to outside services. The system is still able to do what it was designed to do, but nothing outside of that. It is almost like the system is one step ahead; it knows what we are going to try next. We have a team of hackers on it, though, and when we are able to figure it out, we may be able to build a safe communication grid using the Winter network and its services.

Thank you to all the leads who were able to provide a report out today, please continue to keep us informed.

***

The decorative lawns that flanked the gently curving driveway were no longer a welcoming sign of home, but a training ground. The soft grass was now broken by black- and green-clad pseudo-military defensive forces marching in formation. Farmers who once helped in the fields were now preparing to defend them. The organized units seemed unreal behind the tinted glass of the hospital shuttle.

Three rows back in the long bench seats, I was surrounded by the most broken and battered individuals. All their feelings were locked behind frozen expressions, their eyes cast out to a world they no longer related to. Yet each day they chose to jump into a shuttle that took them deeper into what equated to a warzone to care for people who would most likely die or kill them for a peanut butter sandwich.

It was not long before I understood why they stared out into nothing, not acknowledging what was cast out before them like an alternate reality. The shuttle weaved in and out, avoiding blockades and debris. This was not the town I knew, it was something darker, the black-and-white portion of *The Wizard of Oz*. The streets were lined with abandoned vehicles and garbage, waste that had never been picked up, and the people who were left didn't care enough to do anything about it. Storefronts were left with shattered windows, the openings framed by jagged teeth. Once-beautiful boutiques had been reduced to smoldering rubble, shiny baubles gobbled up by black soot. City parks had been reclaimed by nature, the unkempt grass enveloping picnic tables. The brittle yellow sod of the ball fields edged the dusty unused diamond. Suburban neighborhoods were left abandoned, the voices of children playing in front yards long faded into the sound of nothing. No TVs, radios, gripping traffic, conversations—the hum of 'normal' life had been wiped out along with the people who made the sounds.

Liz's small body sat directly beside me, her hands still clutching her knitting bag. Her soft pink lips were slightly upturned in a contented smile, an ill-fitting expression in this environment. One hand freed itself from her knitting bag and reached for mine. She could feel me staring. Her tiny fingers tucked into my palm as she gave a reassuring squeeze. Her eyes never moved from the forward-facing position, as if she was looking with anticipation to a future I couldn't see while still acknowledging the past in her hand. As quickly as it came, though, her hand retracted to its original location—clutching her knitting bag.

Eli had asked me to bring Liz to the hospital to check on her and the baby.

The hospital was not like I remembered it; it, too, had taken on a darker feel. The parking lot was full of abandoned cars, a strange reminder that many who were gone had never left. Some cars had been moved and positioned as barricades.

The shuttle pulled past the makeshift gate and the ominous-looking security personnel. I recognized my car still parked behind the precariously positioned minivan with back-window sticker people. *They never left.*

The van pulled to the front, and the medical team shuffled out, mind-numbed zombies with vacant, glassy eyes. The collection of pale blue scrubs lined up, one after the other, like prison inmates on work release. I had the urge to pull them back into the shuttle, take them home, and set them free in the field or even just put them out of their misery. *What a horrible place we live in now.*

My hand reached behind me, searching for the cool metal of my handgun—my security blanket. I was reminded of Zavier when he was little—he had a small, fuzzy blanket he carried with him everywhere. When he would sleep, he would bunch it up in a little ball, press it against his face, and breathe it in.

We shuffled past the security guards, many of whom lived somewhere within the safe confines of Winter. The lobby had been converted into an extension of the emergency room and resembled a field hospital. Waves of crying and moaning mixed with the methodical instructions of the medical team.

I gently placed my hand on the small of Liz's back and moved her toward the stairs. We walked past the sea of gurneys and people sitting up against walls waiting for their turn, continuing up the stairs toward the research lab without a look back.

Eli emerged with a grandfatherly smile. He reached for Liz and guided her to the examining room. There was something to be said about humans and communication—we could adapt and shift without directly acknowledging the unspoken. Since Liz had stopped talking, it had subconsciously inspired people to express and respond using nonverbal cues. It was a challenge to think more critically about expression and connection, and thoughtful intent, but there was something that bridged a gap when you shared a common language.

Liz patiently sat through the exam, following every command without hesitation. Eli took several vials of blood, carefully labeling each.

"Liz," he finally said, breaking the silence as his pen stopped in mid-stroke.

Her gaze rose from the vial she had been intently watching, to meet Eli eye to eye.

"Liz, we have yet to see a successful birth. We have heard of a couple of newborns surviving elsewhere, but since the virus hit, most babies don't live very long after they are born... We are working to understand why this is happening and how the nature of the virus seems to impact reproduction, but I can't be certain that will happen in time for your baby. There are risks with every pregnancy in normal circumstances, but there are even greater risks now." His bottom chin quivered, and I could sense his fear and apprehension—and his deep concern for Liz, who, to him, was family. *One big, happy family.* I was proud he had held steady thus far.

Liz took a deep breath, opened her knitting bag, and pulled out a small pair of handknitted booties. They were pink and tiny, one slightly bigger than the other. She smiled with all the confidence in the world.

I reached out my hand and placed it on Eli's shoulder. "So...we are adding a girl to the family?"

Liz's smile grew from ear to ear.

Eli caught my meaning. "Well, then, let's see if we can get this little girl to cooperate and allow us to hear that heartbeat." Eli reached for the small doppler.

The energy in the room shifted to that of hope and determination.

Eli didn't have to search long before the rapid *whoosh* of galloping horses erupted from the small speaker. For a split second, we were a grandfather, an aunt, and a new mom celebrating the excitement of a new life. The moment stopped time, and there was nothing in the room but the beating of that little heart.

***

Eli walked us toward the lobby. He had been staying at the hospital working in the lab most nights, and it was good to see him. *I miss him.*

As we neared the top of the stairs, I could hear the screams of the nursing staff. My pace quickened, and soon I was sprinting, leaving Liz and Eli behind. As I hit the bottom of the stairs, I could see the bodies below, two in scrubs lying out like starfish. Pale blue fabric had growing maroon stains spooling from the collars down to their chests, the pooling blood merging between the two forming a heart.

"You let her die!... You…you killed her! All of you! She was all I had left, and now I am going to take you all with me!" a panicked male voice boomed out across the lobby. The screams and moans were replaced by whimpers and muted cries. The security team had their guns drawn and pointed at a tall, disheveled man near the nurses' station. In his arms was a small frightened nurse, the blade of a rusty machete digging into her neck. Her toes were pointed, and her arches stretched as she pushed up to relieve some of the downward pressure. She clung to his arm, trying to hold the blade steady, her eyes pinched shut, the corners wet with tears.

I put my arms out and slowly walked away from the stairs and to the center, toward the nurses' station.

"I want to hear about what happened to her and how I can help," I said softly. My heart was racing, and I could feel the throbbing in my neck as my mouth grew completely dry. *Take another step.* "Why don't you just let her go and…" His eyes were lost somewhere else. And then, with a single, rapid, seamless motion—

"NO!" I reached out, lunging toward him, unable to stop him as he slit the woman's throat. The moment slowed as her throat slid down the blade and her body folded delicately to the floor, a feather floating gracefully through the air.

I felt a gentle tug from my waistband, and before I could turn, the loud *pop* of my gun erupted in my ear.

My eyes locked with his as I watched the bullet pierce his chest. His tall form stood still, then wobbled and dropped in a thunderous clatter beside the lifeless nurse. My ears ringing, I turned to see Liz still pointing my gun at the man who now lay lifeless on the floor. I reached across the barrel, still warm from being fired, and closed my hand around it. Without resistance, Liz released it. She gave me a nod, walked out the front door, and hopped in the shuttle, knitting bag in hand.

***

The ride back was a blur. The ringing in my ear was a welcome distraction and almost gone by the time we returned to Winter. The shuttle had barely stopped before I jumped out. I went straight for the cellar. Now called the Bat Cave. *My sanctuary.*

We had turned most of the space into an armory with a portion dedicated to training. I spent a lot of time below the stairs, mostly by myself at night when I couldn't sleep. Working out helped me to clear my head. During the day, a few of the security leaders and I trained together. *More like, I get my ass handed to me.*

The cool air hit me as soon as I began down the stairs. Before I even got to the bottom, I was lifting my shirt, revealing my sports bra. I could feel the anger and frustration bubbling up against the back of my tongue. *Why did he have to kill her?*

"Fuck saving the world!" I rushed the bag, kicking and punching with everything I had. I could feel the muted slap as each punch hit the bag, and the blood was rushing as I forcefully exhaled with each kick. The suspension chain began to rattle under the relentless attack.

"Why…did you…have to…kill her? You cowardly…weak son…of…a bitch!" I grunted and growled. "Why…did you…take her!" Each syllable was full of disdain. Rolling back in time, everything began to spill out, every crappy situation of the last months blurring together. "Why…did you…not come…back for us?!" *Why did you not come back for me?* My arms weakened, and the anger turned to sadness.

The bag bobbled, I was slow to respond, my guard dropped, and it punched back, sending me to the mat. Breathless, I lay flat on the mat, the cool surface feeling amazing against my sweaty back.

"Sounds like a hell of a day, *Ms.* Winter. Maybe you should crack open one of those bottles of wine. Wait…we both know how that ends. And I would hate to have to pick you up off the ground…again." His voice was a cocktail of sarcasm mixed with arrogance, and a touch of annoying, condescending wit.

"Fuck you, Hutch."

"Well, if you insist…" He smirked slyly and reached his hand out to help me up from the mat. I took it, only so he could see my overexaggerated eye roll. *Your wish.*

He was slightly unshaven, and there was something about his unkemptness that brought out the best in his features.

"What brings *you* to the Bat Cave?" I said with emphasis, to draw attention to the irritation at his presence in my voice.

"I will be gone in a few. We just got a few cases of ammo, and I wanted to…"

"Don't you have people for that?" He let a long pause build between us; my snarky-ness was not returned in the usual volley. No queen of the castle, serf, or glass tower jokes. He is not quite himself.

"Ya…uh…um…how are Liz…and the baby?" his voice stammered out.

"So…you heard." My defensive demeanor softened. He *was* here for a reason.

I stepped a little closer. "She is doing okay, Hutch, and so is the baby. Eli is keeping a close eye on them. We heard the heartbeat today."

He averted his eyes and fumbled with a small box of ammo. I could see he was trying to prevent me from seeing the tears build. I avoided going into detail about Eli's concerns—something told me he already knew. I stepped close and ducked a bit to catch his eye, then I reached out, touched his fumbling hand in a futile attempt to offer reassurance. His hand slowed then stopped; he lifted his head slightly, returning my gaze. His hands were warm and worn, rough. I held my hand against his for maybe longer than necessary as I felt the pull of gravity pulling my body toward him. He reciprocated. I could feel his flannel shirt brush up against the bare skin of my stomach. He was so close that we were sharing the same air space. The familiar smell of vanilla drew me in.

A flush crept up through my cheeks, and a tingly sensation built in my stomach. *Longing.*

He sensed my hesitation, closed his eyes to sever the connection. He brought his lips to my forehead, kissing it with tense force. I gasped slightly at the contact, as if I had been holding my breath. He pulled back, leaving me motionless and unsteady as he walked away.

He paused on the first step, and without looking or turning back, spoke. "Maybe *Tom* is not the man you think he is"—then he continued out of sight.

***

The flak jacket fit looser than how I was sure it was designed to fit, but it would have to do. My go-to pistol was positioned in the hip/thigh holster to make room for the rifle I needed to carry. Necessary accessories for this type of meeting. I pulled my dark hair up into a messy bun, far from the casual mom look I rocked in the board room most days. *Not as badass as Lara Croft, but still...*

The logistic team had made mention of a small band of children collected by a teenage girl somewhere near Shoreline Lake. Hutch had tried to get the girl to bring the children to Winter, but she'd refused. She traded with a few of the logistics guys to get some basic supplies, including Tylenol and triple-antibiotic ointment. He assumed one of them might need medical attention, but she was skeptical and gave him very little information, and nobody could blame her. Things had gotten pretty bad, and there were a lot of pretty sick people out there, willing to do pretty sick things.

I had been asked by the council to try to retrieve them.

The desperate hunger for the sound of growing children had taken over the camp, an instinct so primitive, the reassurance that our species would survive for generations. We needed something to symbolize that this was not the end of us all.

As a mom, my heart was flooded with panic, knowing what was out there and that these babies were in the middle of it. Many of the Free Nationalists had taken up positions around the harbor. They were not normal soldiers—many were militants, tyrants, looking to annihilate everything and everyone in their path, like hitting reset—including resetting society back to a savage, lawless state.

"Mom, are you going out with the team?" Asher's voice broke the silence and echoed off the stone walls of the makeshift armory. He had become accustomed to finding me here. He had grown so much; he was tall and thin like his father. *He looks so much like Tom.*

"Yes. There is a group of children we are hoping to reach before something bad happens to them." I laced up my boots, using crisscrossing patterns, a simple order.

"You have been going out a lot with the security team. Have you heard anything about Dad?" My fingers paused, and I could hear hope strangled by heartache in his voice.

Tom and Asher had been best friends, and Asher worshiped Tom's every move. I was always outnumbered by the 'three amigos.' Every waking moment had been about the boys since the moment they were born. Tom was the stay-at-home dad when they were newborns; he took the night shift with them. He lived and breathed his boys, and they loved him for it.

Tom worked from home often as they got older, and the boys' schedule was perfect for him. He always said he did his best work at night. He could work with our international counterparts in India and sleep when the boys were at school, and later be there to cheer them on at whatever activities they participated in after school. I managed everything else: the company, the family schedule, the routine. He was the chairman of fun and the ultimate dad.

I couldn't imagine what he must be going through without them. *Or me.*

"No, sweetheart, I have not heard anything more. But I will keep looking, I promise."

"I am going with you." He became impatient with me, like I was not doing enough.

"Asher, it is really dangerous out there, and I need you here to keep an eye on your brother."

"If it's so dangerous out there, then why are *you* going?"

"We are trying to help as many people as we can and make sure this community is taken care of, including you and your brother." I could sense his growing emotions begin to spill over their banks. My heartaches—I could feel his loss. Fifteen (and a half) and nearly an adult, and I couldn't explain all of this to him. I couldn't tell him to grieve his father, that I was not even sure he was alive, and it was not like a divorce, because there was no separation. There *was* no closure.

Tom couldn't be dead, and yet if he lived, I knew he would have come back to them. *Me.* If he could have.

"What!? So, you pick them over us?... Just leave *us* as orphans! Dad leaves us, and now you leave, too..." His voice had shifted, hand-picking each word to inflict the most damage possible.

"...How could you let him leave? What did you do to keep him from coming back?"

"Asher, your father did not leave us because he wanted to. He would never leave you boys. If he had a choice, he would come back, I know he would." I was blindsided. Lost as to how this started, I felt his anger, so raw and unprovoked. I find myself grasping at anything. How could I make this better?

"You...you're always telling him what to do. Telling everyone what to do. He wanted to get away from you!" His lower jaw quivered with desperation, looking for anyone to blame for why life had changed, for Tom's disappearance. I was jealous of his uncontrolled fury; I wanted to be angry, too. How good it would feel to let it all spill out, raw and uncalculated. This was not acceptable behavior by any stretch of the imagination, but maybe he was right. Maybe this *was* all my fault. I was sure I deserved this. And I had nothing else to say to fix this. So, I just let him go on. *Take the hit.*

"And now you are telling me what to do. I am old enough to take care of myself! It's not like you are around anyway, always down here or out with the security team. Dad was the one who took care of us."

"Asher..." What I needed to say escaped me, the right words flitting around in the stone room, out of my reach. There were no words that could defend me now—the daggers dug deeper, closer to the heart.

Final shot.

"I hate this place, and I hate you! I wish Dad was the one who had stayed with us at the hospital." *Me too.*

The flag of defeat inched up the pole, unfurling in the wind. My mind caught in the snap of the fabric tugging at the rivets, clacking against the metal pole. *I know, baby. I miss Daddy, too.*

***

My mind wandered through the abandoned vehicles and homes along I-280, imagining the oblivious people who had once owned them, visually exploring the corporate campuses that had been bustling businesses, thinking about our 'normal' life and how there was nothing left of it but grit and bones.

Normal life now packed an AR15 and a handgun, and wore a flak jacket. And I was a single mom failing miserably at raising teenage boys during the apocalypse.

I could feel the truck slow to a stop, and my rifle shifted slightly. The team started to clamor about, as mumbling voices collected on the outside of the trucks. I grabbed my backpack with a few wish-list items from the last negotiation, and a chocolate bar to entice her with gifts. I hoped my day took a turn for the better. I had been eaten alive by the last teenager and I could use a win.

We stopped in the parking lot of the Google headquarters, hoping someone nearby had seen the kids. Several diehard Googlers had stayed within the campus. Even with the degradation of the internet—almost catastrophic at this point—they continued to fight a war of their own. I was surprised the Free Nationalists had not set this place ablaze. *Unless they are on the same side.*

They had been feeding the children like feral kittens, bits and scraps, so that they almost did not even seem human. The last sighting had been over two days ago—and that was of just one of the younger ones.

We followed the lake toward the 101. Businesses had been picked through, left mostly in ruins. A system of trails snaked along the waterfront. The pools around the slough were green with algae, accompanied by the sour smell of decay. There were still a few bodies along the waterfront, just more waste no one felt obligated to dispose of. The temperature had begun to drop as we moved into fall; however, it was not yet cool enough to provide relief from the smell.

From the periphery, across the parking lot, I saw the curtain rustle at what looked to be an adult care facility. I casually signaled to the security leader to check it out. There were a few trucks parked out front, neither looked like they had been abandoned, and both looked worthy of investigating.

We broke into search teams. I took my place with the entry team. At the entrance, I lifted my rifle into ready position and followed the signal. The cool metal rested close to my cheek. The automatic door was slightly ajar, the putrid smell of death still hanging in the air. I snuggled close to my rifle to quickly replace the awful scent with the familiar smell of gunmetal. The slow crackle of heavy boots on broken glass and debris broke the silence of the empty lobby.

During the first outbreak, the elderly had been the first to go. Unfortunately, many of the care facilities could not keep up with disposal and let the bodies decompose where they lay. That could be the reason for the bodies by the slough. I imagined these ailing, fragile figures breaking free, looking for a quiet place to die in peace.

The leader signaled the lobby was clear. The sweep team branched off down one wing and we took the other.

We moved down the hall, sweeping each room as we went. *Body. Body. Empty. Body.*

The leader signaled to halt. I fell in at the rear. My hands began to sweat and my heart was pounding behind my ears. In the stillness, I could hear the muffled sound of a tiny voice. We advanced toward the sound.

Without warning, the sharp pop hit the side of my face from an open door. The soft tissue of my cheek crushed against the hard bones in my face. I stumbled, caught off-balance. I could feel a large arm wrap around my neck and squeeze. I pushed my chin down, forcing pressure on his forearm, then I jumped and grunted, trying to free myself. My rifle fell to the side as I reached for his arm to free myself. He scrambled to put pressure on the chokehold, arching his back, lifting me from the ground, pulling me into the room.

Gunfire erupted outside the room, and the sweep leader shouted orders to take cover and return fire.

I clawed and pried my hands between his arm and my throat. The light began to fade. *So easy to just fade away.*

With a quick shot, I dropped my fist to his groin. He loosened his grip just enough for me to take a reverse elbow shot to his sternum.

Without thinking or hesitation, my pistol was drawn, and I squeezed the trigger. The loud pop kicked back against my hand. The gunpowder smelled metallic. A direct hit to his stomach. A look of surprise washed over his face as he crumpled to his knees, clutching the growing red stain on his shirt, smearing it into streaks as he tried to stop the bleeding. My expression remained emotionless and callous.

I stepped to the doorway; the gunfire was done, and the sweep team had assembled in the hall.

There were four down, including one of ours.

"Ms. Winter, there are three in the room."

By the looks on their faces, I knew it was the children. I left my new friend gurgling on the floor, never looking back.

A young girl, maybe fifteen, was half dressed, gagged, and tied to the bed, her beautiful medium-brown skin exposed and covered in welts. My heart sank, as I saw Liz's face standing at the fountain in a T-shirt covered in blood. I wanted to throw up. And then the rage washed over me.

"She is a fucking baby! Get her untied and covered up!" I shouted without a specific direction.

As I turned, the team leader passed by me to cut her free, while two more terrified faces looked up from the corner. Their little hands were tied together. They might have been nine and ten, one boy and one girl, trembling and filthy.

I stomped out of the room and back to where I had dropped the guy. He was scooting across the floor on his stomach, his blood trail smeared behind him. With every ounce of energy I had, I kicked him in the face. He rolled to defend himself and looked directly up into the barrel of my pistol, my unforgiving face just beyond it.

"What the fuck is this? You are monsters!" Charged energy made it hard for me not to pull the trigger as I saw the bloodshot whites of his eyes.

"Look, I am just the broker." He shifted his arms up in defense.

"You broker children!?" The muscles in my jaw tightened as I clenched my teeth, unable to contain my disgust.

"We all do what we need to do—to survive." He stopped squirming and he began to stammer.

"Who do you work for?" I growled out.

"Anyone who will pay us. Destin's guys will take anything." His cavalier answers told me that what he did was not out of desperation. *Fucking scum.*

"Who is Destin?"

"This is pretty much his territory now, and whatever they want they get. I bet they will have a good time with you, sweetheart."

I could feel the cascade of tension pass down my arm, compressing my fingers as I pulled the trigger one last time.

I exited past the team. They did not move, no sound, no judgment. I squeezed back through the opening of the automatic doors, happy to feel the open air on my face. The sour smell of the slough was a welcome change compared to the confined smell of long-decomposed bodies. I was stumbling down the front walk to the row of trees at the edge of the parking lot. The retching was building behind my teeth. I grabbed the trunk, steadied myself, and the rough bark grated against my palms as I slid them down, no longer able to contain the contents of my stomach.

***

Cami, our collector of children, led us to an empty office building. Somehow, she had kept nine, including herself, alive, one as young as a year old. She told us she had found the baby in a car shortly after the outbreak. There was no one in the car, as if someone had just walked away. She had turned the breakroom into what looked like a daycare.

It didn't take much to convince her to move her small colony to Winter, with the promise that she could leave at any time.

As the team loaded up the children, I paid one last visit to the local vigilante cyberhackers left at Google.

M. LaVon

The War Around the Corner

I flung the door of the truck open and dropped my boots to the paved driveway of Winter, each step a command on its own.

"Get these kids to the infirmary, and call Sarah. They need to get checked out."

Liz came across the driveway and reached out toward me. My eye and the side of my face had begun to turn purple and black, and that, along with some scratches, made me look like hell. I was sure I smelled like vomit, too.

"I am fine, Liz, thank you. We have some new children to look after. Can you make sure they get fed? And have Sarah check Cami out—she was with some pretty bad guys." I paused long enough to ensure she knew what I meant. Turning away from her, I continued my tirade. "I need the security leaders in the house—now! And someone get me Hutch!?" I sent people scrambling, fully aware that I was barking orders and I didn't care. I had flown past nice hours ago.

***

Security Leader Briefing:

We are now officially in Free Nationalist territory. They are collecting all the assets and resources they can as they fight against the National Guard and US military forces. And they are not doing it peacefully. They are taking out the smaller communities and saving the bigger co-ops for themselves. We will see more people coming to our gates who have been pushed out, seeking refuge. It won't be long now before other supplies run out and the war will come for Winter. I want a full report regarding our defenses, vulnerabilities, and supplies by the end of the day. No one will breach our perimeter: Shoot first; ask questions later.

The full council will convene tonight.

If necessary, I will work with our logistics team to start negotiations.

***

Hutch swaggered in as the security team exited. Recognizing the sense of urgency, he paused at the door.

"Shut the door," I barked.

His natural arrogance faded as he took one look at my face and rushed over to me.

"What is going on? Holy shit, Cate! What happened to you?" I was caught off guard by his concern. Before I could pull back, he reached for my face. I sucked air between my teeth as I winced. And retreated behind the desk.

"Don't worry about it. I am not your problem." My voice was still terse and commanding.

Under his breath, I could hear, "…You *are* my biggest problem." His smirk was gone, and his defenses were up.

I scowled in response. "What do you mean by that?" My blood began to boil. I was angry, and I was looking for a fight. I couldn't help but instigate a war I knew I could win.

"Nothing, Cate." He crossed his arm, closing off.

"Do you have something you need to tell me, *Hutch*?" My question was dripping with accusation.

"What are you looking for, *Cate*?" Sensing the loaded question, he put up his defenses.

"You're not exactly a construction manager, are you?"

"Not exactly." His eyes narrowed as he glared down at me, completely annoyed.

"Then what are you?"

"Just a guy who makes connections."

"The guy from Google seems to think you make more than connections. He says he knew you from before, and you are the 'go-to guy'." I came back around, standing between him and the desk.

"What is your point, Cate?" His patience was gone and his irritation was obvious.

"You lied." He shifted to the other foot, his eyes downcast. He was completely annoyed with my allegation. And I didn't care.

"Look, I didn't lie about the logistics or construction. I was military logistics before, and when I got out, I started working construction. Well...I made some connections for some people..."

"You failed to mention you are an arms dealer!"

"Look, princess, you don't have a problem if I supply your little kingdom, but all of a sudden you've found your moral compass?!" He worked hard to strike every condescending chord possible.

"You have known all along what we are dealing with, and you didn't think to tell us? *Me?* The only reason *Destin* has not stormed in here is because you are supplying them with guns!? And God knows what else!"

"How do you think this works? People don't do stuff for free!... And I don't have to tell you anything. I am not one of your puppets, and I am not *Tom!* Save your domineering routine for him. Oh wait, that's right. He dropped your ass."

Maximum damage.

My turn to return fire. "What? Are you dealing in people, too? Did you have anything to do with the people who kidnapped Liz?" I could see the veins in his neck bulge out. The rage was tearing out. *That's right. Let the monster out. Come and get me.*

He moved forward, pressing hard against me with his chest pounding against mine. Forcing me to the edge of the desk. I held tight to him, my fists clenched and my body rigid, letting him know he did not intimidate me. Soaking in all his hatred. His skin was on fire, and every inch of him was solid like rock. He could crush me without even thinking about it. *Crush me.*

"Liz was taken because of your high-and-mighty, arrogant stunt, and she is only alive because of *ME!* They only let her live because of *ME!*" I knew he was right, and that I deserved everything he said. His words were molten lava bubbling out, annihilating everything in its path. "Destin can have you for all I give a shit. If it wasn't for Liz and the baby, I would let him burn your little *empire* to the ground. At one point, I thought you were worth fighting for, but you spend so much time worrying about fucking *Tom*, you're blind to what is right in front of you. I hope you get what you deserve, *Cate.*" *There it is, final shot.*

I held solid until he was out of the room. And then I fell to the floor. *You win, Hutch.*

***

Winter Council Meeting, Security Review, November 8, 2025

Current state (Cate Winter): The fighting continues. The United States government is still losing ground to the Free Nationalists. The constant cyberattacks on both the government systems and networks nationwide have crippled any chance for reparation. The West Coast is waging a cyberwar, and we appear to be deep in the war zone. On-the-ground fighting continues to be near government strongholds and valuable supply routes.

The southeast has suffered irrevocable damage, and the fall weather has brought several tropical storms and hurricanes into the Southern states, including nearly decimating Florida and parts of eastern Texas. Subsequent flooding carried disease, and with the lack of supplies and no national disaster response, there were a number of casualties as a result. From what we have heard, people migrated north, taxing what resources were left in those areas, causing even more widespread violence. The war for power has merged with the war to survive.

The population decline has been staggering. We lost approximately 38 percent to the virus alone. After the war, natural disasters, attrition through injury and disease, starvation, and the nonexistent birth rate, we estimate the numbers will grow to be closer to a 56 percent decrease of the US population by the end of the year. And this will continue to climb.

The greatest direct concern for the Winter community is protecting our resources and the health of our people. There is no assurance that we will remain safe here. Many of the communities around Winter have suffered significant losses, if they have not been completely eradicated by the Free Nationalists and associated parties. Those that are still standing are being strategically allowed to do so.

We have just learned that our current 'friendly' status has been dependent on ongoing negotiations and concessions between the Free Nationalist and our logistics team—this had been kept from the council at the discretion of the leader of the logistics team. I am sure the oversight was done with the best of intentions and out of caution. I, as I am sure the council, appreciates all the work the logistics team has done to ensure this relationship. However, we would like to review the stipulations of this agreement and establish a more transparent conversation going forward.

In the interim, we continue to increase our security and work with our neighbors to establish safe zones.

In other news, we were able to bring nine children from the outside to Winter. We will be working on their community placement after they have been screened by the medical team.

***

Hutch stood at the back of the room, his back to the door frame, looking down as he fiddled with a key. I couldn't help but watch him. Before I ended the report, he looked up, held my gaze, shook his head, and left.

***

Jared caught me as I exited the meeting. He was frantic and concerned and out of breath. "Cate, can we talk?" His voice was low, and he was acting hypercautious.

"Uh...sure, Jared, armory?" He shook his head. I raised my eyebrows and shot him a perplexed look. "Library?"

He started walking without confirmation.

We walked through the door of the library, and he took one last look down the hall, ensuring an all-clear. "Jared, why are you being so weird?" I was completely lost and caught off guard, again, apparently today's theme.

"Cate, I think we have a problem with the WMS network." He was practically whispering.

"What are you talking about?"

"You know how I have been monitoring the network traffic and activity at our data centers?"

I nodded to acknowledge my recollection.

"I was amazed that so many hospitals were able to consistently access the system despite what's been happening in many areas... Even our own hospital has experienced significant downtime. So, I dug around and pinged a few IP addresses, and some appear fully operational. And some have even increased their use of the data centers."

"So?"

"The IPs all appear to be based in Florida. Don't you think it's weird that there is practically no infrastructure left in Florida, but their *hospitals* are doing great?"

"Your point?"

"Cate, I don't think hospitals are the ones using the network—I think it is like a pseudo dark web." His look of 'duh' was slightly irritating.

"Who would have access or the ability to do that?"

"*I* don't even have that kind of access, and no one's been able to hack it. The person would have to have an intimate knowledge of the system and our infrastructure."

A nervous sensation washed over me, and I felt a little lightheaded.

"And Cate, there is something else."

"Oh geez, what?"

"Someone here has been able to access the network."

"I thought you said you weren't able to hack it?"

"We have not been able to hack it, but that doesn't mean someone else who knew what they were doing could not use it."

"Monitor every WMS employee account and figure out who is accessing the system."

***

The mornings were a lot colder now, and we had had a fair amount of rain. It left an earthy smell in the air. I welcomed the change of the seasons and enjoyed a morning jog around the estate. People began to stir, opening their windows for the day and heading out for chores as early as possible. So many were pulling double duty between sustainability and security. It still had a small-town feel, people waving and greeting each other. People sharing the morning news over a cup of tea.

I wove through the fields and down the alleyways, through the orchard and past the training units, and then made my way back to the house. A few people passed through the kitchen on to their morning tasks, and I was left alone briefly to fix a cup of coffee, a luxury reserved for mornings after those nights with little to no sleep. Yesterday had been a lot to digest.

Zavier came down and kissed me on the cheek. "Morning, Mom." Always the happy-go-lucky guy.

"Morning, sweetheart." He had also grown. He resembled my side of the family, for sure, the spitting image of his great-grandfather. Zavier was much shorter than his brother, with darker features.

"Is your brother awake yet?" The warm coffee was just what I needed to start the new day.

"He was up before me, might be down working out." My stomach dropped.

And then I dropped my coffee.

Like Father, Like Son

The pack was heavy and shifted uncomfortably on my back. The paper map was crumpled in my pocket. It should be a straight shot to San Francisco.

I knew it was him when I saw him hit the system. He had always said that no matter what, I could find him online. We used to play hide-and-seek online, but he could never hide from me for long. He had once hacked my school's network and sent me funny messages during computer class. I laughed so hard out loud that I had to say I'd sneezed.

He taught me the alphabet from lines of code. I would sit on his lap as he wrote line after line. The gentle clicks of the keyboard would send me to sleep, my head against his chest. When I got old enough, he would let me type out the string. It wasn't long before I was sitting beside him with my own computer, chasing him around the network, searching for Easter eggs.

I didn't know why he had not tried to directly contact me, but I didn't care. Soon enough I would be with him. He had probably gone to our house and couldn't find us.

Mom was going to be so mad when she woke up, but when I brought Dad back, she would be happy again.

The tree line was sparse and hard to use as cover. I skirted through neighborhoods where possible. It was eerie—there was hardly anyone on the streets. Abandoned cars and broken glass were everywhere. I saw a few people, but they just stared at me. Using the side streets was taking too long. I needed to make up time if I was going get to San Francisco by dark.

The rumble of trucks crunching through the broken glass and debris all over the road came up behind me, and I quickly ducked into a gas station. The store had been cleaned out. Broken containers and empty wrappers covered the striped concrete. The fridge was wide open, not one soda left. The looters had even taken the scratch tickets. I did find a pine-tree air freshener and a pack of gum. I tucked into a corner and waited them out. The newest wave of looters went through all the cars and sucked out every droplet of gas from each of the tanks at the station. I had eaten the whole pack of gum by the time they left, around 3 PM.

I had made it almost to the airport before the sun started going down, and there was NO WAY I was walking around this place after dark.

When we used to pick Mom up from the airport, Dad sometimes would take us to the ballpark to play catch while we waited. We would watch the planes land, and if we were really early to meet her flight, we would hit the ice cream shop down the road.

It was getting close to dusk now, though, and I was getting nervous. Most of the city was without power, and it was getting dark fast. The Crowne Plaza was the closest hotel to the ball field. I snuck through the empty lobby and quickly made my way to the stairwell. I pulled out my flashlight and jogged up the stairs two at a time for as high as I could go. After catching my breath, I searched my way through the hall. To my surprise I found an open room, a cleaning cart parked in front of the door. I slid in, did a quick search, and quietly closed the door, locking it behind me. I realized this was the first time I had stayed in a hotel by myself overnight.

The room window opened to the mostly dark city, the view stretching down the 101, facing the airport, and including a decent view of the water.

I pulled up a chair to the window and pulled out some of the food I had grabbed on the way out. The room was completely dark, except for the light of the rapidly disappearing dusk sky. The descending darkness made any lights easy to spot. It was super strange, but one runway was still lit.

Several vehicles moved down the 101, including several trucks. I could see a few buildings with their lights still on—they must be running on solar power. As soon as it was completely dark, three planes landed in a row on the lit runway. An hour passed, then three more. Several more large trucks moved down the 101, heading to the airport. I watched for a few hours, then finally crawled into bed. I could hear the planes land, and soon I fell asleep.

***

The sun broke through the window, and I kicked off the covers. I moved back to the window and grabbed a granola bar. The morning was quiet—no planes, no trucks, nothing.

I quickly packed up my gear, then slowly and quietly opened the door to the hallway. I cautiously made my way back down the stairwell and out through the main lobby. Like a ninja.

I considered making my way to the train tracks, hoping for more places to duck into along the way. I rounded the corner toward the parking lot and walked right into a group of scavengers.

Without losing a second, I turned and sprinted away.

"Hey you!" I heard them cry, but I was running with everything I had toward the water. I scaled the fence at the ball field and dashed across the street and down the trail. *Oh my God, they are fast.* In no time they were closing in on me. I darted back through the parking lot and briefly lost my traction on some loose gravel. I bit it, big-time. I scrambled to get up, and the chase was back on. They were within arm's reach. We tore back down a trail near the powerlines and out into a parking lot. And there the truck was waiting for me. I was surrounded.

"What'cha running from, kid?" A large, overweight guy was standing in front of the truck, his T-shirt far too tight. In his right hand he was holding some sort of knife. Another guy was just leaning against the grill.

"Come on, kid, why don't you come with us? We can give you a ride."

"You've got to be kidding me." Had I said that out loud? They circled me, but I went on. "Look, I am not sure what you want. You can have my pack, there is some food in it." I found myself not knowing where to look, as they were all around me.

"What are you doing out here alone? Don't you know this ain't no place for a kid," the sprinter chimed in. I should have pushed on through last night.

"Ya, I think you are right. I will just get out of your way." I tried to break the circle, sidestepping the group.

"Stupid kid." They were on me, grabbing at my backpack, ripping it off me. I pushed—shoved—whoever I could get my hands on. The big guy dropped the hammer, nailing me in the face and dropping me to the ground. I tucked into a ball. They kicked and punched me. I covered my face, but it didn't seem to work. One after another, after another. The gravel of the pavement was grinding me and turning my skin to hamburger with every shot. I could taste the blood and feel it dripping down my face. I was going to die on the roadside. I would never see my dad again. *I should have listened to my mother.* Big Papa dropped one good kick to the face and I saw stars. I thought I wore them out—or I was dead.

They took my pack, jumped in their truck, and were out.

Oww, my ribs—I could barely breathe. I tried to get to my feet but I stumbled back down. The blood was clouding my vision. I rolled up on all fours and pushed up to standing. I was pretty sure I was bleeding to death on the inside. I made it about fifteen feet out of the parking lot, tripped on a curb, and ended up lying partially in the road. I thought I would just rest there.

I was in and out, but the road didn't feel that bad.

A flicker and a face appeared. *Oh crap, not again.* He hoisted me up and threw me into the back of a truck. Well, at least I was not going to die on the side of the road.

***

The blue sky and soft, fluffy clouds melded with the haze of blood in my eyes and danced overhead, making shapes in my dreams, interrupted by the deep dark blackness. The muffled voices brought me back.

"I believe he is one of yours?" The truck shifted back into gear.

The canopy of familiar trees broke up the blue. Crap, Winter.

Like Mom

The guards at the gate buzzed the house. An unfamiliar truck pulled up, out climbed a tall man with dark features. He was young and handsome. He looked up, then nodded, acknowledging me. He stepped to the back of his truck.

"I believe he's one of yours?" I looked at him, confused, and stepped toward the truck.

"Oh my God, Asher!" I climbed into the truck.

"Hi, Mom." He was covered in blood, and he looked like he'd been in a bar fight and taken a couple of bottles to the face, but nothing critical.

"Get the medical team out here now!" Within seconds Sarah and a couple of nurses came rushing out, lifting Asher and whisking him away.

"Where did you find him, and how did you know to bring him here?" I could feel the tears begin to well.

"Airport, he had this on him." He handed me a printed map, with Winter marked as "home" and San Francisco as the "destination."

Liz came to the door, urging me inside. "I can't thank you enough for bringing him home. Liz, can you take care of…?"

"Kavik," he said.

I moved up the stairs. "Make sure he gets food and water for his trouble."

***

Asher was sitting up on the examining table, his shirt off. There were welts and scratches everywhere, but he was awake, talking through his fat lip.

"He is pretty beat up. I'm sure he has a broken rib and a mild concussion, but for the most part, he's just bruised and he has this cut over his eye. He did good protecting his major organs. He is lucky." The limited level of alarm in Sarah's voice calmed me. But then the mom-anger set in.

"Asher Thomas Winter, what were you thinking?! We have teams all over the area looking for you... You could have been killed... What were you planning to do? Just run off to San Francisco, join the Free Nationalists?!" My hands were flaying wildly, and I couldn't think of what to say next. Then the tears began to fall. I wanted to scoop him up in my arms and cradle him. What had happened to my baby? I felt panicky, I couldn't catch my breath, and it all just came out like a waterfall. My arms and legs began to tremble. Sarah swooped in with a chair. That was where I lost it all.

"I can't keep anything together—not my family, not this place!"

The sobs were painful, deep and jarring. Sarah backed away and let me implode, as I spiraled into my emotional breakdown.

"Do you think I wanted your dad to leave? Do you think I wanted any of this? Do you think I want to do this by myself? HE LEFT ME! He left me dying in a bed by myself. When I woke up, I woke up ALONE!... I am the one who was left to take care of you. I am the one still making sure bands of militants don't take you out to a field somewhere and beat you up and leave you for dead or worse!"

My livid tirade brought me to my feet. I was still crying like a crazy person. I could feel the presence of a crowd gathering, but I was past the point of caring.

"I don't sleep. I can't hold anything down. This world has gone fucking batshit crazy, taking children and women, and killing whoever is left. I am so angry all the time, and all I want to do is punch something! And SOME PEOPLE are dead-set on putting me in my place... Even Hutch thinks I am a control freak who was abandoned by your father... Yes, your dad 'DROPPED' my ass, but what you don't know, what you don't realize, is your dad... your dad... If it wasn't for me, your dad would have been serving time in a FEDERAL PRISON! I got him through college, I gave him a job that DID NOT INVOLVE HACKING THE GOVERNMENT. I bailed him out, I took care of everything. Your dad was on house arrest when you were born! And I am still the one covering for him."

I was *that* crazy person. Catching my breath, I sat back down.

"Asher, I loved your father, I still love your father. I knew who I married. But don't think for a second I have done nothing to keep this family together. Your dad needed ME."

"Mom." Zavier's small hand rested on my shoulder. Shit. I bowed my head. My thirteen-year-old was now the voice of reason. *A new low in parenting.*

"Let's go for a walk and let Asher get cleaned up. You guys can talk more later." Asher's eyes were as wide as saucers; he was shocked beyond words. I'd crushed him, Tom's hero image crumbling before us both. *I am so sorry, baby.*

Several people from the search team had gathered in the hall. They'd had the pleasure of front-row seats to my nervous breakdown. Mom of the year. *Carry on, nothing to see here.*

As I walked out of the infirmary and around the corner, there, perched nonchalantly against the wall, was Hutch. I clenched my teeth and narrowed my eyes. As usual, he was fiddling with his keys, his head slightly down, the messy wave of hair tousled down, shading his eyes. I paused, looked to him, my tear-soaked face red and blotchy, framed by my unwashed, disheveled hair. "Happy?" He slightly lifted his head so I could see his eyes. Zavier urged me on.

***

There was a chill in the room, and I avoided getting out of bed again. Tom's empty spot was dark and cold. Not that it had ever been warm when he was there; he spent most nights in his office typing away. He was so far from me that sleeping alone became normal. I stared at the pillow imagining he was there, much like I had done back when we were home. When he was there, we could talk all night—well, he didn't talk much, but what he did say was profound. He was brilliant and witty, always waiting for the right moment. There was no sense of arrogance about him; he was far from cocky. He was handsome and mysterious, easily disappearing in a room full of people. I understood everything about him. Or at least I thought I did. We could talk without talking. And when he looked deeply into my eyes, I could feel him in me. He was everything I was not, and I needed him to balance me. *I need him.*

I knew he was not coming back for me, but it hurt too much to let him go.

Liz snuck in and filled the void in Tom's spot. She reached over and wiped the tears away. She snuggled close, pulled me in, and stroked my hair, letting me cry it out until I fell back to sleep.

***

Asher's voice broke in, waking me. "Mom? Are you ever going to get out of bed?"

"What time is it?" I said from my groggy fog.

"Time to get out of bed— It has been two days, and it is around five o'clock." His response was full of sarcasm.

"Five in the morning? Or the afternoon?"

"Afternoon. And you need a shower. I brought you coffee, I think you need it."

"Okay, I am up."

"Mom?" He paused, his insecurity flooding out. "I'm sorry."

"No, Asher, *I* am sorry. I lost my cool. I was just so hurt that you would run off like that, and I was so scared. I don't want you to hate your dad. He loves you and your brother so much." I sat up against the pillows.

"I know. I went out there looking for Dad. I thought you would be happy if I brought him back."

"What made you think he was in San Francisco?"

"I have been following him online, tracking him. I have been watching the WMS network in case he accessed it. I saw his signature on a bit of code, and it pointed to a system in San Francisco."

"You hacked the system? How?"

"I know Dad's code. I have been writing it since I could handle a keyboard."

"How did you know it was him?"

"Dad's hacker alias is D3ST1NY."

Fuck. Just then it hit me.

Destin.

What to Expect

The soft yarn slid through my fingers, around and down the shiny knitting needle. The rhythmic *click* of the metal surface was steady and routine. The motion of the rocking chair moved in sync, soft waves keeping me going. My shoddy attempt to learn to knit a blanket had resulted in two different-sized booties, one hot pad, and a random scarf. When I showed the booties to Eli and Cate, I thought for sure they would laugh. In reality, their expressions were priceless, and I was dying on the inside. If we only had Pinterest. *1st row: Knit 75.*

I grabbed a pregnancy book from the library, assuming it had been Cate's. It now sat on my little nightstand. There was nothing in the book about what to expect when you survived a pandemic, were held captive by militants, and had been impregnated by a ruthless tyrant. Or how to prevent your baby from dying when the survival rate was dismal. But apparently, she was the size of a carrot. That reminded me to write to the author.

Adam insisted I move into one of the tiny homes. He said my blue tent would not be good for the baby. Not that he had any experience with babies, but it made sense. In an attempt to compromise, he painted the interior blue for me. It was a nice soft blue. I had a silent laugh, because it seemed ridiculous, dressing up a tiny house in a makeshift trailer park during the middle of the apocalypse, but I it seemed to make him feel better.

I was pretty sure these people had lost their ever-loving minds. It was like when I left, I had taken any sense they'd had with me. My internal playlist kicks on for a chorus of "I've Got a Lovely Bunch of Coconuts", the *Lion King* version, where Zazu is held captive.

If I had been gone any longer, Cate and Adam would have killed each other for sure. Well, Cate would have definitely killed Adam. He had an inherent talent for driving people to homicidal ideations, and I knew he was egging her on intentionally. He had it bad for her, he couldn't even keep his head on straight. I had been so close to telling him to take a cold shower before he hurt himself. And she was on the verge of major collapse or total annihilation, one of the two, and anyone in her wake was going to be sorry. I was surprised she had not hunted Tom down and ripped him to shreds already. *2nd row: Knit 8, Purl 3, Knit 5. Repeat.*

That guy had another think coming. What husband left his wife half dead in a hospital bed, no text, no hacked email, no ruthless band of pillaging mercenaries to deliver the news that he had ran off and joined the dark side.

After the incident with Asher, I wasn't sure she was going to come out of it. But now she seemed more determined than ever to build an army. I wasn't sure if it was to defend Winter or to take out Tom. It would be one hell of a show regardless. Me and you, peanut—front-row seats to the biggest War of the Roses ever. *3rd row: Knit 3, Purl 5, repeat.*

***

The gentle knock broke the silence and startled me. With both fuzzy slippers down, the rocking chair stopped. I laid my project to the side and shuffled across the floor. Slowly opening the door, I could see him. He was nervous and shifted back and forth, running his fingers through his shiny jet-black hair. Then he quickly put them back in his pockets, arching his shoulders in a partial shrug. Shy and timid, childlike, and handsome as hell. It was amazing how long one could stand in awkward silence.

I gave him a little smile to let him know him that coming by was cool. He gave a half smile in return. He took two steps back, and I swapped out my fuzzy slippers for more outdoor-appropriate footwear. We had gotten a bit more rain lately, and there was nothing more sad than wet fuzzy slippers. I grabbed one of Adam's old flannels off the hook by the door and followed him out.

We walked through Winter. We stopped by the stables and grabbed a couple pieces of fresh bread. The lady who lived two tiny homes down from me baked the bread in a brick oven behind the stables—simple bread with a little sea salt, but delicious. She brought it down to the stables to trade, but because I had my own 'bun in the oven,' she slipped me a few pieces when I came by.

The bread was still warm and smelled like hot stone. I liked to watch him eat it, his expression sated and kind of cute, each warm bite bringing a little smile.

We stopped by the training ground and watched Zavier and Asher spar. Since Asher had gotten his ass kicked, he had been training nonstop, and, like his mom, he was a quick study. It was no match; Asher had a good foot on Zavier. With one quick sweep, Asher dropped Zavier to the ground.

Asher spotted us and turned to say hello, and Zavier reached over and hooked Asher at the ankle, bringing him to the ground. Kavik almost choked on the last bite of bread in a fit of laughter.

They both sprang up and came to say hello.

"Kavik!" Asher welcomed him excitedly. "I am so glad to see you again. I still can't thank you enough. What's up? What brings you to Winter?" Without letting Kavik answer, Zavier jumped in. "Are you coming to work here? Where have you been staying?"

Kavik shrugged his shoulder, obviously overwhelmed by all the questions. "Um... I just came to say hi..."

"That's cool." Asher nodded in a dude-to-dude kind of way.

"Um, uh, I should be going, but maybe I can come again sometime." He reached up, sweeping his fingers through his hair. He looked to me, and I smiled. I would like that.

***

Adam must have heard that I had a visitor. He had been hovering over me like a watchdog. I had been really hurt when he'd first disappeared after I came home—he had never been good with emotional situations. But the overcompensation and the literal 'big brother' act was driving me crazy. I wished he would go stalk someone else, like Cate. He had brought me a cradle, which was nice, but oh my God, I needed him to give me some space. I knew he was just hanging around to see if Kavik would come back. It had been a few days, and I wasn't even sure if he was coming back.

I had finished knitting my first blanket. Not exactly square, it was a weird green color, and not as pretty as the one I'd brought home, but at least when I looked at it, I got a good laugh. I hoped my daughter would have a good sense of humor.

My baby bump was coming along nicely. I thought I could feel her flutter around, but maybe it was just gas.

My thoughts were interrupted by a gentle knock on the door. I jumped up. I could feel a new feeling, maybe giddiness mixed with nervousness. I opened the door with a big smile. Ugh—it was just Cate. Sad face.

Reading the shift in my expression, she stepped inside. "Uh, what is that all about? Expecting someone else? You seem disappointed to see me." She gave me a sly smirk. I rolled my eyes in return.

"Sorry, I am not a handsome young man… Yes, I heard. You are all the gossip. And more importantly, it is driving your brother nuts. And I am loving every minute of it!" She gave me a wink and a sarcastic giggle. I smacked her in the shoulder and smiled back. I was blushing.

She gave an overexaggerated "Ouch!" followed by a dramatic wince.

"In other news, Eli says today is the day for an ultrasound!" We hugged in shared excitement.

"He brought it here, um…after the last time… So, yay! lucky for us!" I gave her a look like, 'What? He doesn't want me to kill anyone at the hospital again?' And closed with a 'whatever' shrug.

"Eek… I am so excited." She was like a proud aunt, and it made me smile. Cate was far from a ray of sunshine most days.

With a silent giggle, I showed Cate my finished blanket. She put a hooked finger to her chin and cocked her head to the side as if trying to figure out what it was or what to say. In a failed attempt to contain herself, she blurted out a slight laugh and snorted. She *snorted!* I couldn't help myself, and an out-loud laugh jumped out. It startled us both, and then we were both laughing loudly.

Through her laughter, she stammered, "You know, if the baby poops on it, at least it will be the same color." She was crying from laughing so hard. I was, too.

Just two giggly girls again.

***

Eli was in his usual lab coat, distinguished and scholarly. He was very silver-fox *GQ* in a nerdy kind of way. I wished I could have met his partner, Christopher. Cate had told me so many stories about them, like storybook uncles. Christopher was apparently hilarious, an eccentric artist type. I would have loved him. It would have been such a contrast to Eli's Southern, conservative nature; they must have been one amazing duo. All the same, Eli was like a father to me, and I loved him.

I ran and gave him a big hug.

He chuckled, hugging me back. "Cate must have told you we'd try to do another ultrasound today." I nodded anxiously.

"Well, let's start with the basic exam. And I would prefer it if your heart rate and blood pressure were not through the roof." He gave me a mock-scolding, trying to get me to calm down.

Eli checked me over from head to toe. As he'd expected, I was right on track.

He flipped on the machine and dimmed the lights. The screen cast a gray-blue light against Eli's features. He placed lubrication on the probe and positioned it on my baby bump. Cate was at my shoulder, and I could almost feel her energy, her fingers intertwined with mine. Eli wiggled the wand about, and the pixels formed into little shapes. And there she was—he held the probe steady and we took in her little face. Her little button nose was perfect.

Eli systematically measured each appendage, her head, her body; he checked her blood flow, her heart, her brain. She was amazing—and perfect. And she was a girl.

I was glowing. We were all glowing.

The lights went back on and Eli took some more blood, his research continuing. As the blood filled the vial, I could see his gears turning, the weight of the world on his shoulder.

Before I left, I hugged him one more time. His familiar, warm, and welcoming arms encircled me. I knew he needed her to survive as much as I did.

Back in my tiny house, I crawled into bed, the soft blue walls around me comforting. My hands gently stroked my stomach. My voice came out in a whisper, "Sonia, sweet girl, you are strong. You will make it."

***

Orange spiced tea was the perfect way to start a fall morning, and it was just right to enjoy during a slow stroll through the stables before I helped out with crop care in the high tunnels. People were setting up their trade tables filled with dried herbs, warm bread, eggs, handmade crafts both personal and unique, canned sauces, and signature dishes packaged with care. At the end of the day, the tables would be replaced by entertainment, music, games, and people telling stories. I wondered if Adam could find me one of those baby wraps so I can take Sonia with me wherever I went and she could enjoy mornings like these, too.

Speak of the devil, there was Adam—like I was not going to notice him stalking me. He was resting against a wall of one of the stalls. I walked straight over to him, my expression less than enthused by his stalkerish behavior.

"What!? I was just checking up on you."

I crossed my arms in feigned annoyance.

"What? Okay, okay... Go about your business. I just want to meet the guy."

I rolled my eyes.

"Does he know about the baby?"

Ugh. I looked down at my shoes.

"Didn't think so. You want me to tell him?" *Yes, I want to give you license to terrorize this poor guy.* I shook my head in an adamant 'no.'

And playfully pushed him.

"Fine." He smirked and sauntered off, letting me go about my work in the high tunnel.

The work in the high tunnel was simple, mindless, and repetitive. We used the main crops to feed the community, and some people had started growing specialty items in what looked like a pea patch. I had never even grown a house plant before, but I thought I liked farming.

The hokey chorus of "Now I'm a Farmer" by the Who turned my stubborn focused pursed lips into a slight smirk.

***

The afternoon burned off the chill, and it was a perfect day to sit and watch the security units train. Like a lounging lizard, I laid out on the rock wall in front of the estate, letting the sun wash over me. Eli had me on a pretty strict schedule: light work, eat, rest, light work, eat, rest. Repeat.

A familiar pickup truck pulled around the fountain and came to a slow stop. Kavik hopped out. He sent me a nervous smile as he strolled over, stopping short of the wall. He was wearing a tight T-shirt with a faded album cover on it—a guy who liked music. I couldn't help but stare. His hotness was very distracting—I had no control over my hormones, and I could feel myself blush.

"Hey. Uh. Hi," he stuttered out. I smiled and slid off the wall.

I felt jittery and nervous.

"You... You want to go for a walk?" I smiled again and nodded. My dorkiness was so embarrassing. I couldn't keep my cool.

Before I could make a complete ass out of myself, Adam came bounding over. OH MY GOD. He seriously had issues. I was slightly annoyed but grateful.

"Hey, you two. Liz, I am so glad I had a chance to catch you! I wanted to go over a few things with you." I glared at him hard enough to burn a hole through his face.

"Oh hi, who's this?" He acted fake surprised, looking at me and holding his hand out to Kavik for a handshake.

"Uh hi, Kavik." He was squirming but mustered a firm shake of the hand in response.

"Oh...Kavik, the hero who saved Asher? So great to meet you! I am Adam, but everyone calls me Hutch. I'm Liz's big brother."

"Hi." Awkward silence. Adam put his hands on his hips, slightly sticking out his chest in a Superman pose. Oh, brother.

"So, what brings you back to Winter?"

"Um, I came to say hi. Liz was really nice to me the other day..." He trailed off, obviously not sure what else to say, looking over at me confused. I returned his look with an odd side smile.

"Well, let me take you around the property and introduce you to some folks. Liz, you don't mind, do you? We will be back in a bit. Com'on, Kavik." Adam slapped him on the shoulder.

"Uh. Okay." They took a couple of steps, Adam already transforming into Hutch. Kavik looked back and I mouthed, 'Sorry.'

I camped out on the front steps of the house. Kavik's truck was still out front. Cate plopped down beside me. "Your brother got to Kavik?" She tucked her knees to her chest, crossed her arms over the tops of her knees, and rested her chin on her forearms.

"Yep," I squeaked out, my facial expression full of anxiety. Cate reached her arm around me, pulling me close. "It is good to hear your voice again." And we sat in silence.

After about an hour, they came from across the drive. "Um, it was good seeing you, Liz, um, uh… Have a good night." Kavik hopped in his truck and pulled out.

My eyes narrowed as I stared down *Hutch*.

"What?!" His arrogance bubbled out like a natural spring, and he shrugged his shoulders like he had no idea why I was upset.

I stood up, crossed my arms, and stomped into the house.

Cate came up behind me. "Now you've done it," she said to Hutch and followed me into the house.

"What?!" he said again as we disappeared past the oak entry.

***

The air in the high tunnels was warm and humid. The rows of mixed crops had sprung up from the soil, the vivid green foliage speckled with a burst of brightly colored vegetables. I harvested what was ready and groomed what was needed.

"Hi." Kavik's voice interrupted the rhythm. To my surprise he had come back. I greeted him with a warm smile.

"I have something for you. Can you come?"

I shot him a perplexed look, but I stood and followed him.

We walked silently from the fields to my home. On my front steps, I saw five bulging bags. I looked to Kavik. His hands were in his pockets, and he seemed nervous. When I walked over to the bags, I could see yarn spilling out, in every color and texture imaginable.

"Hutch said you like to knit. There is a craft store by my place. It has been pretty picked through, but I found some stuff in the back. I didn't know what color you would like or what kind of yarn you use, so I just grabbed a bunch. There are some other needles and stuff there, too." This was the most he had ever said to me since we'd met. My mouth agape in surprise, I could feel the tears collecting in my bottom eyelids.

"Um, if you don't like it..." His nervousness morphed to an apology. He reached for the bags, scrambling to right the situation. I reached out and touched his arm. It was firm and flexed, and he stopped and lifted his head. "Thank you," I said with the utmost sincerity.

"I have to go..." he said, softly retreating. A sudden feeling of disappointment washed over me. He turned. "But can I come back tomorrow?"

"I would like that." We both smiled.

***

The tail of the long blue scarf draped against my legs, the end tassels softly sweeping the floor as the chair rocked back and forth. I was focused on adding the last few touches to the opposite end. The air had a sharpness to it these days, and I thought he would appreciate the sentiment. My head was adrift—I was daydreaming, lost in the sweet moments we had shared over the last few weeks. Each day he pulled me further away from the current of the deep blue sea.

"Sonia, sweet baby girl, I think it is time we talk about you."

Tonight was the community Christmas festival. Winter was alive with energy. There were even cookies. It was like taking a step back in time—the people had banded together to decorate and prepare a special meal. We had a choir and a band; they had all been practicing festive selections.

Last tassel.

"What do you think? I think it's my best yet." My voice was still strange to me, a reminder of who I used to be. I was working to get used to it again. I had so much I wanted to tell and teach Sonia.

***

A familiar knock on the door brought me to my feet. The wooden door swung forward, revealing him standing on my steps, the soft light of the interior casting a warm hue on his face. The makeshift alley behind him was full of activity, friendly faces passing by. He was handsome in his best work jeans and a slightly oversized dress shirt I am sure he scavenged from somewhere. He was carrying a small package.

In his usually apprehensive way, he passed me the gift. In return, I passed the blue scarf to him. His expression transformed from anxiousness to admiration. He quickly wrapped the scarf around his neck, bunching the fabric into gentle blue waves.

He nodded to me, signaling that it was my turn. I opened the small box, exposing a set of brightly colored toy keys.

"When I saw the cradle… I just figured…and my girls loved those." The sadness washed over him, and he looked away, his face showing the deep anguish only a parent could bear after losing their children. "I am sure she will love them, too."

Whoville

The smell of roasted nuts and cinnamon carried through the air, pulling us forward by the nose. The promise of hot cocoa was almost irresistible. My boys were on either side of me as we made our way from the house to the stables. They were nearly grown, and I felt the urge to pull them back and stop time, but I knew it was futile. Asher, a few months from sixteen, towered over me. I was positive he would be over six feet tall when he finished growing. I looked up to find he had decided to grow a mustache, and I wondered if it had anything to do with a certain young lady who was new to Winter, and about his age. Zavier, on the other hand, was thick and average height. I was grateful he still had his sweet baby face.

"Go ahead, you two." I gave them the green light to go find their friends.

"Thanks, Mom!" they said in unison, giving me a peck on either cheek.

I walked the rest of the way alone. The lights were mesmerizing, twinkling with a newly found purpose. Someone had cleverly decorated a couple of the pines near the stables like Christmas trees. So many people had gathered between the stable and the barn, many holding candles with round paper disks at the bottom. I walked around the back of the crowd, observing and enjoying the moment.

My grandmother loved Christmas; she always made a big deal over the holidays. She would say, 'There is nothing more powerful than the spirit of the season. It inspires people to give of themselves and think of others. *And open their pocketbooks wider.*' She would then give a wink. She had no problem putting Winter at the center. For Cici, it was about maximum impact. She had hosted so many charity events, big parties supporting whatever meant the most to her. She raised millions.

This was a perfect way to honor her memory and that tradition. *Miss you, Cici.*

Eli stepped to the front of the barn. His usual lab coat had been replaced by a Christmas-inspired sweater.

The crowd hushed in a massive wave. His deep Southern voice carried over the crowd.

"I have come to Winter every year for as long as I can remember, even before the events of late. I found comfort, friendship, and even the love of my life here. Cecilia Winter, our town's namesake, was my best friend, and she would bring everyone together to celebrate the season. I hope she is looking down today and is as proud as I am of the community we have built. This is our day to celebrate—it is our day to give thanks. You all have worked hard to overcome tragedy, to ensure our resilience, to secure our future, and I am thankful to serve every day beside each and every one of you. 'Glory to God in the highest heaven, and on earth peace to those on whom his favor rests.' That's from Luke 2:14. Wishing all of you many blessings and a merry Christmas."

With a flick of the switch, a star on the front of the barn lit up, the soft yellow bulbs inspiring the crowd to join in "We Wish You a Merry Christmas." Song after song we sang, and collective joyous laughter and merriment filled the air. *Straight out of a Hallmark movie.*

I found my way through the stable, caught up in the taste of hot cocoa, savoring the slightly bitter chocolate and sweet milk. I weaved back through the makeshift alleys, the sound of the caroling fading to the background, the radiance of the Christmas lights glowing behind me, making everything in front of me seem dark as I worked my way back to the house—the dividing line between good and evil, light and dark, happiness and despair.

A familiar dark figure was perched on the steps. I didn't acknowledge him as I ascended past him.

"Hey."

I stopped. "What do you want, Hutch?" My eyes locked forward as I spoke, my words infused with disappointment.

"Cate...don't." His hand reached out and grabbed my wrist.

"Don't what, Hutch? What do you want from me?"

"Just don't." He let go of my wrist.

"Don't *what*?" My agitation was building.

"Hate me." He took one step up backward to force me to look at him.

"Ha, I think the feeling is mutual." I crossed my arms.

"Come on, you know that's not true," he whined out.

"Every opportunity you have, you find a new way to tell me how much you hate me. You exhaust me," I said, exasperated.

"I never said I hated you. You're just…well, a lot to deal with—and kind of a bitch." It was too dark for him to see me roll my eyes, but I did it anyway.

"Oh, for fuck's sake. Thanks, Hutch, you have a way of making a person feel special. It's Christmas, so can we save your bullshit for tomorrow?" I moved up the stairs. He sprung up and caught me before the threshold.

"Wait, that is not…not…how…er…that is not what I meant. And you know it." Looking down at me, he put himself between the door and me. He reached his arm across, bracing against the frame, keeping me from entering. I paused.

"Cate, you are…"

I didn't want to hear it, not now. "Please, Hutch, I am tired." I pushed my chest against his arm in an effort to move past. His arm buckled slightly, and he released the frame, grasping my shoulder in an almost embrace. I avoided eye contact. The anxiety built, and my heart was racing. His arms around me sent butterflies wild in my stomach. He gently turned me to face him. He took a step toward me, resting me against the polished oak frame, bringing himself closer, his chest aligned to mine. I couldn't help but look up.

His breath caught, and I could feel his heart pounding in his chest, his body trembling, so tense, as if at any moment we would explode, ripping each other to pieces.

He brought his lips to mine, soft at first, and then with force. I reciprocated. His energy electric, I caught fire. I took in every second, every mean and hurtful thing he had ever said, and I gave it back, pushing my lips hard against his. *I want so much more.*

I pulled away and pushed out of his arms and into the house. He stayed in place, still braced by the solid oak.

"Cate." His head was down, and he didn't look at me.

I couldn't look at him, either.

"I don't need any more criminal masterminds in my life." I stood and held that in my mouth, tasting every hateful word, regretting every dagger as they took aim and rushed toward him. And then I disappeared into the darkness.

All lies.

***

The breach alarm sounded, sending me flying out of bed. I quickly slipped the flak jacket over my sports-bra-tank-combo and yoga pants, grabbed my pistol from the nightstand and the assault rifle from by my door. Then I moved to wake Asher and Zavier.

"Asher, make sure all the kids get to the armory. Zavier, you know the drill, get the kids settled. Neither of you open the door until you hear 'A to Z'."

"Mom, we're good," Asher said in a man's voice. *When did that happen?*

The security units were already responding. I could hear the distant sounds of gunfire coming from multiple locations. The command team assembled in front of the main house.

"Someone tell me what is going on!" I shouted.

"We have several breaches in the co-ops," Kevin chimed in.

"Tell me something I don't know," I growled.

"It is an organized assault. These are not scavengers," he elaborated.

"Detailed status?" I commanded.

The unit commander spoke up. "They are on the outskirts of the co-ops. We have lost several team members, but we have held them back. On the south end we are funneling them to the lower ground, so we can take the advantage as they progress."

"I want them out! Send in the incendiary team. Show them we are not playing. Make it happen." The commander relayed the order. Explosions could be heard in in the breach zones.

Within minutes a commotion at the gate had caught my attention. Gunfire broke out.

"They are pushing through the main gate! Defensive positions!" Kevin shouted.

Waves of security teams scrambled into position along the driveway. The sound of trucks rumbled closer.

The loudspeaker crackled, "Cease fire, cease fire, this is a peaceful occupation. Cease fire, cease fire, this is a peaceful occupation. Additional resistance will result in further loss of life."

"Hold your fire! Remain in defensive positions!" I commanded.

"How did they get to the main gate without us knowing? I want all unnecessary personnel to find safe cover. Kevin, if they get aggressive, give the order to light them up."

Kevin relayed the instructions. The convoy pulled down the driveway and lined the loop.

A man jumped out and looked to Kevin. "Are you in command?" Kevin held steady.

"I am," I said intentionally loud and came down the stairs into view. *Of course, he would assume the one in command is a man.*

Several team members followed suit, jumping from the trucks and taking counter-defensive positions.

The man returned to the vehicle and opened the door, obviously, their commander's lacky.

The man put one foot out, and then the second, still shielded by the door of the vehicle.

But once he stood, I knew instantly—tall, thin, familiar.

Tom.

***

His eyes were cast down as he fidgeted with his hat. He was dressed in all-black, pseudo-military gear. *My supervillain husband returns.*

"You've come to serve me papers? Or to murder, rape, and pillage?" I said with true disdain.

He moved toward the steps as if he were welcoming himself home. "Hi, Cat, I thought you would be happy to see me, but I see you have not lost your charm. It is good to see you are well. I like what you have done with the place."

"What are you doing here, Tom?" I had thought I would feel differently in this moment, all heartbroken and sad, but the black hole of anger sucked any weakness away, suppressing it deep within the void.

"We need to talk, Cat. Can we go inside?" He lowered his voice so just I could hear it.

"Call off your assault teams."

He complied. With a flick of his finger, he gestured to his guy and he radioed the men to fall back.

We walked through the foyer and into the library. His presence brought a chill to the room.

"What are you doing here, Tom?" I asked again, stepping behind Cici's desk, hoping for her strength—and maybe a defensive position.

"Cat, you need to understand what is going on here."

"I understand perfectly, you fucked-up— Again, Tom. You left your children and your wife. You are a murderer, a rapist, and a terrorist, and you are singlehandedly destroying everything in your path. Not to mention starting a cyberwar. Am I missing something?"

"Cat." His voice was mildly condescending.

"Don't fucking call me that. We are beyond pet names." My jaw was throbbing with tension.

"Listen, this is bigger than us, and I had to make a choice." His voice was low.

"You chose to abandon your family—to wage a war?"

"The government knew about the virus and could have done something, but it suppressed the information, letting millions die. They let you and the boys almost die. They even had plans to target areas to spread the disease."

"Your family didn't die, Tom. You can't even pretend this is revenge—and the government didn't make this virus. It evolved."

"Yes, but they could have prevented all of this. The demands were clear: Come clean and establish a new government or go to war. We have allowed businesses to destroy the planet, and we are paying for it now with mass extinction of our species. Corporations had their hands in everything, hiding the truth from everyone and lying to avoid liability. It is time someone held them accountable!" Now he was barking at me.

"Two wrongs don't make a right, Tom. The few who survived are now dying in *your* stupid war and at the hands of *your* militia." I matched his bark.

"All wars have casualties, but it is for the greater good. Those who deserve to live will survive." The shallowness in his voice was cold and soulless.

"'Greater good'? There will be no one left by the time you're done. Your son was almost killed a few weeks ago when he went out looking for you. My friend Liz was held captive, raped, and tortured for over a month. People are kidnapping children and selling them. How are you okay with that? How can you expect me to be okay with that?"

"Don't be on the wrong side of this. You will regret it." His temper was not so contained.

"Is that a threat?" I scowled, furrowing my brow.

He hesitated, then turned around and walks out. I was on his heels. *Don't you dare walk away from me.*

He stopped at the top step, looking forward. "This property is being seized to support the Free Nationalists—"

I cut in before he could finish. "You've forgotten yourself, Tom, and you have obviously forgotten who I am. Winter is mine. You and your people will not set foot on this property again."

His eyes narrowed as he turned to face me. And then his sarcastic smirk returned.

"Disobedience will not be tolerated. Those who oppose will be detained and executed." In a sick way, he appeared to love the idea of punishing me.

"Really?! I should have let them lock you up. I got you your freedom, Tom. If it wasn't for me, you would have nothing. Your threats mean nothing to me. I know who *you* really are. And you sure the hell are not taking Winter away from me."

Quick as a lightning strike, the sharp smack of his backhand caught me by surprise, and I could feel the instant swelling from his knuckles across my cheekbone. Without hesitation, I pulled my pistol from my waistband and pointed it at his forehead, dead-center. Without looking I could feel Hutch to my right and the entire convoy, guns drawn at me.

"Try me, Tom."

Tom opened his palm, trying to settle his men.

With a sardonic chuckle, he said, "New lapdog? Hutch, is it? Playing both sides, I see. That can be dangerous. Just between us guys, she likes it rough." His smile grew from ear to ear. This was a game to him.

Two can play at this game. I showed him an ear-to-ear grin in return. "Let's put it this way, *Tom Destin*. I have my finger on the self-destruct button for your precious network. If you don't think I have access to everything you transmit using the WMS system, you are sadly mistaken. We have been watching your every move, 'Destiny.' Each data center is booby-trapped. A flip of a switch, and they are gone. And I would be happy to grant your friends in the government access to the system to know every last detail of your master plan, troop movements, what's happening in Florida, and so on. I thought it was interesting, and I am sure they will, too. You may have noticed a bit of lag when we were creating backups… You can have one or the other, your choice. Your cyber empire or our simple farm."

Out of the darkness, two faces appeared.

"Daddy?" Asher's voice was confused.

"Mom? Why are you pointing a gun at Dad?" Zavier was concerned.

"I was just showing him my gun. Dad just came by to wish you both a merry Christmas, isn't that nice? But he has to go now, right, Tom?"

"Yes, boys, I will see you both real soon. I just have to take care of some things, and then we will be back for you and Winter. Love you two." Tom signaled his team to roll out. "I will see you again, Cat. Oh, and be careful out there, things have gotten really dangerous. I would hate for something to happen to you or someone you love." The convoy pulled out, and I holstered my weapon.

***

"Oh my God, you are so hot when you go all badass." Hutch spoke under his breath, trying to lighten the mood.

"Bad timing, Hutch," I said, exhausted.

"Do you really have all that stuff on the Free Nationalists?" he asked, sensing my bluff.

"Nope. We are pretty much screwed." *He is going to annihilate us.* "Can someone get me Jared?"

No Precious Gift

Behold, children are a heritage from the Lord, the fruit of the womb a reward.—Psalm 127:3 (KJV)

Another birth with a fruitless delivery; Christmas brought no miracles. I was grateful I was able to make it back to the hospital in time to deliver yet another newborn into God's gracious hands.

There was no predicting God's will. He gave and He took away. I had seen only two live births, only to watch the infants fail to thrive.

We had not been able to determine the distinction between full (permanent) or partial immunity to the virus. We had tested several parents whom we assumed to be immune; they had survived the first exposure, and both had no symptoms, both had antibodies present and were able to conceive, but the pregnancy would still terminate shortly before full viability, producing a still birth.

The virus must alter the blood group in some way, leading to SFTS secondary disease of the newborn (SFTS-NB).

Upon further necropsy examination, we discovered the fetuses carried limited antibodies when tested and they were anemic. They appeared pallid, but were mostly normal upon external examination. There was moderate edema within the internal organs. Their hearts were enlarged, and the lungs were underdeveloped. Fetuses who reached gestation were unable to breathe on their own and died shortly after birth, even with intervention.

There was some sort of undefined incompatibility between the mother and the fetus, an antigen-antibody incompatibility, causing the production of maternal antibodies passing through the placenta affecting the newborn. I just needed to find a compatible pair, a compatible mother and child to compare and synthesize the antibodies.

At twenty-one weeks, Liz's baby showed no signs or abnormal measurements of the internal organs, and the heart and lungs appeared normal. In the fetuses who made it to a live birth, the edema and heart and lung abnormalities began to present shortly after twenty-eight weeks. It was in God's hands.

***

The sound of flash grenades was deafening, startling me from my lab chair. Additional explosives shook the equipment from my desk, sending me to the ground. The smoke wafted through the lab, making it hard to catch my breath, the toxic haze choking me. My ears were ringing, causing my head to spin. My disorientation made it hard to get to my feet. They were on me, dragging me from the lab, descending the stairs, the lobby floor below a sea of bodies. Blue scrubs were swimming in pools of red. My captors were a black mob of tactical gear.

They dragged me out the front, stepping over the security detail, into the parking lot to an awaiting van. The sun had set. They shoved me in the van, slamming the doors behind me. I knew it was only a matter of time before they took over the hospital. I could never have imagined how it would be taken. I could not have imagined this.

The van's motion and the effects of the smoke turned my stomach. My head was throbbing and my ears ached. I moved to the side to try to steady myself; having no window or light was disorienting.

It was not long before the van came to a jarring halt, flinging me forward. The driver and passenger doors alternated shutting. Muffled voices came closer to the back door. I huddled in the corner of the back seat defensively. The doors were flung open, and two soldiers climbed in and pulled me out of the corner, slamming me face-first to the ground. One was behind my back with his knee to the center of my spine, wrenching my arms behind me.

"This is not necessary. I am not resisting." Every black man's story.

"Shut up, old man!" A fist met the back of my head, bouncing it off the metal of the van's floor. Flashes of light sparked in my vision. The two lifted me under the shoulders, dragging me to my feet, moving me out of the van. I was at the docks.

"What do you want with me? I am of no value to you." My throat was dry and sore.

"You're nothing to me, old man. I would have killed you like the rest of 'em," one of them mutters while we progressed toward a waiting boat.

"Don't mess around or I will throw you over."

The white and red emblem of the Coast Guard patrol boat was unmistakable. They took me belowdecks and secured me for the short trip across San Francisco Bay. I had very little time to speculate their purpose before the boat arrived at its destination, Alameda Island.

***

The room was dark and vast. I was assuming it was part of the old airfield or maybe a maintenance facility. The chains and shackles used to secure me to the chair rattled and echoed against the metal sheeting.

My friends were back.

"What makes you so special? Another black man who thinks they're somethin'. Not sure what the boss wants with you... I think you're nothin'." With that, his fist made first contact across my cheek, dropping me off the chair. "You think because you're some kinda doctor, you're better than us?" A quick kick to the face scooted me back. I clambered back to the chair, pulling my chained hands to the seat, trying to get to my feet. I didn't want to go out lying on the ground like an animal. There was nothing I could say or do to stop this. Resist or not, the beating wouldn't stop. Racial hatred ran so deep.

"Stay down!" The fist was like a steel rod to my ribs, forcing the air out of my lungs in a harsh cough. I imagined my father on the roadside in the deep South; he had done nothing to those men. There was no greater crime than being a black man in a white world.

The closing shot to my temple sent me back down to the ground. I could see Christopher's happy face waiting for me. I was okay with going to be with him. *Lord, I am at peace. Bring me home.*

***

I woke with my face still pressed against the chilled concrete. I could feel the facial fractures; my mandible was swollen, and there was dental instability at my gumline. My breathing was labored, and painful, perhaps internal bleeding was causing a pleural effusion. I would monitor for signs of lung collapse.

The long squeak of the door echoed across the hollow nothingness. They were back to finish me. *I am coming, Christopher.*

"Eli." I knew him, but it was not the friendly tone you would expect from an acquaintance.

"Tom?" Uncertainty wavers in my voice. I fought to push my arms underneath me to get a better look, to confirm I heard what I saw. Tom was a ghost.

"What's going on, Tom? Asher said he knew you were in San Francisco, but we assumed you were being held captive." He grabbed the chair and spun it around, straddled it, and leaned his arms on the backrest, facing me.

"Asher is a clever boy. I look forward to having him with me… I saw Cate and the kids last night. She is looking well. I can't thank you enough for keeping them alive for me while I…had other things to take care of."

"Tom, what are you talking about?" My question was free from accusation—I was trying to remain nonthreatening.

"Cate has always been fierce, and I always found that sexy. There was something about her dominating nature that did it for me. Seeing her last night so enraged brought back memories… Oh man, I will miss that." There was something in his demeanor that had shifted. Tom was family to me, but this was not the Tom I had known for close to sixteen years. There was something wicked in his eyes. Something sadistic.

"Why am I here?" I was still confused. Nothing about this made sense.

"I need your help. Cate has been a bad girl, digging around in places where she has no business digging. And you are going to help me secure those assets. Sorry about this, old friend. I tried to warn her. But she can't keep her mouth shut and just make it easy. She wants to play, so let's see what's she's made of." His sinister grin was callous and determined. *He is going to kill that girl and enjoy every second of it.*

"You don't have to do this, Tom. I am not sure what you're into, son, but I know—"

He got up from the chair and started to walk away, then paused. "That is where you're confused, Eli. This is exactly where I want to be. This is my war." He projected his voice forward, echoing back, making his proclamation seem eerie and evil.

"But she loved you…" My voice came out shaky.

"Which makes this even more fun." My heart sank. The devil had gotten this boy.

My two new friends came out of the shadows, evil minions lurking in the darkness.

"Go another round, but be careful not to kill him. I want the seriousness of the situation to be clear when she sees it. Bring the pictures back to me when you are done."

The Lord is my shepherd; I shall not want. He maketh me to lie down in green pastures: he leadeth me beside the still waters. He restoreth my soul: he leadeth me in the paths of righteousness for his name's sake. Yea, though I walk through the valley of the shadow of death, I will fear no evil: for thou art with me: thy rod and thy staff comfort me. Thou preparest a table before me in the presence of mine enemies: thou anointest my head with oil: my cup runneth over. Surely goodness and mercy shall follow me all the days of my life: and I will dwell in the house of the Lord forever.—Psalms 23 (KJV)

What's Mine Is Mine

"Ms. Winter, there is someone at the gate requesting you. He says you're expecting him? They're in a black SUV, and I wouldn't describe them as friendly."

I looked around the drawing room at Kevin, Liz, and Hutch. We had just met with Jared to work out a cyber-strategy. The blood drained from my face, leaving just enough room for me to take a deep, exasperated breath.

"Are they in full tactical gear? What do we see around the perimeter?" I asked from behind the table.

"Yes, there are a lot of unfriendlies in position around Winter co-ops, but no aggressive movement. Two full convoy units about a click back from the gate."

"I want all units in defensive positions. Hutch, Kevin, you are with me. Liz, if the alarm sounds, get all the children secure." Liz nodded, then reached out to me offer reassurance.

"Are you sure about this, Cate?" I could tell by Hutch's tone he was apprehensive.

"Tom is back, and I know him better than he knows himself. I need to buy us more time. He needs to think there is something in it for him... Just trust me."

I slipped out of my oversized sweatshirt, leaving me only in my sports tank, showing off my well-defined midriff. I spun my hair up into a messy bun. Hutch's eyes widened in delight and confusion.

Tom had always been a sucker for me straight out of the moms' yoga class. On days he worked from home and the boys had practice, I would come home from class, still sweaty and disheveled, and he would lay me out on the kitchen island. Through so much of our lives he sat back and watched, let me drive. But not our intimate moments—that was when he loved to take charge. Maybe that was the real 'him'—raw, animalistic, sometimes brutal. I thought it was just a fantasy thing. But sometimes I could feel the anger behind him, spilling out into the moment, the way he looked hard into me afterward. Maybe he was telling me then what I was seeing now.

The knot gathered in my throat, a bit of resentment mixed with degradation, with an added dash of slut shaming.

We walked down the driveway, slow and casual. I was not interested in them thinking we were at their beck and call or made nervous by their presence. *Or desperate.* I was freezing in my sports tank and capri yoga pants, my dark hair still up in a disheveled messy bun, mimicking my fresh-from-the-workout look.

The cast-iron gate peeled open, revealing the black SUV just beyond. Kevin signaled to the gatekeepers to guard the castle. We walked toward the SUV, and the tinted window rolled down, exposing the obscurity within.

"Here, kitty…kitty." Tom's condescending voice purred out, like nails on a chalkboard. *Stay focused.* I opened my palm to Hutch and Kevin, motioning them to hold back, then moved to meet Tom at the window. He held up a manila envelope through the opening. I didn't reach for it. I knew what was in it. He had Eli and he was hoping to get in my head.

"Thank God you brought 'the papers.' I thought you would draw this out, and I would have to get one of those pit bull lawyers. You know, the ones who take you for every last penny, including your record collection. Lawyers are like cockroaches. I am sure *they* survived the apocalypse. I wonder if they take chickens as payment? I am willing to go seventy/thirty on the time share in Hawaii, but nothing less… Oh, I hope the Free Nationalists have a good pension and dental plan. I might want to get some post-divorce work done on these babies." I teasingly lifted my breasts up and casually leaned against the SUV, playing my hand. *I am not scared of you or your army; in fact, you are a joke to me.*

"Your sharp tongue has always had a gift for creative sarcasm. I might have to put it to work one last time when this is all said and done… When I take Winter, I might just have to take you, too." He stole a hard, long look. *The sick fuck is not kidding.*

"You done? You need me to get you a tissue? Cold shower? I hope you are still good with self-service, because the only action you're going to get is dreaming about this ass. It's a shame... That shit is so tight and firm nowadays, not much to do around here but work out... My squats are on point." I watched him squirm in his seat, as I fake-fanned myself. How was that for a shift of power?

"You challenging me?" he said under his breath.

I leaned a bit closer to the window and dropped my voice to a sultry whisper, scanning him from top to bottom.

"You look a bit uncomfortable, *Mr. Winter*. Are you feeling okay? Let me help you out. Do you see that big, tall, handsome guy back there? He is fucking the shit out of *your wife*, e...ver...y... night." I looked back to Hutch, passed an exaggerated wink, and waved. Hutch squirmed uncomfortably. "While you were out waging a war, I moved on. Can't leave a girl alone for too long, you know." His face was fuming. Tom had always been territorial and extremely jealous. I needed to drag out his game as long as I could—I needed more time. *That's right, Tom, focus on me and what you want to do to me.*

I pushed up with both hands from the window frame, presenting a clear view for him directly down my cleavage through my sports tank. The chilly winter air had made the girls a bit more perky and firm. I spread my legs a bit and arched my back in a mock reverse stretch. Being sure to open my mouth slightly, I glanced back. "What's the matter, Tom? *Cat* got your tongue?" I gave him a little smile.

He reached and pulled at his pants to adjust himself.

"Need a little help with that?"

The anger shifted to a smirk. He wanted to play. *That's right, head back in the game, Tom. You have competition.*

"On second thought, let me hold on to these 'papers' a little longer. We have unfinished business to take care of first." He set the envelope back down on the seat next to him.

"Suit yourself." I turned, making sure he got a good look. He needed to see the rest of the show.

"I am coming for you, Cat."

"I know you are, Tom. I will be holding my breath," I said from over my shoulder. Both Kevin and Hutch were in shock, not sure what they'd just witnessed or heard. As I passed Hutch, I whispered without moving my lips, "Cradle my ass in your hand, nice and deep along the center. Make sure he gets an eyeful."

"Uh, what!?"

"Do it!" I said in a commanding whisper.

Hutch's hand dropped in position, and I blushed, then I playfully leaned into him. I could hear the SUV peel off. *Done, your turn, Tom.*

I heard the clank of the iron gate closing behind us.

"Hutch, you can let go now."

"Oh, sorry." He dropped his hand and moved a couple of feet away.

"Someone please give me a coat," I said, shivering.

"I don't know if I can…" Hutch coughed and pulled his coat down slightly in the front.

Kevin scrambled and pulled his coat off, quickly putting it around my shoulders.

"Uh…oh…sorry, Hutch." The flush filled my cheeks again.

"I'm good, thanks." Hutch lets out a slight squeak.

We walked the rest of the way to the house in silence. I could tell Hutch was getting more agitated with each step. As we passed the threshold, he was in full Hutch mode.

"What the…fuck…was that? Your husband is a ruthless murderer, and you are acting like you are going to bang him in a bar bathroom?!" Agitation had progressed to full-on livid. Kevin and Liz cleared the floor and ushered us into the library.

"This is not your concern, Hutch." I didn't know why I'd thought it was a good idea to take him with me on this.

"What do you mean, this is not my concern? You just told your incredibly jealous, militant husband we are playing hide the salami, while putting on a soft porn show, and closing with my hand up your ass!? Not to say I didn't enjoy the last part." Liz gave me a curious look, and I shrugged my shoulders.

"We need more time... Tom likes games, he really likes...games. He needs to focus on something other than killing us all." I knew this plan would work—getting Tom to focus was the whole reason we had ever worked at all.

"I don't know how Tom thinking about you riding his freedom pony will help us?"

"It just will."

"How!? You are crazy—do you want him to come for you? I don't want..." Hutch was losing his patience.

"Shit, Hutch, let it go! It is not always about what you want. I would rather him think and plan how he is going to *fuck* me, than take my kids and then kill me and everyone I know and care about, including you!... He is super-jealous when it comes to me, and he will do anything to get what he wants. I need him to want me alive. Just until we can crack WMS." I was running the show, but there were certain lines I knew never to cross with Tom, and me with another guy was at the top of the list. Tom had gotten another year on house arrest for beating the crap out of some junior who gave me his number. I didn't know it until I had to bail him out.

"What was in the envelope?"

"Pictures of Eli." The thought was like a stab to the heart. It was like shards of glass cutting through the deepest part of my soul.

"How do you know?" He softened.

My energy was gone. "Because if I were him, I would go after what I love the most. We know they took the hospital, and we have not heard from the medical team in two days." I could feel the tears filling the space between my lids, building in heaviness, then I let them fall. I was defeated, exhausted by the weight of it all. I slid down the wall, tucking my legs into Kevin's jacket. Liz grabbed Kevin, giving me space, and passed a scolding look to Hutch, silently telling him to fix this.

Roses or Rifles

I slid down the wall next to her tiny body completely engulfed by Kevin's jacket. I wrapped my arm around her, pulling her close to my chest. I could feel the tears soaking through my shirt. Her hair smelled like fresh oranges and was soft against my face. I couldn't help but reach up to gently pull down the messy bun, and she let me. It fell, the dark, shiny silk draped past her shoulders. I ran my fingers through it, watching the strands separate and divide, exposing my skin beneath, cloaking my hands in its angel softness. I kissed the top of her head. I was unable to resist the urge to bring her to me.

The small metal tag on the zipper of Kevin's coat glided up past her knees and coasted down her legs as it split open, freeing her from below, like releasing a butterfly. Her legs unraveled from its confines. The yoga pants showed off her fit form, and I could see why Tom loved it so much when she wore them. What I didn't understand was how he could not want every part of her.

I shifted my grip under her arms, and in one quick, swooping motion, I brought her body over mine, her legs on either side. Kevin's oversized jacket was still around her, enveloping us both in its cocoon. I brought her into my chest, tucking her in, her mostly bare torso warm through my shirt. In my arms, she felt so small. I grabbed her from behind her knees and slid her up as close as possible, wrapping one arm around her from inside the jacket, my forearm against her bare skin. I let her quietly sob as I stroked her hair, holding her, periodically kissing the top of her head.

I could stay like this for a lifetime. She was raw energy, drawing me in. She was a relentless force. And she would be my downfall. *Oh God, please let her be my downfall.*

My hand moved from her hair back to beneath the cocoon. My two rough hands took turns tracing the exposed small of her back, following along the elastic band of her sports tank, the tip skimming just underneath the edge. She made me want to write poetry and shit.

Her head tilted slightly, showing her forehead. I accepted the invitation and brought my lips down to meet it. I worked my way to the bridge of her nose. The salt of her tears stained my lips, letting me experience her anguish. I slid a hand free from the jacket and tilted her chin to me, leaving her lips unprotected.

I worked my lips to hers, parting them, sharing breath. I could feel her heartbeat accelerate, and mine followed suit. Her back stiffened, pulling her cheeks from my chest and my lips from hers, forcing my hands to gather at her bend, feeling her hips below. Upright, her eyes locked to mine.

Panic set in.

Please don't leave, please don't leave. I was pleading with my hands and begging with my eyes for her not to push me away. My expression saddened at the thought of her leaving me. Every time I got close, she pushed away. And every time she pushed away, it killed me.

But she was a master poker player and she could read me. I needed her to read me. *I need you, Cate.* I had no secrets. I didn't care, I wanted to tell her everything.

Her hips shifted slightly, encouraging me, leaning into me. My hands skated back around her, crisscrossing her body and pulling her back to me, folding her in.

She brought her lips to mine, kissing me with purpose, her soft vulnerability evaporating. She was full-on Cate—powerful, strong, deliberate. Everything was to be done on her terms and I had nothing to say and wanted for nothing. Her fingers found their way through each button of my flannel shirt and worked even further down, leaving me bare, and baring herself, bonding us skin to skin. She led me without hesitation, and I followed her for every beat. Her eyes locked to mine, reading every expression, learning every secret. Lost in the moment, lost in her, I wanted to profess my undying devotion and make a complete fool of myself. *Play it cool, Hutch.*

Without warning, her expression turned to tearful anger, and I couldn't help but feel there was more to all of this.

Each riled-up motion seethed with revenge, the weight of it all pushing her heart further out of reach from me. I could feel I was losing her. Her palms were flat to my chest as if she was pushing me away. I held her hips tight against me, desperate to bring her back into me, wanting nothing more than for her to stay in my arms, desperate to make her forget Tom.

But she just wanted to even the score, with each short, assertive burst.

Her grip tightened, and her breath quickened. No matter how hard I tried, I couldn't help but let her take everything from me.

My pained expression was met with a long, exaggerated blink, until one final, cold look sealed my fate as she lifted away, leaving me shattered on the floor without a word. The emptiness was amplified by the rush of the cool air as she exited the room.

My arms were vacant.

She'd gone from delicate butterfly to ruthless killer, and I had walked right into it knowing I would be the one dying in the end, the casualty of a war I was not even fighting.

***

I planted my feet on the rug next to the small leather library sofa. My head was still reeling, confused and heartbroken. I was positive she had just given me the 'thanks, but not interested' rebound screw.

I was hoping the morning-after walk of shame went unnoticed, because I needed to clear my head before I had any further human contact or I might just say something stupid. *Let's be honest—that typically happens regardless.*

I ran my fingers through my unruly mop and buttoned up my flannel, my train of thought periodically lost, tracing the path her fingers had taken. I sprang up, jumped a bit, shook out my arms. *Shake it off, you know where you stand—in the friend zone. Or more like a frenemy.*

I opened the door of the library and peered slowly around the corner. The hallway was clear, and I quietly moved toward the door. I could hear voices in the drawing room and I worked to exit unnoticed, pulling open the large oak door just enough to look out and squeeze through. I placed one foot over the threshold followed by the other, slowly closing the door behind me.

"Hey."

Startled, I jumped. "Jesus Christ! Liz, you scared the shit out of me!... Liz?" I grabbed my chest to add some drama. Her tiny body was perched on the rock wall, her baby bump starting to really take shape. She must have been waiting for Kavik. I dug the dude—he seemed pretty solid, the Coast Guard type.

"Walk of shame, not your style." Little sisters sucked, such a pain in the ass.

"That talking thing new?" Oh man, it was good to hear her voice.

"I'm trying it out." She jumped down from the wall and met me at the bottom step.

"So, did you tell her how you feel?" *Ugh*, I squirmed, suddenly feeling incredibly uncomfortable. I looked at my shoes and drew imaginary circles with my work boots. *Pishh, what feelings?*

"We didn't really talk, per se, but she made it clear she wants nothing to do with me." I tried to cover up my disappointment with a long look across the driveway, finding a random focus point and crossing my arms to show I really didn't want to get into it.

"You must have said *something*—she is murdering the bag downstairs." Her eyes tracked my sight line and continued, "She is going through a lot. Tom is one sadistic fuck." I knew he was; I had run some guns for him a few months back and walked in on some crazy shit. I wasn't sure how Cate had ever gotten mixed up with him or how he had played father of the year for so long. He was not going to stop until she was dead—until we were all dead.

I looked to her, her sight line still focused off in the distance, her arms crossed. "Adam, she is playing a dangerous game. Don't let her do anything stupid."

"I know, she is totally self-destructing. Tempting the lion, wearing a juicy steak as a T-shirt." Just the thought made me want to rip him to pieces. Losing her to him, such a piece of shit. The anger boiled up like lava from the center of the earth, ready to destroy everything. I wasn't sure why I cared; she was not even mine.

"I wouldn't get in her way, just help keep her out of trouble." She spoke with all seriousness, and with clear expectations. I was not really sure how I could stop her, and there was nothing between us to make her listen to me.

"Good talk." I leaned into the wall.

Kavik's truck pulled up just in time to break the awkward silence. He jumped out and was obviously nervous about something. He looked concerned and maybe a bit paranoid. He walked to Liz, and she stood to greet him. A brief hello and he gave her a quick peck on the cheek. That was new. I gave Liz the side-eye.

"Hey, Hutch, you got a second?" His hands shifted to his pockets, and Liz looked between us, a little confused.

"Uh, sure…" I returned the look of confusion and waited for Liz to offer her approval. She nodded in consent.

We walked down the path toward the stable. He looked back and smiled at Liz. He was almost trembling, a kid who had just wrecked his parents' car. *Oh my God, I hope he doesn't ask to marry my sister. I am not ready, and I think I might puke.*

"Hutch, I think I might have moved one of your people a couple of days ago. The old guy I saw give the Christmas speech." Distracted, it took me a second to digest what he was saying.

"What do you mean, you 'moved him'?" What the hell? This little shit *should* be scared.

"Like I told you, you know, I work for the Coast Guard out at Alameda… We were occupied by the FN, and some of us stayed on." The little punk was completely avoiding eye contact.

"Kavik, are you telling me you are a FN solider?" I was holding back the urge to strangle him.

"Not exactly… I'm more of a contractor." This guy, who was just casually hanging out with my sister, knew the Free Nationalists wanted to kill us all.

"Are you trying to get intel on us?" Cate was going to lose her mind if she found out. "Why are you here?"

"Hutch, it is not like that." He scrambled, sensing my temper beginning to boil.

"What the hell is it like, then?" I subconsciously clenched my fists and looked over to Liz, who was watching intently.

"I was heading to the docks to move some stuff across the bay when I ran into Asher, and that is why I came here. Then I met Liz… Dude, I wouldn't have said anything about the old guy if I was…" He swayed back and forth, and his hands moved up from his pockets to his hair, pulling at the jet-black locks. "Hutch, I love your sister."

"FUCK! Keep her out of this! She loves Eli like a grandfather, and if anything happens to him…" I spoke through gritted teeth.

"Look, Hutch, my point is that I am not here to gather 'intel'; however, I think someone here is. I heard some guys talking about 'Queen Cate's Castle'." As he said the words, a shiver ran down my spine.

"Our last few scavenger crews have met with some resistance, and I am pretty sure we are running out of friends." I knew he was telling the truth; our time was running out.

Kavik broke my train of thought. "You know, not all of the guys at Alameda are FN. They are not all bad guys—they are just guys who have lost a lot and were promised revenge. But many have seen enough and are now ready to move on."

I turned to Liz and gave a cheesy, overstated wave to ease her death stare.

"I need some time to think this shit out. Can you find out if Eli is alive, and how much support we have over in Alameda? In the meantime, I have to go see a guy about some guns." Kavik stuck his hand out to shake like bros. I hesitated, then took the gesture. I hated that I liked this guy.

***

I crossed the field we used as a shooting range, past the empty casings, over the hole-ridden collection of cans, and zigzagged through the solar field and out onto the old racetrack. There were less eyeballs on this side of Winter.

I approached the small tan pickup, the smell of horse shit still alive and well, soaked into the fabric. I thought they had used the vehicle to move horse shit from the stalls back when this place was still open. I was almost positive they even piled it up in the cab. But for quick trips around, it's still my preferred mode of transportation and less obvious than our bigger trucks. I pulled the visor down, dropping the keys into my hand, and started up the gutless wonder.

There were a few places I liked to look for business deals, and the seedier, the better. Unfortunately, it was mostly FN scum out there these days, but it made for good intel and business leads—a couple of drinks and those guys would spill every last bit. I rolled my tan manure bucket down

University and onto Centennial, easing to a slow stop just past the Old Pro. In an act of defiance, I took my place in front of a fire hydrant; it wasn't like there was such a thing as fire response anyway.

Making my way inside, I counted heads to make sure I was not incredibly outnumbered.

A short-haired blonde was behind the bar. Ex-Marine, she topped the brutal scale, tough as nails, and she did not hesitate to make sure you felt like a worthless piece of shit, too. But she had a weak spot for homemade bread and produce. She also had a keen understanding of what everyone was up to.

The day shift was more for business and less for the 'other' stuff.

Goods in tow, I made my way to the bar.

She nodded and rolled her eyes in artificial irritation. "You again."

"Nice to see you, too, Roxy. Is that how you greet all your favorite customers?"

"If I had a favorite customer, it sure the hell wouldn't be you."

"Well, that's a bummer. I might just need to take this fresh rosemary bread someplace else." I flipped the towel from the top of the box, revealing the perfect golden round loaf and greens beneath, then dramatically turned to leave.

"I might have a beer with your name on it."

"I need something stronger." Surprised, she reached for the bootlegged unmarked jar of moonshine from below the bar and poured me a shot. I put the large box on the counter close enough for her to smell the loaf. She was almost mesmerized as the rosemary wafted in the air.

She sifted through the box, noting its contents, which included veggies, bread, grains, a scarf, and, toward the bottom, one box of ammo and two letters: one to some folks over the fire line and one to someone in Seattle.

As I sipped the acoustic alcohol, she casually took the box to the back, returning with it mostly empty.

"You might want to keep your box. I made you a quick snack for your troubles." Looking around the bar, watching for eyes, she set it back on the counter. Without overtly looking, I could see one small bag and a few envelopes inside, one addressed to Winter and the other to me.

M. LaVon

"How are things in your part of town?" I said to initiate small talk. She was a master of telling people what they needed to know, without telling them anything at all.

"Business is good. We get a lot of soldiers these days, new faces moving through. They are pretty hardcore types with interesting appetites for entertainment. Less and less locals, most people moving out, making room for them, you know. Hear they are going north, closer to Canada, where supplies are better." We, too, had heard and noticed the movement of the troops. I was not surprised that Canada was working to establish itself as an ally to the people. It was just a matter of time before the FN pushed across their border; the presence of the FN in Washington was already a big threat.

"Canada, huh? I hear the winters up there are pretty harsh."

She wiped the counter with a wet rag, focused on each even circle. "Yeah, I suppose... I have never been there myself, but I hear a lot of guys in here talking about the winter—true Californians, I guess, not liking all the stuff winter brings with it. They would sooner never have a real winter. There was a guy in here just last night with a lot to say about the weather. Talking about how winter will end soon, and he couldn't be happier." FN forces loved to brag about their potential conquests, and with most of the locals moving out, we were getting pretty close to being on our own. And we were even closer to being the next one on the list—nothing like being sitting ducks.

"We have been pretty lucky with the mild weather so far, makes for good farming..." I said, slowly turning the glass, careful not to overreact to the info. The clear liquor swirled around, coating the glass.

"You might want to watch your crops. I heard it might get kind of cold next week, would hate for you to lose anything." It might be time for an exit strategy; I knew she was right. Cate would be harder to convince.

"Hmm, good tip... It's not as easy to predict the weather these days without a reliable news source."

"We had a few Stanford types come by for our special last week. I think they may know a bit about farming and weather. You might want to track them down for a spring planting strategy."

"That is great advice. Thanks, Roxy." I took one final swig from my glass to clear out the bottom, then collected my box and headed to my truck. Stanford was only a few blocks away.

***

Stanford was far from the bustling campus it once was. Much like everything else it had suffered from the lack of upkeep and general neglect. From what I heard, there were a number of scientists, professors, and academics who still stayed here, even producing an underground newspaper of sorts. It was a big campus, and it wasn't easy to figure out where to start. By instinct I pulled up to the student and visitor information center, but it was relatively empty, aside from a couple of unaffiliated squatters passing through. I wove a trail through the buildings, passing a few people who seemed not willing to talk or help, rushing past, eyes averted. I eventually stumbled into the library, which was strangely abuzz. People were moving in and out—I must have found the hive.

I approached to gawking stares, stalled figures unsure of why I was there. I felt my chest puff up and my heavy boots planted solid on the ground, presenting myself for inspection. I could never quite shake the solider out of me.

The entrance of the Hoover Institution of War, Revolution, and Peace was surrounded by ornate stonework, and the heavy wooden doors, aged over a hundred years, swung wide as I entered. I was greeted by even more stares, a foreigner in a foreign land. It must have been obvious that I was not an academic. People were shuffling between the stacks, faces in books on tables, heavy debates building between serious faces surrounding maps.

I forced out a gruff cough, artificially clearing my throat, and it all came to a screeching halt.

"Can someone point me to who is in charge?" I asked generally, to anyone who would answer.

"Who's asking?" A slightly cocky young man, with thick, horn-rimmed glasses, seated at one of the tables piped up.

"Adam Hutchenson."

"You FN?" he quickly replied.

"Does it matter?" My patience with this situation was running thin.

"It's okay, Sam, he is with Winter." A younger guy, whom I could only assume was a professor, stepped out from between the shelves. He had a slightly disheveled appearance, but he seemed oddly put together: corduroy dinner jacket over a button-up shirt and sweater vest. His small bow tie seemed slightly out of place, but he looked perfect all the same. He reminded me of a young Dr. Henry Walton Jones Jr., also known as Indiana—my all-time childhood hero and lifelong inspiration.

"Dr. Jones, I presume," I said, as serious as possible. I just couldn't help myself.

"How did you know?" he asked with a puzzled look on his face and waited patiently for my reaction. Without missing a beat, "...but my friends just call me Indy."

For a quick second, he had me, then he proceeded to shake his head. I was pleased he'd caught my obscure reference.

Noticing my smirk, he put out his hand. "Hutch, correct?"

"Well, now I do feel left out. You apparently know who I am, but I have no clue who you are."

"Fishel Ades, Fish...or Professor Jones, whatever you prefer."

"Okay, Fish. What is all this about?" I gestured around the library. I was still unsure why I was there or why there was important.

"I am really a history professor, historical strategies of war mainly...or I *was* a professor before the academic infrastructure crumbled. What you just walked into is the Hoover Institute of War, Revolution, and Peace. And unofficially we are the historians for this war. We have been tracking as much as we can from all sides, documenting movements and monitoring activity. This is an unprecedented event in the history of civil wars." His nerd heart was all aglow.

"What do you know about Winter?" I said, breaking the excitement.

"We have mutual associations and similar ideologies." We made our way to a small corner, the old paned-glass panels, warped and rippled, made the courtyard outside appear dreamlike. I turned my attention back to the young professor.

"Ideologies?" My head ached at the prospect of this conversation turning geek-a-rific.

"We share a desire to survive. Destin has ensured we will suffocate here. They have closed off all of California, leaving us with no supplies and no support. We are running out of options. It is time for a better strategy if we are going to turn the tables."

"What do you mean 'turn the tables'?" I asked, leaning in.

"There aren't that many of us left here. After the virus hit, with the close quarters of campus, many students and faculty didn't survive. Those who did survive left in droves, trying to get home to their families.

"The first few waves might have made it out, but then we started hearing stories of violent gangs and militants taking out anyone who was trying to make it out of the state. Unarmed students didn't stand much of a chance. We heard of girls raped and taken captive, then killed, young men tortured or forced to join. Those who stayed did what they could to survive, some joining other communities. I think we even had a few who joined Winter.

"For a while we counted over eleven communities who really made significant progress, including yours. Conditions weren't perfect, but basic infrastructure was being rebuilt. We watched Winter influence trade, supply lines formed, and basic communications were getting through.

"For the most part, the FN left everyone on the inside pretty much alone, focusing on building up places like the base at Alameda. From what we have been able to tell, there are several of these pseudo bases up and down the coast. The Bay Area is just one hub, which Destin controls.

"But things started to shift a few months ago. There were more local raids, forcing people out, and increased activity at SFO, troops coming into Alameda and large convoys to both Reno and Fallon, Nevada, heavy coastal defenses. We have observed several large ships come through and head back out... But even more interesting is the movement toward Seattle."

"Seattle?"

"Yes, there is a heavy push north, and I don't think our northern neighbors like the prospect of the FN trying to redraw the border lines. Canada was hit hard just like we were, but the inner turmoil was significantly less. I think they are letting us implode, waiting to see what's left after it all shakes out. However, they have been providing some supplies, and they are allowing refugees over the border.

"They are well aware of the FN presence heading north, and without a solid government in place here, there is nothing stopping the FN from engaging Canada. The Canadians would like to see Washington in the hands of a less-threatening neighbor, and they might be willing to provide a little assistance to the right neighbor. The last thing they want to deal with is hostility at the border."

"What does this all have to do with Winter?"

"It has more to do with Cate... People talk about Winter as the beacon of hope. It created a survival chain, which many people relied on. Winter and what it stands for...it's like we might come back from this..."

"Not anymore—we are just as much on our own as everyone else."

"We know... They see what's happening now as 'Tom's' fault, caused by a tyrant ex-husband who would kill his own family to advance this war... It is not the best way to gain support for a cause."

"Okay, so say what you say about Winter, and Cate, is true, so what?"

"Don't you get it? Winter matters; Cate matters. They need a leader they can trust. They don't trust those left in government. Destin made sure of that with his propaganda. And they sure as hell don't trust the Free Nationalists. We need to rebuild." His nerd flag was flying high above him.

"Destin will kill us all before he would ever let that happen." The memory of Cate's face, tired and crying after her meeting with Tom, pressed against my chest, clouded my thoughts.

"Destin was smart. He let everyone first think we could make it work. We banded together as indefensible communities, and he let us do all the work. Then his guys came in and took what little everyone had left and slaughtered anyone who stood in their way. But he also shot himself in the foot. He is not Robin Hood saving us from a corrupt government; he is just a power-hungry, ruthless killer." His expression morphed into exhaustion.

"So, what do you think his plan is?"

"It is not just *his* plan that we are concerned with. Destin is for sure a super villain, but he is just one player. The FN has successfully dealt the final blow to what we knew as the United States, ensuring that nothing would go ever back to the way it was. They took total advantage when our country was on its knees. From what we can tell, there is nothing substantial left. Those still fighting on behalf of the United States are not even sure what they are fighting for anymore.

"None of this is surprising, with the state of the nation prior to the outbreak. We were divided before the virus..." His long pause gave me time to think about how things were before.

The United States had been the 'divided states' for some time. Already plagued with the reality of climate change, superstorms battered the east and southern coasts, droughts leaving many of the plains states useless and barren, unpredictable weather patterns making farming impossible, out-of-control pests laying siege to our forests leaving them dead and dry—the list was so long even the scientists had stopped keeping a tally of problems to solve. Every time something new happened, the government was so taxed it was next to impossible to respond to it all. Many small coastal cities had become wastelands even before the virus struck.

That was nothing compared to the unrest that came along with our environmental problems. Social wars on all sides, riots, violent protests, poverty, police states, not to mention the government coverups protecting big businesses—no one was culpable, and no one was held accountable. Tom blamed the government, but I blamed us all.

Cate was right. We had been lulled into a fantasy—that we would weather whatever came, desensitized to what was acceptable, making even the worst scenario normal.

"We are all responsible for what happened, but we have an opportunity to turn things around." He continued letting his optimism squeak out from behind his weary features. If anyone could make it happen, she could. For a brief second, she was all I had on my mind.

"How can we turn things around? Because what I am seeing tells me we are pretty much fucked." With equal pessimism, I pushed it back.

"Trust me." he said with a glint of sarcasm. Touché, Dr. Jones, touché.

***

The ride back to Winter felt long, and I had the overwhelming urge to shoot shit. Fish was a man of many great and crazy ideas. I was not sure how I was going to convince Cate of everything that needed to happen next. I was really not sure I really even wanted to. And I was still unsure how I was going to tell her I had to leave. The only thing I knew for sure was that he was right about Cate. I would rather have been dead than be without her, and she was worth any sacrifice I could make.

I was lost in thought as the little shit bucket rolled to a stop. I grabbed the box out of the cab, and the small bag shifted, revealing the note addressed to me below it.

Hutch. Have Cate. Google twinkies for more info. Roxy

I opened the small paper sack. Twinkies.

M. LaVon

Twinkies

The end of the world brought about the most interesting economy. Paper or digital currency quickly became worthless. The value of food and essential services became the primary means of exchange. Dehydrated kale chips could get you eggs, eggs could get you bread, bread could get you yarn, a scarf could get you Twinkies, etc. The combinations were endless, but you had to be strategic with what you wanted or needed, or you would end up missing the exact combination, leaving you with nothing of importance.

Hutch had a sixth sense about what would work, like a kid with a Rubik's Cube. He could walk into a room full of strangers and arrange in minutes a ten-person chain that end with exactly what he wanted in his hands. It was a sport to him, or maybe an art. I liked to watch him work. He had a certain grace to him, almost political, but not as sleazy.

We had stopped running scavenger parties. It had become too dangerous since Tom had decided Hutch's gunrunning services not worth the trouble. It could also be related to him screwing his wife, or at least what I had led him to believe. Thankfully, Hutch was much more charming than Tom's minions, and some people were still willing to barter.

We worked to keep a low profile, maintaining small and discreet parties. Sometimes it was just me and Hutch. He made it a point to keep quiet. He had barely said a word since the other night in the library. He avoided me at all costs unless it involved business. *I guess he got what he wanted.*

We pulled up to Google headquarters. It felt odd pulling into a parking spot, more a force of habit than a necessity anymore. It wasn't like there were many people on the road these days. Gas had become scarce; Tom's army had taken pretty much every last drop that was hiding in California. Our stockpile would soon run out, as well. We had been able to keep the fuel trucks filled for a long time, siphoning from parked cars, abandoned gas stations, and industrial areas, but others were quick to follow, leaving not much at the bottom of the tanks. Supply lines had also stopped as other regions dried up.

The glass automatic doors hissed open, and the air rushed out as we stepped through, the compressed hiss replaying when the doors shut behind us. Beyond the lobby was a small reception area and a few interactive screens. Strangely, a receptionist welcomed us from the desk. "Hello, how may I help you?" Her voice echoed in the empty space. She was wearing a headset and appeared to be managing calls. I started to open my mouth, but— "One second, I will be right with you." She raised her finger, pointing in the air to ensure we understood that we were on hold. She looked down at the screen and clicked about. Hutch looked at me curiously, and I returned his looks with equal perplexity.

"Yes, thank you for waiting." She smiled, patiently waiting for a response.

"We are here to see…um…someone about Twinkies?" I asked with a bit of trepidation.

"Is she expecting you?" the woman replied.

"I am not sure…but I brought…some?" Again I spoke with trepidation.

"Ah, yes, please have a seat. She will be with you shortly." She pointed to the lobby waiting area.

"Something tells me we are not in Kansas anymore, Dorothy," Hutch said under his breath, as if he was reading my mind.

I sat down next to him, hanging on to my bag of Twinkies, clutching them like elderly women used to clutch their oversized handbags filled with special tidbits: tissues, nylons, half-eaten candy, hot pink lipstick, and a checkbook.

I watched as the receptionist fiddled about. She was younger, maybe twenty-five, and dressed in a skirt, blouse, and heels. I could see she was packing in her waistband. Made me think of mine, something I never left home without.

She straightened the refreshment area, artificially lining the tea bags, coffee straws, and napkins. She never offered us a beverage.

Without much more delay, another young woman emerged from a side hallway. Her Hello Kitty T-shirt was perfectly white, and she wore black leggings underneath, and ankle sneakers. If I had to guess her age, I would have said she was no more than fourteen. She approached and presented herself with a slight bow.

Hutch and I instinctively bowed in return.

"Hi, I am Akemi." She let out a slight giggle at our awkward bow. "You need help? Come to my office." She directed us down the hall to a very large office with a nice picture window. Perhaps it had been owned by a former executive. Now, beanbag chairs, board games, and puzzles took up the space in front of a large glass desk. Several oversized monitors branched out forming a wall, their long octopus arms stretching out from the desk surface. Stuffed plushies of all shapes and sizes lay stacked and piled everywhere, as if she gathered every possible character Googlers had stashed throughout their campuses and placed them around. Besides being a bit creepy, it was happy and cheerful, and I kind of liked it. Hutch, on the other hand, looked like a cat in water. And he wanted out of the plushy bath.

We plopped down in the beanbag chairs, sinking down into a very uncomfortable pose that only a beanbag could offer, and tried to look casual. Akemi sat behind the desk, unphased by our obviously contorted positions. We could barely see her behind the monitors.

"I see you brought the Twinkies." It was hard to take her seriously from this position—that and we were dealing in prepackaged baked goods.

I got the feeling that we were to pass over the Twinkies first, then talk business. I held back an internal chuckle; Twinkies really had survived the apocalypse, and they had significant street value.

Taking the hint, I passed the yellow cream-filled cakes to her, and she set them gently aside.

"Thank you..." She nodded. "How can I help you?"

"I have a bit of a situation going on with my ex-husband." The words sounded absurd coming out of my mouth.

"You understand this is not a law office, Mrs. Winter?" she said as if I was describing a simple dispute.

"Understood, he is in my network and I need to get him out. He is using it to advance *his* war. I would like to send him back to his dark web roots."

As if she couldn't resist, she reached for the sack, rustling the paper as it opened, taking out a single Twinkie. She gently peeled apart the clear cellophane wrapper, exposing the spongy surface. She took a single bite, revealing the creamy middle. I was a little fuzzy on cyber-dealing, but something felt out of order with her consuming the payment prior to the delivery of service, but she appeared more than pleased, so I rolled with it.

"So, you want to wage a cyberwar on your ex-husband?" She seemed to already know the answer to my problem, and she didn't need to wait for a response. She was looking down, staring longingly at the Twinkie. She pinched little pieces of uneven cake and gently picked the little bits from the ends of her fingers, sucking them into her mouth, leaving the eaten end almost perfectly halved, like it had been cut with a knife. She gently folded the cellophane back over the cake and placed it back in the bag. She was methodical, almost obsessive. I watched intently, lost in the routineness of her movements.

Hutch forced a cough, catching me off in space and bringing me back to the conversation. "Cyberwar? Aren't we already in one?"

"No, technically we are not. What's happening is one sided," she said very matter-of-factly, almost like I was extremely naïve—and she was right.

"But what about the government?" As I said it, I could feel the obvious absurdity in what I had just said.

"The government was just a balance on the scale; their cyber presence was 'tolerated,' like the person who is picked to play only because you need twelve players." Suddenly I understood that she was more than she let on, and far from a teenage girl.

"How would this be different?"

She paused before she responded, avoiding looking at me. "There is a cyber-ecosystem. We all play a part, good and bad... Your husband, D3ST1NY, is a bad man, who has shifted the balance and must be stopped before he destroys us all." I was not sure how she knew Tom was my husband or why it was important to her, and I didn't know enough to ask.

As if sensing my questions, she went on. "We all know who you are, Cate. And we all know how you saved those kids. And now we need your help to restore the balance."

"How am I supposed to bring *balance*?" Hutch looked down, shifting and avoiding engaging in the conversation—leaving me on my own.

"We know what you are willing to do to take him out. You have a lot of people behind you, here and on the other side."

"The other side?" Everything began to feel foreign—my little dispute with my ex was now front-page hacker news and at the center of a digital world I had never meant to be a part of.

"The Free Nationalists have made a lot of enemies, but they have a lot of friends, too." Her childishness was wearing off, and the soul of an old woman who had seen her fair share of awfulness emerged. "We want to help you, Cate." I had no idea what she was talking about—I just needed help getting Tom out of the WMS network.

I leaned forward in my beanbag chair, and Hutch unsuccessfully attempted to do the same.

"Who is 'we'?" I was not sure what I'd just walked in on, or who she thought I was or what I was capable of, but I realized I had been greatly overestimated.

"You don't need to know the logistics of it all. Just say the word, and we will make it happen. We are an ally to Winter." As she talked, she half-looked at her screen and clicked a few lines of gibberish, then looked back to me, not missing a beat. "Cate, he will come for you. And there are a lot of people counting on you. You need to have a plan."

"Not if I get him first." My voice was weak, sour with intent, and suppressed by the reality of him getting me first.

"Let us help you." Her features were stoic and full of significance. I couldn't help but wonder what all she had seen hidden in all those ones and zeros.

***

My head was spinning as I exited the large office at the end of the hall. I didn't understand a fraction of what Akemi had said or what was happening. Her skills were beyond my comprehension—even for me, who grew up in tech. What I did understand was that Tom had been operating as a black hat hacker for a number of years, disguised in gray and reassuring me it was for the good of the company and the good of the family.

Even after I had bailed him out countless times, he went so far as to change his name so he could have a normal life. So he could be a normal dad, not living behind triple-paned bulletproof glass talking at the end of a handheld receiver. I now knew he had never given up being Tom Destin; Tom Winter was just the mask he had hidden behind. All fake—just like his love for me.

Memories came flooding back, of Tom's face glowing behind his laptop screen. The late nights he spent without me in his office. There had been a growing gap between us over the last few years. He had been focused on researching what I thought was our next new release, but now I wasn't so sure. I felt like he was living a double life, leaving me to only see a perfect dad, feeling like a failure as a wife as I watched him drift further away from the 'us' I'd once known.

I could feel myself sink deeper into my hatred of Tom. The hall felt longer than it had when we had walked it before, and I had the urge to run down the length of it, run outside and scream.

The sound of feet against the polished floor was irritating, like marching soldiers.

We rounded the corner, and to our surprise a collection of Googlers greeted us in the lobby. The receptionist was pleased with herself. Their energy was faint, like a fading pulse, waiting for a charge.

"They are here for you," the receptionist whispered.

"Why?" I whispered back.

"You're Robin Hood… They want you to say that we will overcome tyranny, blah, blah, blah." She had cupped her hand over her mouth and was artificially smiling.

"I am not their leader," I said through gritted teeth.

"You are now, so make it count." She gently raised her arm to quiet the crowd, which had started to mutter, "We are with Winter." I glanced through the sea of cotton hoodies, character T-shirts, and flannels, then smiled and nodded. I had no great speech planned, no amazing, inspirational monologue, no words to describe how we could overcome tyranny.

"And we are with you…" was all I squeaked out in return. I was working hard to hold back the nervous quiver in my voice.

This was not the turn I'd imagined today would take.

***

The ride back was mostly silent, eerily so. Hutch kept his eyes straight forward, avoiding any opportunity for conversation. That was fine, I didn't feel much like talking. Everything was overwhelming and surreal. How had I gone from a mom protecting my boys, to a community leader, to leading a counter-rebellion against the rebellion?

***

The truck pulled into the old racetrack; the stalled momentum shifted me slightly forward.

Hutch worked to pull the keys from the ignition and tucked them into the overhead visor. I pulled the handle on the door interior and pushed on the door with my foot. The slow, sharp metallic squeak of the door broke the silence. I lifted myself up and out with a new weight on my shoulder, one so heavy it was hard to breathe, hard to stand. I was unsure of what I had just done or how it was all going to work out. We might all still very well die.

I lost my footing, my head swam, and I swayed against the truck. Maybe it was the gravity of the situation hitting me or the putrid smell of manure emanating from the truck. I rested against the cool surface and worked hard to collect myself.

"You need to pull your shit together, Cate."

"You need to shut the fuck up…Hutch."

"Cate, he is going to kill you if you don't. You are smarter than him, and you have more to lose than him. People are depending on you." His voice was uncharacteristically stern, with a mix of soft and tender. He was right.

"I don't know what I am doing. I am not a general. I am not a leader." My mouth was dry, and my voice was raspy.

"You were the CEO of your own company. You have fed, protected, and provided for an entire city when people outside of Winter could not. You have saved thousands. And you have now set off a chain of events and it is too late to take it back."

"Yes, but that is different. This can get them all killed." I spoke in a whisper, as if I said the words out loud, they would come true.

"They would have died anyway." His usually candid sarcasm peeked through. "Cate, they believe in you… *We* believe in you… Maybe it is time you start to believe in yourself before your self-doubt is the end of us all. Now, get over it. This is just the tip of the iceberg, and we've got shit to do." He caught the corner of my eye, which was hidden below my arms, and he shot me a smirk followed by a wink, followed by a come-hither gesture.

"Nice speech. Did you get that off the back of a Wheaties box? You going to start singing 'Eye of the Tiger' next? Did you know about what they were going to say?"

"Maybe a little," he said playfully. "And...there may be someone from Stanford who may want to talk." His face was laden with guilt.

***

I followed him back through the field, past the solar farm and back into the core of Winter. The familiarity of home was comforting. I breathed it all in deep, filling my lungs completely.

I reached over and playfully pushed Hutch. He was supportive in his own way, a little unconventional, and not always the most sensitive, but it was effective. He took the push like a champ, and for a second, I thought he would not reciprocate, but before I knew it, he had picked me up and twirled me around. We were spinning and laughing, squealing. The world spun in place, and for a split second the weight lifted and I was weightless, flying, arms outstretched. One final spin forward, and we slowed to a stop. I slid down the front of him, landing perfectly while leaning into him, his arms still around me. Our hearts pounded in unison. There was something about him that brought me back every time. He saw me like no one else did, and he challenged me without restraint, making me want to be more than who I was.

"Mom?" I quickly stepped back, startled and perhaps a little embarrassed.

"Asher. Hey, sweetheart."

"What are you doing?" Every word, without hesitation, was full of painful judgment, piercing daggers.

"Nothing, it is not what it looks like—right, Hutch?" Hutch's hands in his hair translated his discomfort. "Yes, it was nothing," he croaked out. There was something in his expression that said it was not nothing to him, making my heartache even greater.

"So, what, you've replaced Dad? With...him?" At nearly sixteen Asher is almost eye to eye with Hutch, and his jealous temper brought Tom right back to the middle of it all and me right back to reality. And the weight pressed back down all at once.

"Asher...that's enough. You're treading in territory you have no business being in," I said. His fists clenched, boiling over. And my heart broke a little, watching a young Tom fume over what was 'his.'

"I can't believe you would do this to Dad! Cheat on him! So, what, are you getting a divorce now, too?!"

I was taken aback. What delusional world had I let him live in?

"Asher? One, your dad left us, *he* left *me*. Two, this is nothing to be concerned with." I looked over to Hutch. He raised his eyebrow and half coughed.

"Dad said he was coming back for you, for us, that he just had stuff to do… How could you do this to him?"

"Asher, that isn't what your dad meant. He has no intention of us ever being a family again." I was exasperated.

"You liar! This is all your fault in the first place. I hate you!" I knew he meant every last word, whips cutting deep into the flesh. He was charged up and stepped closer.

"Asher, man, you need to calm down, son." Hutch calmly offered a word of caution.

"'Son'!? Who the fuck are you to tell me what to do?!" His rage was resentful, uncontained, and frightening.

"Asher! That is enough!" A last-ditch effort to assert any parental control.

"What?! What are you going to do about it? Ground me… Ha! You can't tell me what to do, either." He stepped close enough to tower over me. I stood my ground. I could feel Hutch's eyes locked on Asher.

"Asher, back up, dude." Hutch's voice turned deep and threatening. And without warning, Asher lunged at him. Unbridled anger spilled over and flooded to the ground in a knotted pile of men. With little effort Hutch flipped him facedown, his hands restrained behind him. There was something in his movement, the effortless fluidity, skills that even with all my practice I had yet to master. Clues to who or what he was. "I ever see you threaten or intimidate a woman like that again, young man, I will take you out. I don't care whose kid you are… Now, go take a walk and cool down." He flung him up and gave him a final push, sure to stand between him and me. We watched him walk away until he reached a safe distance.

Without turning to look back at me, Hutch said, "You have a hothead on your hands."

Holding back tears, I replied, "I know. Just like his dad." I took a moment to catch my breath.

Still avoiding eye contact, Hutch continued, "Do you really think things between us are 'nothing'?"

"Hutch..." He turned to look at me, but I kept my eyes downturned. I paused too long, though, leaving too much air in the space between us, giving him more than enough time to come to his own conclusions. He turned to walk away. I tried to make up the time. "It's complicated...and I have a lot of stuff to figure out...and the boys..."

"You don't have to do everything yourself."

"I know, but this fight is between Tom and me..."

"There is more at stake than what's between you and Tom, and it is time that you share the load."

Avoiding the subject, I shifted the topic. "Hutch?" He turned back one more time, and his eyes told me he was hoping for more than I could offer. "You did more than just logistics for the military, didn't you?"

"Yes..." It was now him who looked down. "I have a lot of sins to atone for." Without any more detail, he left me to wallow in the empty space between us that I had created out of excuses.

M. LaVon

The Edge of Normal

The crack of the bat smacking against the ball brought me back to when things were normal. I watched the ball soar deep into the field, ducking beneath a row of veggies. *Home run.* My shoulders swung through, lining up the warm yellow wood against the horizon. The buttery setting sun in the winter air reflected against the polished surface. I paused, taking in the feeling before sliding the bat down through my palms. My hand wrapped around the smooth finish felt natural and comforting.

I had missed the excitement of rounding the bases after a hit like that, digging my heels into the dirt. The momentum carried me across the bags, engulfed in a cloud of dust and chalk as I slid into home, then I ran into the dugout, guys slapping my helmet, jumping up and down.

I missed my teammates, guys I had known since T-ball. I missed tournaments that would last all day and the barbecues after. We would have been planning the spring season now. I missed when Asher and I would play catch late into the evening until my arms were so sore it felt like they would fall off.

I missed being just simple Winter brothers, A-Z.

And shit, I missed chocolate cake and hot dogs and cheap greasy pizza and Sour Patch Kids and cartoons.

I missed Mom just being Mom before she wanted to save the world. I missed Dad being Dad before he became a supervillain trying to destroy it.

I missed Asher wanting to hang out. He barely went out of the house these days, holed up in his room all broody and lame. He had probably hacked some ridiculous dark web porn site.

Mom was always in the cellar working out; she only slept in small intervals. And Old Man Eli... I missed him, too. He'd always said I reminded him of Uncle Christopher: 'You have the soul of a writer.'

My thoughts drifted as I worked my way through the crops in search of my one remaining ball. The last one had had an unfortunate incident involving a cow that led to its untimely demise—the ball, not the cow. The well-worn leather had rolled deep beneath the leafy foliage, but I scooped it up and tucked it into my glove, folded it under my arm, and retreated to the loft in the barn. *My lair.*

I headed to my favorite spot, the edge of the loft opening, overlooking the stables. It was like being on the edge of the world with one leg dangling over. I pulled out the shabby, tattered, hand-signed copy of poems by Robert Frost. I had snagged it from Cici's library. I wondered what Mr. Frost would have written about this.

As we watch the world descend

From greatness to the end,

Tragedy a common friend

As loss without mend.

We wear our losses greatly

As we count our blessings daily,

Only to have them taken,

Left without a decent piece of bacon.

I laughed loudly to myself, folding back the worn paperback with Mr. Frost's face on it and replaying the verses in my mind. The rhythmic words filled the hollow spaces, taking the place of all I missed, leaving me lost in someone else's reality. Past the tip of my sneaker, I could see her, interrupting my thoughts and stealing my attention. Her hair was pulled back in a slightly disheveled way. It looked natural and cute. Her medium-caramel skin accentuated her short, curvy stature.

I watched her make her rounds along the outskirts of the stables. She was welcoming and friendly, with three little ones in tow, following behind her like a little caravan of tiny people mimicking her interactions. She was patient and kind with them, encouraging them, teaching them to network and seek out resources. Little ducklings.

I was lost in her, and Mr. Frost's words faded away, falling to the wayside.

I wondered if this was how the birds felt, perched high in the trees, admiring everything below. They gathered apples and congregated next to the first row of tiny homes. The setting sun, orange and yellow, highlighted her full cheekbones. The shade of the trees left a crisscross pattern, vanishing in little bits as dusk took hold. The pieces of her wispy hair swayed as she giggled with her little gang. I couldn't help but smile while watching and listening to their antics. Without warning, she glanced up; I had forgotten I was not entirely invisible, and I faltered and almost fell out of the opening. I caught myself mid-wobble, and rolled back through the hay door. My lack of grace and coordination was impressive.

"Smooth, real smooth. No one likes a stalker, Zavier. Why don't you come down and join us?" I could sense the sarcastic humor in her tone. The flush in my face burned as I tried to compose myself and spring back to the opening.

As creepy and inappropriate as it might have been, she was how I would have imagined my mom to be as her younger self: funny, pretty, sarcastic, a natural leader.

"Why don't you come down? We have an extra apple." she shouts up to me. My fingers were crossed that she couldn't see my rosy cheeks.

As I tucked my feet in and prepared to make my way from the loft, Asher steamrolled around the stable. He was so tall and thin, like Dad; he had really grown. I must have bubbled up from another end of the gene pool. He was much more developed, too, whereas I was still...well, asserting my maturity with wit and charm.

Asher wrapped his mighty tree branches around her shoulders and faced the sunset, followings its rays to infinity, leaving me lost in the shadows of the loft.

Cami snuck one final look back at me over his massive arms, her doe eyes sharing in my disappointment. I gave a half wave as I watched my brother build his wall, just like in Mr. Frost's words. Maybe good fences make good brothers, too.

***

Through the secret door I creep, down the stairs I slowly peep, to the mat I sneak, only to watch her sleep. —Zavier Winter

I had taken to lurking—no one saw me anymore anyway. They were too busy with everything else. I didn't mind so much, there was plenty to observe. No one really expected much of me in the shadows. I made my way to the cellar to check on Mom. This was where she went to work out her thoughts.

Finding my place at the bottom of the stairs, I crouched, folding my legs to my chest. I crossed my arms, resting my chin on them. She had fallen asleep on the mat again. When she was able to sleep, this was where she was, late at night, hunkered between the guns and the wine.

She was huddled into a ball; I was sure she had worked herself to the point she passed out. Sometimes I thought she came here to torture herself. It killed me to watch her literally beat herself up, but it paid to see her sleep. If she didn't, she just wandered around, checking and double-checking everything, as if she knew something was coming.

I was the only one left to watch over her, and I was sorry for that. Asher would never have chosen her over Dad.

And me, I am not much. The only thing I was ever good at was now inconsequential—a solid hit to the back fence was not worth much in this scenario. Well, unless I had a gun in my hand, but Mom wouldn't let me keep one with me. She always said, "You'll shoot your eye out, kid." I guessed that was a reference to some movie from back in the day. Hutch sometimes took me out to the field to fire a few rounds. He sucked down a beer, or a few, and lets me take down the cans. Every time, he was like, "Hot damn, kid, you could hit the eye out of an eagle." Hutch was cool, and it was too bad Mom thought he was a 'piece of shit.' He told me to keep watch over her, and I would never do any different. When he talked about her, his eyes lost focus and he was lost somewhere else. I didn't think he was a piece of shit.

She stirred a little, shifting slightly against the cold surface. I quietly grabbed her blanket and tucked her in, like every other night I did after the first time I'd found her. When she woke, she would simply fold it and put it on the bench. I wonder if she knew it was me who tucked her in, or maybe she assumed it was a magic blanket fairy, like the one that picks up the socks.

Up the stairs and through the corridor, I found my way to Cici's world, mystical pages bound in leather. At night I was out of the shadows, moving freely without anyone noticing. *Mr. Frost, maybe I too have become acquainted with the night.*

***

M. LaVon

Loud voices flooded past the door. I startled awake; I must have dozed off. I peeled my slobbery face from the leather of the library sofa. I could feel the wet slob caked around my mouth as I tried to gather myself up. In the scramble, the book that lay beside me dropped to the floor with a thud, tumbling into the morning light that seeped through the small window. It caught just right on the glossy cover, making it sparkle and shine. I froze and waited, making sure I was not heard.

The voices were familiar—and it was not just any voices. Asher and Mom were at it again. He seemed to be picking a fight about anything these days. *The air is too hot, the winter is too cold, Dad left us and it's her fault, she did not stop the end of the world.* Blah, blah, blah… Ugh.

I slipped Mr. Frost into my back pocket and stretched out. I gave an exaggerated reach high above my head to delay my inevitable entry into the warzone. I hesitated at the door to the main hall, the cool door handle resting in my palm—to open or not to open, that was the question. No one knew or cared I was in there; I could stay and live someone else's life all day, or I could walk out into the crossfire and hope to prevent bloodshed.

I tightened my grip on the handle, gently turned my wrist until the click told me to pull. The smell of fresh, crisp air seeped into the staleness of the room, cutting into the dusty and comforting smell of the library, reminding me there was a world outside these walls that was real.

Mom and Asher had the front doors open, one foot in and one foot out past the threshold. Asher towered over her, and she looked so small next to him. I was not sure when it happened: One moment we were little, and the next he was not. Mom's voice quivered, telling me it was time to jump in before she said something that would put her in the cellar for weeks.

"Hey, Mom, Liz said there was a nine AM community meeting you needed to prep for?" I said with all the innocence I could muster.

"Where is she? I don't remember anything scheduled for this morning." Her voice was unsure but acknowledging. She turned her attention back to Asher.

"Asher, we are not done here. You need to get a handle on your attitude. Your behavior yesterday was not acceptable. And I don't know what you are doing online all the time, but you need to be cautious, there could be consequences." Her voice was scolding. "Zavier, will you run and get Liz? I am not sure what I should be prepping for." Confused, she headed into the drawing room.

Asher looked to me with a sullen expression. "What the hell, dude?" He turned his aggression toward me.

"Can you just cut her some slack? You don't have to be a total d-bag all the time."

He was unamused with my meddling and stomped off. I imagined his giant figure ducking through the doors like an oversized troll.

Now to find Liz to have her help me out with a bullshit story about how she'd gotten the date of the meeting wrong.

***

Liz did not hesitate to corroborate my alibi that it was a misunderstanding, a simple mistake of "pregnancy brain," whatever that meant. She said Mom would get it. She gently squeezed my shoulder for good luck, I guessed. She was amazing, everything I imagined an aunt would be. I had spent many evenings sitting on the floor of her tiny house reading whatever as she knitted away. The rhythmic clicking of the needles was nice. She didn't say much, but I didn't mind.

Packing the news for my mom, I headed back from the stables to the main house. The trail to the house was well worn and easy to follow without even looking.

I felt a tug on my back pocket. With a swift yank, Mr. Frost was set free from his denim holster. I took a moment before I spun around to catch the culprit. About five-foot-nothing, Cami stood there, proudly holding Robert hostage.

"Poetry, huh? I wouldn't have pegged you for a poetry guy. Aren't you, like, a jock?" Cami's sweet voice was tainted with a mix of her trademark sarcasm.

"Oh, she can read. I thought the leader of the Lost Boys would need remedial... What can I say... I am a complex character with many layers. Didn't anyone ever tell you stereotyping is rude?" Not my best comeback, but it would do.

She snarked out a quick laugh—more of a laugh-*huh?*—at my witty rebuttal.

"Yes, well, I was not always the leader of the Lost Boys." Her usual zinger was replaced by a long pause, telling me she was thinking of how things used to be.

"You know, I can always tutor you with my genius if you ever so desire." I worked hard to embellish my offer with a pretentious tone.

She punched me in the shoulder, and I howled and whined for effect.

"You want to play catch?" she said, breaking the banter. I could see she was serious.

"Huh, I never pegged you for a jock," I said mockingly.

"My dad and I played catch a lot, and I've played softball for as long as I can remember…" Her voice trailed off, lost in remembering.

"Sure, let me grab gloves and a ball."

I rushed in and told my mom about the mistake, but she had already moved on to something else. A brief acknowledgment and a wave sent me on my way.

I ran through the building, grabbed two gloves and a ball, and headed out to the lawns flanking the driveway. The steady volley cleared my head of everything but us in that moment. It felt familiar: The world was not ending; there was no war, no virus, no fighting; everything was normal. I could almost remember the taste of Sour Patch Kids.

For Every Season

My internal playlist shuffled to "Turn! Turn! Turn!" and The Byrds remind me that there is a time for everything, and this is Cate's time to hate.

The crazy look in her eyes told me that this was the end. She would end Tom, even if it meant the end of her. How do we quantify the lives of those whom we loved? Was the life of my brother, my best friend, my love, or the man who would save my baby worth more than stopping a madman from killing us all—especially after we had lost so much, almost to the point nothing was left.

I watched her kiss her boys good-bye, and Zavier clutched on to her as if he could read every step she would take in her face. He was so much like his mom, a deep thinker wrapped up in feeling every moment. Asher stood conflicted. Since Tom had come to Winter and left him behind, he had grown more introverted and distant, the wedge between him and Cate growing tenfold. It was slowly killing her, her inner torment hidden behind her stoic features. Her worst nightmare was that Asher would choose Tom.

Adam came to me, kissed me on the forehead, and then hugged me with all of himself. I whispered to him to bring them all back to me, every last one, including himself. We had lost too much for good-byes to be a modest gesture.

Before they all left, Kavik and I took one last walk around Winter. He reached for my hand, and I let him have it. It was rough, but he was gentle, weaving his fingers between mine. As we parted ways, he turned to face me, brought my fingers to his lips and kissed them, then thoughtfully rested his hand on Sonia's little bump. There were no words between us, but he said so much.

Their plan was simple: Get Eli and stop Tom.

How could we have been so foolish to think it would be that simple? We weren't warlords, we weren't militants, we weren't trained killers, we were just people hoping to be on the right side of humanity. Cate thought she knew Tom well enough to know he wouldn't risk the lives of their sons, and maybe also deep down, he loved her enough to spare Winter.

But Tom had no intention of letting this go. He was hellbent on leaving his old life behind, severing any connection to who he once was and who he was now, or maybe who he had always been. Cate, for all the good she thought she was doing with him, just helped hide what he truly was.

***

They came early. The breaches crashed down like waves on a rocky shore, exploding into chaotic sprays, taking everyone and everything out to sea. It was like the entire military force of the Free Nationalists rode in on those waves, the horseman of the apocalypse. It was merciless carnage. Tom was not kidding when he had said he would come for Winter and wipe it off the face of the earth without so much as a second thought.

What did it represent—what threat were we? We were just simple farmers.

From the front steps, I watched the evening sky glow orange and yellow with the spreading flames. The sound of distant explosions boomed, echoes scattering the livestock. We were surrounded, with nowhere to go. Some people had attempted to flee through the front gate, only to be executed on the spot. The screams floated up from the stables, voices bouncing against the rock walls and the stucco façade. This sounded so familiar. We had been here before.

They must have watched them leave. They must have been watching for weeks. They must have been watching the entire time, lying in wait, thinking we never stood a chance. How else would they have known? But why did they not kill the others whom we had evacuated first?

The flames were visible, dragon tongues lapping the air, spitting speckled embers deep into the darkness. Smoke and firelight washed out the stars. We were on an island being swallowed into the mouth of hell.

Save the children—their little bodies were huddled deep in the basement, surrounded only by stone and the grace of God.

I watched the last line fall as the demons came out of the flames, their black silhouettes framed by the yellow and auburn backdrop. The creatures, no longer men, decimated all who stood before them. They walked over bodies like they had turned to stone and lay shattered on the ground. I stood transfixed, my feet remained planted, I couldn't look away. Glass broke behind me as they laid siege to the house. I heard the commander shout out, "I want everyone in the house!"

A cold chill coursed through my body, and the hair on my arms stood on end.

I stepped to the middle of the stairs so he could see me. He stopped, flanked by two of his men. I knew them, too. Their guns were down, and without hesitation I drew and dropped them. I could feel the heat of the chamber as the bullets exited the gun. My trigger reflex knew no restraint.

He drew his pistol, and I hesitated for a second too long. Time became sluggish, until a force behind me collected me at the hip, pinning me against the wall. As the clap of the bullet caught me, searing pain followed in my right arm. My gun went loose, and the metal clacked as it fell down the steps. Zavier's body continued to shield me from whatever was coming. I could feel the rough pulling as Mr. Routine yanked Zavier from me. I reached back, clamoring to hold him with me, but evil had a fierce grip.

"You're lucky your dad is who he is, or I would kill you where you lie, boy. Where is your brother?" The harsh growl told me he was in a mood.

Asher slunk out of the shadows, head down, one arm crossed holding the other at the elbow. All the signs of a child who had just made a horrible decision that got a lot of people killed.

"Good work, son, your daddy will be really proud of you." Mr. Routine patted him on the back. Devastated for him, I laid against the wall where his brother had saved my life, and he avoided looking at me.

"Asher? What is he talking about? What does he mean?" The world had just come crashing down on Zavier, everything cruel and raw. Beads of tears cupped in his eyelids, sparkling in the firelight as he stared at his older brother. "Asher… A— Did you tell Dad?"

Asher was pensive, looked away, the division of good and evil in him indistinguishable. "Zavier, Dad needed my help," Asher whined in response.

"What about all these people?" Zavier's voice cracked under a million tons of pressure.

"I didn't know it would happen like this." Asher was pleading with his brother, to no avail.

"A—how did you think it would happen? Dad abandoned us, became a ruthless supervillain, and now he wants to kill Mom, and you're helping him!? He doesn't care about us... He is just using you...and you're too stupid to see it." Zavier was wise beyond his years. I watched as the most painful lesson rolled out in front of him.

"Dad wants us back, Z." Asher was full of conviction.

"A—Dad is nothing more than a bully, and I don't want anything to do with him," Zavier answered with a look of absolute disgust.

His switch flipped, Asher lashed out, striking Zavier in the stomach and punching a shot to his face, dropping Zavier to his knees.

"Nobody asked you! Mama's boy!"

Mr. Routine slapped his knee in delight. I was sure nothing was more satisfying to him than someone else's pain.

Mr. Routine signaled to one of his lackeys to take the boys to the truck. Asher caught him and whispered something in his ear, and Mr. Routine chuckled and winked. Asher ran back through the house, returning with Cami. My stomach churned, and I held back the puke sensation. I reached out for her. *Don't go.* She looked back, confused, then was dragged off to the awaiting convoy.

"Move out, we got what we came for. Gather at the docks," he shouted to his men. Then he turned back to me. "Now, what to do with you?" He reached down, grabbing me by my hair. His fingers wove in, grabbing clumps, bringing me to my feet. My arm was soaked through, the seeping blood forming long streaks down to my fingers, droplets gathering at the tips, leaving little red polka dots below me.

He was in a mood for sure.

In the foyer, he started by throwing me against the stairs. I scrambled to get back up, and he caught me with a backhand to the ear. I put my arms up to defend myself. He searched and found where his bullet had entered me, pounding the open flesh with his fist. My cries left me without air, taking me back to my knees. He picked me up by my shoulders, tossing me into the beautiful antique mirror. The glass shattered, raining down, crashing in pieces all around me, falling in glittery flecks. His massive hands found my hair again, pulling me back to the stairs—forcing me down, trading my hair for my throat. My arms were flailing, grasping for anything, then he reached down, tearing my pants open in the middle. A choking scream broke as I scratched against the arm he had pressed against my neck. He was not even phased by my growing bump and Sonia beneath it. My hands made contact, clawing, fighting. He pushed up far enough to punch me in his favorite spot, the bone of my cheek still jagged from his hand, crunches biting the tender tissue.

Without delay he got back to his business. His forearm applied pressure, holding me steady, leaving me searching for air. He did not wait, reaching in me, my scream muted and gurgled. The louder I tried to scream, the tighter the pressure; the tighter the pressure, the quieter my screams became. The warm light came for me, flashing white, everything slipping away—except for him tearing into me, ripping into me. *Sleep.*

A distant *pop* brought me back. He stopped, peeled out of me, and rolled to the ground. The light flooded back. The sharp pull of air formed a gasp, bringing me up from the stairs. Kavik rushed to me, sweeping me up.

Mr. Routine squirmed and shifted on his back, looking for anything to defend himself. But it was too late. The shot must have been dead-center to his spine. I could see the rage boiling deep in Kavik's eyes.

I kept his eyes to me. "Let me end this." He took a hesitant step back, as I searched for closure.

Without thinking, I collected a long, pointy shard of glass from the floor. I felt the sharp edge cutting through my palm as I stood, admiring my reflection.

I stood over him like every time he had stood over me as I'd cowered in his shadow, huddled against the wooden panels of that shitty trailer. I crouched, kneeling beside him, the glittery glass crunching under the soles of my fuzzy slippers. He lay splayed out and exposed, vulnerable and helpless. I wrapped my hand around him, still swollen and throbbing, letting him feel my power, my control, soaking up his fear.

With a quick swipe I took back what he had taken from me. I placed it back in his hand, held my eyes to his, watched that sink in, and then took back everything he had taken from all the others. *Sonia.* My face was the last face he saw before I slit his throat.

Lose, Lose

The frigid water of the bay flittered and lapped against the hull. The water split, dividing into transparent waves folding over themselves and then dissolving into the blended mass. Tiny white bubbles danced in our wake. The dark night sky was twinkling with diamond stars. Hutch sat beside me, his features warm and distinct in the moonlight.

Much more handsome than when his mouth was moving.

When life was normal, a trip on the bay would have been the beginning of a beautiful date night. Now it was like marching to your death with your closest friends.

The ripples of the water in front split into two, paving the way, the murky abyss calling us closer. The shoreline welcomed us with baited sarcasm. *Here kitty, kitty. Come closer, come closer.*

I imagined the fireworks as we arrived, fanfare displayed through rebuked affection. But the shore was shrouded in black and without resistance, our landing without reproach. An invasion without confrontation. *Shit.*

The ship bounced off the buoys, jilting and jumping us about, the squealing plastic squeezed out as it was compressed between the ship and the dock. The swagger of the ship settled as the large metal platform hovered against the wooden deck.

I dropped a boot to the planks, fully anticipating it would be shot off, but nothing. It was too late to think this was too easy, too soon to retreat. *Come get me, Tom.*

Kavik came to the handrail. "The team is just past the guardhouse. They will escort you where you need to go."

"Kavik, go back to Winter. Make sure they're okay, something does not feel right. Tom would never let it be this easy. If all is okay, come back for us. If not, we'll find a way back."

He nodded, we unloaded, and he sped off. The boat left a trail of rippling foam as it made its way back across the bay.

The hair on my arm stood to full attention. There were limited defenses—not that our small team of invaders was worthy of a full assault, but a couple of warning shots across our bow would have made me feel better.

We worked our way past the docks and to the guard shack as instructed.

A young sailor was waiting huddled in the four-by-four booth, terrified and apprehensive. He was not much older than Asher. I might have been old enough to be his mom, or at least his really cool aunt.

I eased into the booth, and he pushed back in response, as if he was virus free and I was a carrier. I held out my hand to steady him.

"Look, they found out and shot most of the 'deserters.' Some are held up on the other side of the campus, but you are on your own." His voice was shaky and nervous.

"Where did everyone go?" I pulled out my calm mom voice.

"After the rebellion was subdued, several trucks loaded up and headed out across the bridge, some took to the water, but went southwest. There were some guys here earlier talking about Building H."

"Building H?" I let my confused face do most of the talking.

"Building H is in the middle of the campus, close to the command center, at the beginning of the old runway." He pointed to a nondescript path away from the guard shack.

"When you say a rebellion, you mean..."

"There were a couple hundred guys looking to take back Alameda, but they did not stand a chance against those animals..." His anxious look turned to disappointment and sadness.

So much for outside help.

We lined up and, like a disconnected caterpillar, cautiously crept across the camp, wherever possible keeping to the buildings' edges. We took our time to peer around every corner, but there was nothing, no one. The so-called rebellion, poorly timed as it was, gave us the perfect distraction. How could trained military guys been that far off?

The grass in the center court was well worn, pressed down by uniform units beating it flat over time. The green was slightly visible, illuminated by blinding halogen lights perched high overhead. The buildings were cookie-cutters, exact replicas of each other, only differentiated by oversized letters and numbers. We scanned the faded military-grade paint looking for Building H. To my surprise, Building H was different. It was much bigger, maybe a maintenance facility or hangar of some sort. I looked to Hutch, who was intently focused on assessing the situation. The security detail were backs to the wall, slightly crouched in the dark and quietly signing to themselves.

We weren't completely alone on this side of the base. There were a few men guarding Building H. We decided it would be less obvious if we moved toward the outside of the court, swinging wide and coming up behind H, and behind the solider guarding the front entrance.

I moved back in line, and the caterpillar inched out, diving deeper into the shadows. We were steadily inching, shoulders a rifle-length apart. Each step was in unison, synchronized, an invisible shell holding us together. The slight shuffle of cloth set the pace, an intimate rhythm made possible by the closeness of the group. The slight chill in the winter air turned our rapid, heavy breath into foggy plumes, like the steam behind a train.

I was so caught up in our movement that when we stopped, I looked at the leader perplexed, only to realize we were there, against the side of Building H.

I could feel Hutch's eyes burning into my back, reminding me this could be our very last moment together, this could be our last moment period. I had an overwhelming urge to turn back to him one final time, to say good-bye, maybe to say I was sorry for everything. But this had never been about us, this was about them, keeping my boys safe, saving them from Tom. It was about building a world for them to live in. This was about saving Eli, who had started this all. This was about putting an end to this.

The team centered around a side entrance, taking defensive breach positions. Just as we prepared to enter, gunfire broke out off in the distance, not from the dockside but the land side. The energy shifted, and a large group of soldiers, once invisible hiding in buildings, crossed the courtyard heading toward the firefight.

The gunfire intensified, lighting up the night sky. The orange and yellow streaks flashed, wiping out the stars. The Alameda rebels must have gotten their second wind or were waiting for something else altogether. Maybe they were waiting for us to get into position. Two very loud explosions sent the guards ducking for cover, their faces lying flat against the tiny pebbles covering the worn pavement.

Taking the chaos as a sign to move, the team leader breached the door and pushed inside. Just past the entrance, the room opened wide, revealing very little inside. *Is this supposed to be a trap?*

Cautious, the team leader moved us to the center, forming a circle of protection around me, like the Secret Service guarding the president. For a moment I felt out of place, no longer just part of the team, Hutch caught my cold stare as I tried to decipher what was happening.

And then it sunk in—my own team was using me as bait to draw Tom out. *This is a trap.* Tom knew I was coming because we had told him so.

Hutch's eyes shifted away—and I know immediately it had been him.

Before I had a chance to say anything, I heard a gurgly voice call out from the shadows. "Cate?" and I knew—the very thought took my breath away. Without even thinking, I pushed out of the circle and rushed to him, sliding down across the concrete on my knees beside him.

"Eli!" I exclaimed. Excitement, panic, sadness, fear, happiness, anger—all at once took over. The tears were without restraint, my hands grasping and clutching at him, trying to lift him and pull him closer to me. A heavy chain was weighing him down. His beaten, emaciated body was almost unrecognizable, but his voice was still the same.

"We are here, we got you. We got you." My voice caught.

"You can't be here, child. You need to go. He wants you here, and he is going to kill you." Each syllable of his warm, Southern drawl was bringing me joy, even if it was meant to be a warning.

"I have missed you so much." Everything around me was gone. I had forgotten where I was or why from my happiness in that moment.

"Cate, you have to go... Don't be a fool." His voice was weary but commanding.

"Help me!" I said, looking back to the team, exasperated. "Take him—help me!"

Two of the team members worked to free Eli from his chains and lift him up. He could barely stand. His arms stretched out across each of their shoulders, Jesus on the cross. His head drooped down; he was unable to stay up under his own effort. "We got you, Eli." The reassurance in my voice sounded desperate.

The team lined up to extricate us. The circle moved back into place. We got about five steps before the first shots were fired.

The guys in front peeled away, like the skin of a banana, leaving the soft supple meat exposed. The spray of blood from their exit wounds exploded before me. The next few shots dropped the team leader and the one to the right of Eli. The one to the left pulled Eli to the ground and back into the shadows near the entrance we had come in, now an exit, dragging him off to oblivion. I stood still as they all fell away. And just like that, it was just Hutch and me in the middle.

The dark figures stepped in from obscurity, parting like the sea. Tom stepped forward from behind his minions, all clad in black military uniforms.

Without hesitation or warning, Tom lifted his gun and landed two into Hutch's chest, point-blank. No lengthy supervillain monologue to give us time to think things through.

As he fell, I couldn't help but verbalize my anguish. "No!" My hand was outstretched to his, and he turned and for a spilt second our eyes locked, and then I felt him slip away.

"So, it's true." Tom didn't even break his stride, charging toward me. He whipped his pistol across my temple, the metal still warm, dropping me to my knees. Specks of light flashed behind my lids, followed by a wave of nausea. The image of the perfect father and husband I had conjured in my mind faded away as the waves passed. Passionate moments, giggling faces, intimate embraces, tender kisses, all evaporated into nothing, all of it gone.

He towered over me, drunk with power. "My, how things have changed." His belt buckle was aligned at my eye level. He reached out and stroked the back of my head, pulling it toward him in a rocking manner, ensuring I understood his condescension, a mock blow job. Pairing his hands, he brought his pistol to the side of my cheek. The metal had cooled, and the smell of gunpowder was more prominent.

A moment of clarity and confidence led me to strike upward, catching him off guard. His arm shot up, allowing me to land an additional blow to his ego.

His gun dropped loose and fell out of reach. He let out a huff, pulling his arms in to cradle his manhood.

I could sense Hutch stir, and still on my knees I shuffled to him, my hands crawling and clamoring across the cold concrete until I reached his warm hand. His other hand was moving to the back of his scalp, feeling for the part of his skull that must have hit the ground first. At the edge of his flak jacket, a growing red stain has formed, framed by pooling blood beneath, presumably seeping from his exit wound. It was hard to miss the scorch mark where the other bullet had landed dead-center in what would have been his heart if it hadn't been protected by the Kevlar.

He croaked out, "I'm fine," and began to stir.

The heavy presence of Tom's men shifted the air in the space around us, as he ordered them to lift and hold Hutch. A sense of panic washed over me, as I fought to hold on to him. He groaned loudly as they pulled up on his bullet-ridden shoulder.

As soon as Hutch was clear and in the hands of the soldiers, the sharp sting of the back of Tom's hand slamming into the already swollen and bruised side of my face caught me off guard and sent me further to the ground.

The shock turned to anger, and the magma at my core boiled and churned. The love I'd once had, a solid unbreakable crust, melted and sloughed away under the intense heat, revealing only vehement disdain and indifference for the man who used to be my husband. My hands folded above the concrete into fists, channeling unchecked rage. He was nothing but a bully, a tyrant, stuck in the body of a man whom I'd once loved, a man I'd once shared the most intimate times, but who now was nothing to me.

Hutch began to resist his captors, engaging in a three-way brawl. Even one-handed, he put up a good fight.

A renewed sense of independence from Tom drove my leg forward in a sweeping motion, leveling the playing field and sending him to the ground beside me.

Desperate to gain the advantage, I staggered to my feet, still slightly unsteady, but determined. I raised my leg to stomp his face, but in a split second he rolled to his guard, reached up and grabbed my foot mid-stomp, twisting my ankle and bringing me back to the ground. Thankfully, he dropped me close enough to him for my fist to make direct contact with the soft flesh of his abdomen. The impact put pressure on his diaphragm, shifting the air, pressing it out from his chest.

I scrambled to put distance between us, crawling away with my chest against the ground. I kicked at his arms, which were still holding my legs. His long, lean, snakelike form struck out as he climbed up behind me. His arms constricted around my throat and shoulders. His legs beside me wrenched upward until we were standing, and his arms threaded around me in a chokehold. My hands instinctively grabbed at his arm, scratching and peeling at them in an attempt to get free. He reached over and pulled my gun free from my back, flinging it to the ground.

"You won't be needing that... Squirm, baby, squirm...I kinda like it... With a single twist I can end you." His voice growled from behind gritted teeth. *He means it.*

My thoughts split over to the ongoing fight between Hutch and the two men across the room, the grunts and howls of hand-to-hand combat echoing across the hollow space.

My elbow dropped to Tom's sternum, and my boot stomped across his foot. Barely fazed, he held tight, pushing me toward the wall, crushing me against it, grating my face against the rough surface. His full weight leaned in, his knees bending slightly, crouching at my level, pressing even more so he could fell his hardness against the soft line of my backside. He was making this all about him and what he craved from me. His arm squeezed around my neck even tighter as he played out his fantasy, the drool leaking from my mouth as I struggled to gasp in air.

"I could take you right here. You should have not crossed me, Cat, you are not the boss here. You are nothing but a weak fucking whore. Now *your man* can watch me rip you to shreds and end you." His face tucked in deeply to the nape of my neck, his hot breath in my ear, cheek resting against my hair. He was breathing in the scent of me, feeding off my fears. *Animal.*

He worked his hand around my torso, pressing the ridge of his palm firmly against my pubic bone, letting his fingers dangle and explore.

"He...is...more...man...than...you...will...ever...be," I gurgled out from beneath his arm. *He is right.* He could end me quickly.

I released my hands, briefly giving in to the chokehold, holding my breath, and pressed up from the wall against him, forcing him to divert his hand from its exploration. He might kill me, but I'd be damned if he got *his* while doing it. He struggled to hold me down.

"That's right, Cat. You know I like a good fight." He stepped back, letting me up from the wall, freeing me from the chokehold to reach for my wrist, spinning me around to face him. I used his own momentum to land a clean hit to his face, only to have it returned full-force. I raised my leg and pushed off from him to gain some distance between the wall and him. His smirk was patronizing, dripping with years of resentment. How could I have missed his hatred for me? My heart broke a little. *Blind.*

I searched for my gun, which was lost in the dark grayness of the shadows. He was relentless in his attacks, like a drunk, abusive husband angered by cold mashed potatoes, reduced to an animal playing with its prey. With every hit, I backed away, hoping to get closer to my gun.

"You are so stupid, Cat, up in your crystal castle ignoring what is going on in the world, comfortable in privilege. Blind to what is affecting those around you, like always. Don't you see, you have no control over how this plays out. You could never make the hard choices that needed to be made." He was a stranger to me, unfamiliar and sinister.

"You are getting played, Tom, they are using you to wage a war. You think they give two shits about your ideologies? This is about control and power…and you are no better than the ones you are fighting against. You are a murderer. Unleashing nothing but suffering…"

"What do *you* know about suffering?! Everything you ever had was handed to you on a silver platter!" His spiteful tone was not surprising, but it still stung.

"And you had no problem taking from that platter! I gave you everything—your job, your house, your kids, your life! If it wasn't for me, they would have put you in prison, and you would have died behind bars."

"Yeah, Cat, that is right. You are the fucking savior. How did that work out for you? As we speak, your precious Winter is burning to the ground. Your arrogance got all those sad, sorry people killed." The bile from my stomach lurched up my throat. I lunged at him, hammering my fists at him, driving my knees into him. I took advantage when he was off balance to land a solid punch to his temple, sending him to the ground. I stomped his face to the concrete, the feel of my boot on the soft tissue of his cheek filling me with momentary delight.

Without pause, he gathered himself up and returned fire, the sex-filled enthusiasm he had earlier replaced by pure lividity. No amount of defense would stop him now. *This is when he kills me.*

Clack, clack, the sound was coupled with Tom clenching his leg and bowing to the ground. Behind him a small figure emerged from the darkness. I followed his line of sight down to one of the remaining soldiers lying on the ground with a shot directly to the head, freeing Hutch.

"Mom, you okay?" To my surprise, Zavier's voice echoed against the empty walls.

Asher burst through the door right after and ran to Tom, propping him up. Tom's face was frozen in shock at Zavier's attack.

"Z– What did you do!?"

"I suggest you both back the fuck up!" Zavier ordered his brother and father in a commanding tone. "No mistake, I shot you in the leg on purpose. The next shot will be to the head." I was completely taken aback by Zavier's authority and his use of expletives.

In the silence, I became acutely aware of the overt fighting outside, and so did Tom. The rebels must not have been as overrun as previously thought. Tom and Asher inched backward toward the exit, Zavier still aiming for his father's forehead.

"Cat, this is just the beginning. If you think you'll be safe, you are sadly mistaken. You will meet the same fate as Winter." Tom was holding on to Asher's shoulder like a crutch.

"Tom, are you really that delusional to think I would let you take Winter? Things aren't always as they seem. Most of my people are long gone. You were so preoccupied with your little game that you might have missed some important details. As we speak, your cyber-empire is under siege, your data centers are destroyed, and your Alameda forces are being overrun. I wonder what your command will think about you when they have to come and save your ass from a simpleminded rich girl and her peasant farmers. Good luck with that." His scowl told me he was not going to let this go.

"You won't win this time, Cat."

"You wanted a war, well, now you got one... And, Tom, my name is not fucking *Cat.*" Zavier held his hand completely steady as they exited the building. As they disappeared from view, the thought of not seeing Asher again broke my heart into a million pieces—he was his father's son.

Zavier lowered his gun, and something about him was more mature and resilient. I regretted not noticing it until now. "Mom, Kavik is waiting at the dock. We need to go." He spoke with urgency.

The fighting was centered around the main entrance, no longer just the Alameda rebels, but so many who had taken sides with the people of Winter. Men and women were coming to our defense, wanting to take back what was ours.

***

I walked across the dock, knowing nothing would be the same from here on out. We were no longer farmers or survivors; now we were soldiers about to embark on a new chapter to reclaim our freedom. Exhaustion was a rolling wave, collapsing over me as we loaded the boat. A sorry lot we were, battered and broken—but alive.

"Kavik, radio to the teams to fall back to defensive positions. Blow the bridge to buy us some time. Let's get this show on the road." I folded into the wheelhouse bench seat next to Eli.

"I don't understand?" Eli was obviously bewildered at what had just happened.

"This is bigger than us now. With that little skirmish, we just joined the resistance, the third faction of a never-ending civil war." My eyes were fixed at starboard, watching the shore fade away as we headed out onto the bay. "After you were abducted, they cut off all supplies and communication. Tom initiated a cat-and-mouse game that was meant to end with the decimation of Winter and, of course, me. He used Asher to get inside information about Winter and the greater communities. This was what gave us the advantage.

"Hutch was able to build a network of resistance sympathizers who not only had the special skills we needed to cripple Tom's efforts but who were willing to orchestrate a pretty convincing coup, giving us the opportunity to get you back.

"Our friends at Google declared a cyberwar on Tom without him even knowing was happening. They were able to track Asher and his correspondence and figured out everything we needed to know.

"With some help from the outside, and some friends who like to blow shit up, Hutch arranged the destruction of all the WMS data centers, rendering them useless."

"What about Asher?" His soulful eyes were sunken in and surrounded by dark circles. His head was full of sweet memories of Asher, childlike and innocent, far from the arrogant and troubled young man he had become.

"I knew Tom would come for the boys, but thankfully Kavik was able to ensure they were safely transported back to me. But I knew Asher would choose Tom—he was never mine to keep. He had made his choice months ago and would have run away from us regardless. I at least know he is now with Tom and not dead on the side of the road. Easier to let him think I am the monster Tom made me out to be." As I said it, the words tasted sour and were heavy, like sucking on rocks.

"So, what now?"

"I hope you like poutine and the rain," I said jokingly.

He gave me a 'Oh, child' look.

"We have made arrangements to move north, to Washington. The Winter Lodge on Orcas Island, the old executive retreat, currently falls in Canadian-occupied territory. They have agreed to allow us safe passage and support while we move our people, many of whom have already begun the journey."

"In return?"

"It's complicated." I was too tired to get into the details of our agreement just yet, and I was not sure I had digested it all myself, either. I was now the proud leader of what is left of the Northwest Territory and responsible for pushing the FN out of Washington, Idaho, and Oregon. We would also partner with Montana, which had been holding its own for some time. Not to mention I was to lead the navy out of Bremerton. We planned to migrate anyone we could behind enemy lines to northern Washington.

I snuggled into Eli's thin body and put my head back against the wall behind the bench. Once I felt him drift off, I snuck out of the wheelhouse, leaning against the railing. Hutch made his way to my side, his arm in a sling and his wounds bandaged.

"Nice work, princess." He nudged me with his good arm, only to wince anyway.

"Why didn't you tell me I was just bait?" The slight hurt in my voice was audible.

"You are never 'just' anything." He turned to grab my attention.

"Then what was the deal during the breach?" My head drooped low to hide my insecurity.

"You mean, protecting you from yourself? Yes, I ordered that. If not, you would have been the first person he'd dropped—well, maybe second, after me." He shared a sly smirk.

He took my silence as an invitation to keep talking.

"Look, there is a reason why they put the commander behind the line. You will do us no good dead. I personally like you alive. And like it or not, there are a lot of people who expect me to keep you alive. I take that job seriously."

"How's that working out for you?" I said, looking at his arm sling with an exaggerated gaze.

"What, this old thing? I thought girls liked boys with scars." I couldn't help but chuckle at his ridiculousness.

***

The sun rose behind the thick smoke now blanketing the area, a muggy orange glow casting an eerie dull hue. The little fire, intended for winter, raged past the co-ops, through the surrounding suburbs, and broke free into the hills above Woodside. In a strange way it was what was meant to be: a good-bye, leaving me with nothing to come back to. We eased past the wrought-iron *W*, moved down the long driveway, through the battered ornamentals, and around the broken fountain.

The estate was broken and partially collapsed, but still stately in a ragged and tired kind of way. The stables and large barn were piles of smoldering ash, the rows of tiny homes, rubble. Our new beginning had been brought to a catastrophic end. I took care to savor each step as I followed them up to the large oak door, which was swung wide open, untouched, and now out of place in the menacing warzone.

The crunch of broken glass between the soles of my boots and the terra-cotta tile echoed in the grand foyer. Blood streaks and smears from what I could only assume a body.

I couldn't leave without saying good-bye. Surprisingly, her library was mostly intact, minus what we had packed and sent ahead.

As I had done so many times before, I let my hands lead me by the fingers around the room, the tips stroking the carved pieces, swirling up and around the curved features. The polished varnish was soft and smooth, cool and warm. The smell of aged books and dust hung in the air, the smell that filled my childhood with beautiful dreams and imaginary places, as I moved to her desk and my special corner. Sitting once more in her chair, I hoped to channel her, her kindness, energy, presence of mind, power, influence. If I could be half the women she was, I might stand a chance. *Sadly, I know I am not.*

"Cate, we need to go," Hutch called from the door in a soft, sympathetic voice. "The defenses can't hold for long, and the ships are waiting."

"Are we sure we have everyone? Our friends from Stanford, Google, and the others?" The idea of abandoning anyone pained me. The FN would surely not leave any stone unturned looking for resisters. I owed it to them to protect them, and I wouldn't be able to protect anyone here once we moved out.

"Everyone who will come," he said sadly, knowing those who stayed behind would not stand a chance.

"Did the bodies get taken care of?" There was a hollowness to my words as I spoke them out loud. I was referring to the people who had stayed to make it seem like Winter was alive and well, to provide the distraction we needed to get everyone else out safely. My head bowed, feeling the tremendous loss. Hutch nodded his head to acknowledge they had been taken care of.

"Give me one more second." As I watched him slip out from the doorway, I took in another breath, as if to breathe her in one more time so I could carry her with me. I placed my palms flat to her desk to feel her one last time and then pushed off with her strength. I whispered a faint good-bye as I exited.

My boots took me back down the grand hall and across the crackled glass, passing me through the oaken threshold one final time. I pulled up my bandana to ward off the thick smoke and took one last look at what had become Winter, the once-stately equestrian estate and thriving city, now decimated to a pile of rubble, the feeling of home reduced to crackling cinders.

"M'lady, your chariot awaits… But you are going to have to drive, my shoulder is killing me." Hutch leaned against the little shit bucket, tall and handsome…hair disheveled, filthy and covered in blood, arm in a sling.

"You look like death…and you're going to let me drive your POS?... Wow, how did I get so lucky?"

"Only the best for you, my dear." He shot me a mischievous glance as he clumsily fumbled into the cab, doing his best to protect his injured side, wincing and whimpering.

"Such a baby," I mumbled under my breath loud enough for him to hear.

"'Hero'. I think you meant to say 'hero'," he playfully responded.

"You need a tissue, crybaby?" I let the lightness of the banter hold back the tears as Winter disappeared in the rearview mirror.

M. LaVon

Good-byes Bring Hellos

The siege of San Francisco was swift, calculated, and deliberate. Our Canadian allies snuck in while the FN were focused on the local uprising. Once we pulled back our ground forces, the FN worked to push the forces farther back across the bridge, only to be met with an unexpected enemy at sea. The Canadian ships, cloaked as cargo and fishing vessels, quickly crippled anything within striking distance.

Tom had underestimated my thoughtfulness, my obsession with details, and my willingness to do what needed to be done. His venomous words bounced around in my mind: 'You could never make the hard choices.' But letting him take Asher nearly broke me in two. A part of me knew he was right—the part that harbored deep-seated guilt, the part that was hidden in the deepest corners of my self, and perhaps the part that would never forgive for what I couldn't bear to face.

I could not kill him; I knew that now. My heart could not separate the Tom I had married from the Tom who wanted me dead. For a brief second, I was a battered wife who apologized for her husband's shortcomings: 'Maybe it was my fault.' The hatred I felt was more for myself, for my own weakness. I had let him beat me, put his hands on me. And I felt I'd deserved it. If it hadn't been for Zavier, I would have let Tom take me, end my life, and maybe it would have stopped it all from hurting so bad.

I replayed every second: My gun was there—I could feel it in my waistband, the cool, hard steel comforting me. I was faster than Tom, I had the advantage, and my will was weak. It was my fault Hutch had taken those two shots. And now, because of me, more people would die.

The ship pushed through the bay. The murky water rippled outward from the bow, whirling and churning. Our wake caused the charred hulls, remnants of the overnight skirmish, to bounce and bob about, each slowly capsizing as their buoyancy failed. Billows of smoke towered skyward from what was left of Alameda. Crumbled buildings and loose debris lined the shore. The bridges were damaged and unsteady. The looming smoke made it difficult to see past our immediate surroundings, conjuring memories of the long-ago San Francisco fog. The mechanical hum of the drones and helicopters brought me back to the present.

If they are able to do all of this, why do they need me? They were doing fine on their own. I was far from qualified to lead.

My self-doubt filled my mind. Kavik joined me, as if sensing my reserve. Holding tight to the edge overlooking the sea, I took stock of the destruction we'd unleashed.

"You did the right thing." And with his subtle quietness, he broke away and disappeared without another word.

The gentle breeze from the movement of the ship made me aware of my damp face. My tears rolled from my cheeks, over the railing and to the sea below. I imagined all of me falling in after them, the cool water taking me to the bottom, a piece of myself staying behind. I could feel the door to my past closing with a hard, angry slam. Good-bye to California, good-bye to my old life, good-bye to who I was, my precious firstborn, my grandmother—and good-bye to *him.* Good-byes made it easy to see how hard I had been holding on to everything from before.

We broke out of the bay into the open waters of the Pacific Ocean, joining the waiting convoy of ships pointing north.

I could feel the burden of sleep heavy in my lids. The last forty-eight hours had been a staunch reminder that I was not as young as I used to be. My body was horrifically sore, with stiffening muscles and bruised features. I trailed the railing to the stern of the ship, the cold metal covered by thick white paint. My fingers evaluated the slightly uneven surface, textured by rust, seawater, and many coats. I skipped my fingertips over the various gaps and openings, pretending they were running legs jumping from one side to the other.

I took refuge between two large supply containers, out of the wind and out of sight. Slipping down the wall, landing against the shiny plastic, I rested my swollen cheeks on the soothing exterior.

I let my eyes flutter and blink as I began to drift, taking as much in as I could before the world went dark. The smoke hung over the land, but the farther we sail, the more it folded away, revealing soft blue skies hanging over deep blue waves. Perhaps it was a new beginning or maybe just another chapter.

The gentle motion rocked me, lulling me to sleep. I let the darkness overtake me.

***

The familiar warmth of the magic blanket was again a pleasant surprise. The mysterious nighttime culprit had yet to identify himself. I had always suspected it to be Zavier, but I was afraid that if I said something, he would feel his little secret was no longer safe and it would scare him away. I thought of his little hands tucking it around me, and overwhelming joy, connection, and pride fill me. It was a simple gesture that meant so much.

The warmth of the sun had been overtaken by the chilly night air. The shore was almost indistinguishable in the blackness. A few lights twinkled as we passed, but the competing starlight made them hard to appreciate. Without the constant light pollution from before, the stars were almost unimaginably real and vivid. I put out my hand as if to touch them, collecting them in my palm.

I willed myself to move below, to be around those I loved so I could remember again why this was all worth it. The stiffness consumed every movement, bringing me to wince and moan with every attempt to move. I could barely lift myself. The adrenaline had long since passed from my system, amplifying my weakness. I ran my fingers over my face to confirm the grotesque swelling that was the source of my throbbing headache.

The stairs leading farther into the ship were steep and hard to navigate with my aching bones. At the bottom, I could feel the nausea building. I grabbed the railing to steady myself. Familiar voices echoed within the metal corridor. *Laughter.* I couldn't help but smile—it was such a luxury.

I worked my way down the hall to what appeared to be the galley. Channeling my inner Hutch, I perched quietly by the door, soaking in the energy.

"Holy shit, kid, you are a natural sniper. Now we just need to get you your own top-tier rifle." Hutch's voice was proud and boisterous. I could feel Zavier blush. He had never been great with direct attention.

"Thanks, Hutch. Mom has never liked the idea of me becoming a gun-carrying maniac. And sure, the hell not like you..." They laughed, and he smacked Hutch's back, like he was just one of the guys. I raised my eyebrows in surprise. *He has really grown up without me even noticing, and now he has quite the vocabulary.*

I moved through the doorway, far enough to be noticed. The mood deflated, and I felt a bit disappointed to have dampened it.

Eli was the first to move. "Um, let's get you some ice..." The look on his face told me I looked just as bad as I felt. They made room on the bench for me to squeeze in. The effort to sit made me wonder if I would need to stay there for the duration of the journey. But then I looked around the table—at Liz, Sonia's bump, Kavik, Hutch, Zavier, Eli. I lived for them and I would die for them. *Forgive me friends, for not killing him when I had the chance.*

I pressed the ice pack to my swollen face; the pressure caused me to momentarily flinch and pull back. Everyone stared.

Looking to Hutch, I said, "Come on, baby, give this sweet thing a kiss. You know you want it." I puckered my ginormous lips, desperate not to let the laughter die.

"Um...uh, well, you know, uh... I have this injury, and I think Eli said no hanky-panky for a few weeks—you know, doctor's orders..." Hutch replied with a sly smirk.

"Wait, you heathens are not pulling me into this mess? You people are grown... Lord, have mercy, give them the strength to make adult decisions...and please let my baby girl choose someone...um...else." Eli exaggerated his Southern accent.

"Uh...you'd better take what you can get, brother. He's right, sorry piece of shit..." Liz jumped in, holding her belly and giggling.

"Ewww. Earmuffs. Please, no old people PDA... I might just vomit." Zavier was glowing with laughter as he made a dramatic fake kissy face, followed by a vomit expression. Kavik watched and laughed, putting his arm around Liz.

I tried to smile and laugh. It hurts so much it brought tears to my eyes, but it was worth every second.

***

The landscape morphed as we made our way north. The California coastline shifted to the rocky shores of Oregon. The small cottages and former luxury lodges lined the edge and were mostly dilapidated by neglect. Summer vacationers were long gone, the concept of vacation lost forever, buried beneath the need to survive. The rising sea level had claimed many and had by now taken over the lowest parts of the beach. The power of the sea was altering our perception of what was ours, its violent act of reclaiming what was once man's world, now pulled back to the earth. Inevitably, the end would not be at the hands of any army; it would be from the earth telling us enough was enough. It was just a matter of surviving until then.

The opening to the Puget Sound was a welcome sight, the deep green hills above the shore were magnificent, almost pristine. The grayness of the sky, accompanied by the unique mist that only Washington could offer, reminded me of being young and traveling here with Cici, and the anticipation of days spent under the eaves of the covered porch, tucked beneath a fuzzy blanket, nestled into the outdoor couch with a never-ending supply of books. *Before I had kids, before Tom.*

The Winter Lodge on Orcas Island was once a 150-acre recreational lodge and summer resort. It was known for fishing, hunting, and its amazing scenic surroundings. The resort was made up of several large buildings, including a bed-and-breakfast, several small cottages, general facilities, and a number of waterfront homes, all with a vintage quaintness.

Cici had acquired the property from a former colleague of my grandfather's and a friend of the family whose health was failing. There had been no one else left to look after the property, and they were afraid it would fall into disrepair without someone taking it over.

Cici was delighted to take it on, and she invited the WMS employees to use it. Many staff members brought their families for the summer. We had also used it as an executive retreat when I was still the CEO.

When we decided to leave Winter and move the community, our Canadian allies offered us safe harbor in Victory, British Columbia. But the council weighed the options and decided Orcas was as good of a place as any for a new settlement.

The island had enough access to essential resources to supply the community, although the reality was that we were going to have to work harder for energy and food. The climate off the Sound was sometimes unpredictable, not nearly as ideal as Woodside. There were direct trade routes with Canada out of Victoria and Washington through Port Townsend and Anacortes. But even more important, it was defensible, and within the protection zone established by Canada. It was hard to wrap my mind around seeking political asylum on our own land, in our own country, and being protected by Canada.

The armada pulled into Deer Harbor, moving into the marina. The larger vessels docked at the end in the deepest water, the smaller ones using any open slips. The large system of walkways rose and fell as the ships settled against them. The pilings squeaked and howled as the metal rubbed the tar-treated surfaces. Several of our vessels were already in port, secured and unloaded. Curious locals had come out of buildings, staring cautiously as we descended on what had been, until two days ago, a sleepy island town. Onlookers held their positions, not willing to yield without knowing if we had come in peace.

I waved Liz over, watching her belly, which had become round and impossible to miss. And I couldn't help but smile. She was my consummate advisor and most trusted friend. These days, wherever she was, Zavier followed. He had a guardian's heart, and I loved him for it.

Several people had gathered at the marina, surprisingly, several elderly people among them. We had lost so many children and elderly during the outbreak, it had become a novelty to see either, and I was sure the locals thought the same upon seeing pregnant Liz and Zavier. The crowd parted at the doorway without so much as a word, making it easy to see which way they wanted us to go.

The offered path led to an older man, silver gray with a thick, short beard, almost Nordic. His wool sweater and rustic appearance were reminiscent of the Old Man and the Sea. He was busy going about his business, less enamored by us as the rest of the people who had collected to gawk.

"What can I do you for?" His voice was deep and strangely familiar.

"My name is Catelyn Winter. I own the Winter Lodge property up the road. This is my colleague Liz and my son Zavier."

"You Cici's girl?" He stopped.

"Yes, Cici was my grandmother. She passed a few years back." I searched my memories for this man's face with no success.

"She was good people... Captain Jack..." He stuck out his hand in greeting. "I operated the ferry from time to time for your grandmother. She preferred coming in on the water versus a float plane… You travel with quite the entourage these days." His eye lifted, looking out the window at the fleet of mixed-purpose ships we'd rolled in on, his eyebrows raised.

"Yes, well…we are less menacing than we appear. Do you know who we need to talk with about moorage? And are there any town council members I should connect with?"

"I manage the marina. We have some guys who can help with maintenance, and we deal in trade, primarily fuel. As for who runs the town, that would be Mama T. She also manages the Deer Harbor Inn, the only restaurant in town. And she manages most of the properties here in Deer Harbor. She would be interested to know how long you'll be in town." I nodded to acknowledge his concerns.

"Thanks, Captain, we will be in town for the foreseeable future, so it would be great to get to know everyone." I looked around, taking stock of the curious faces, then turned to exit.

He called out as if remembering something of the utmost importance. "Oh, and we also have a small country store with all the comforts of small-town living, canned goods, tackle and equipment, seasonal produce, seafood, staples, and the occasional baked specialty… We even have seeds for planting in the coming spring, and some imported goods from Canada." I again nodded and smiled, thanking him for his thoughtful introduction.

We made our way past the small crowd that had gathered to spectate the silent invasion, then walked the short distance to the Deer Harbor Inn. The street was lined with small country cottages with equally small gardens, bordered by split-rail fences. The inn was set back from the main street, down a short rural drive, encircled by a fruit orchard and several yet-to-be-planted raised garden beds.

I could feel the nostalgic relevance radiating from the place. The green outer façade original was thickly painted, most likely full of lead. The door was trimmed in red to match the window frames, complementing the hometown vibe.

As we drew closer, I could smell the warmth of fresh biscuits and real bacon. Cici and I had once come here for lunch; I had homemade split pea soup that was to die for. My mouth began to water at the thought. Liz must have been thinking the same—the look on her face was pure exuberant excitement.

We walked up the ramp toward the front door. It rose high enough for us to take in the majestic orchard and surrounding lush green landscape, even in the dead of winter.

I pushed the door open, revealing the simple sweetness inside. The walls were decorated with family photos and historic information about the orchard and the inn. A few locals slowly sipped their coffee and tried, without success, to refrain from overtly staring. We grabbed a table close to a window to take in the view.

An older woman approached the table with a few handwritten menus and water. Her posture was hardened and guarded, knuckles swollen with arthritis and lips pursed with permanent irritation. "What brings you in?"

"Biscuits," Liz blurted out with a quickness and verbal authority unlike her. I let out a little giggle.

"Please excuse my friend. Her little one is doing all the talking these days." I gestured to Liz's bulging stomach. The lady smiled and warmed to us. "Actually, excuse us all," I went on. "It has been a while since we have been in a real restaurant and we might have forgotten how to act."

"Don't worry, our food ain't anything special, but it is warm and fresh." She looked back to Liz. "Mama first... Biscuits? Gravy or jam? Farm-fresh eggs? Some potatoes?" Liz almost jumped out of her chair to hug the women. "Yes!" she proclaimed, and the lady grinned from ear to ear. There appeared to be a kinship in food and the appreciation for it.

"And you, young man, cheeseburger and homemade fries?" Now it was Zavier's turn to leap out of his seat. I thought I might have seen tears forming.

"Yes!" He looked to me and I gave him a 'mom look'. "Um... Yes, ma'am... Thank you."

"And you?" she asked.

"Soup of the day?" I asked, unsure what I was getting.

"Beef... Well, deer barley, and a grilled cheese sandwich." My lips were wet in anticipation.

"Sounds lovely." I smiled as she turned away. "Oh, and can you tell me where I can find Mama T?" I added to try to catch her before she headed to the kitchen.

"That would be me. Let me get you all fixed up and then we can talk business." Without waiting for a response, she disappeared behind the swinging doors. A young girl, about Zavier's age, came and shyly offered us coffee and tea.

As we waited, I slowly sipped my coffee and nodded slightly to the locals still staring at us. They appeared flustered at my acknowledgment, and they nodded in return, but then looked away.

It wasn't long before our food arrived. The wafting smells engulfed us. Delicacies from the finest restaurant could not compare at that moment. Everything was full of savory goodness. We gorged ourselves on what tasted like heaven until we were completely sated. I could feel Mama T watching us from across the room, pleased with how satisfied we were with her creations.

As soon as our plates were empty, she made her way back to the table, this time with the young girl, who cleared the table as she joined us at the fourth chair. As she sat, the last customers exited the restaurant as if taking an invisible cue.

Without hesitation, Mama T jumped right in. "What brings an army to Deer Harbor? Are you some of those crackpot Free Nationalists?"

"We are...well...more of an independent...um...organization. And no, we are not Free Nationalists." I was careful not to lay too much on the table to avoid potentially complicating the situation.

"'Independent organization'? Are you some sort of commander?" I had not exactly thought of a title for myself. That might be helpful in the future to avoid the question altogether.

"I own the Winter property about half a mile past the marina," I said, hoping to direct the conversation.

"Oh, the old lodge?"

"Yes. It was my grandmother's place and I inherited it when she passed."

"I am sorry for your loss. But why come here now?" She had a clever way about her and was intent on steering the conversation back to the way she wanted it to go.

"Well..." I looked to Liz, who seemed completely comfortable with me figuring out what to say. "The Free Nationalists are working their way up north, and they intend to take Washington as a territory. The former government has been unable to gain ground to take the Pacific Northwest back."

"What does that have to do with you and Orcas?" Her matter-of-fact tone makes me nervous; I had not developed a platform to articulate this whole crazy idea just yet.

"We were pushed out of California by the Free Nationalists. Our community is made up of about two thousand people. We had no place to go, and we would not have made it through the eastern lines. Our allies and Canada offered asylum and safe passage out of the Bay Area. We have an agreement with Canada and the former US government to defend the Northwest Territory from the Free Nationalists. I am the de facto commander of the group." I steadied my voice and hid my nervousness. "We intend to make Orcas our base. It is currently out of reach by the Free Nationalists, and we would like to keep it that way."

"That will not be enough." Her curt insight was surprising—and she is one hundred percent correct.

"Why do you say that?"

Her face twisted and contorted, evidently trying to compute my obviously stupid question.

"You say you have about two thousand people on an island? And you think that is enough to defend against hundreds of thousands of murdering savages? We hear all about what's going on down there." It did sound a bit crazy when it was repeated back to me.

"The hope is to recruit a suitable force that can retake the Northwest with the help of our allies." My lack of confidence bled past every word.

"The looks on your faces *literally* tell me you have gotten your asses handed to you a few times. You ladies need to get your shit together." I had gotten so used to my face being hamburger, I might have forgotten I looked like Frankenstein—Liz, too. We looked like two MMA fighters. "Let's get your people settled, and then we can work it all out. We have some open spaces at the WorldMark and a few of the smaller resorts. Plus, what you have over at the lodge. We will need to get creative when you start bringing people in, but we will figure it out. And we will make a true commander out of you yet." She was quick and organized—I admired that.

She walked us back down to the WorldMark, and I left Liz with her to sort out all the housing logistics.

Hutch had made quick work of getting everything unloaded, including the shit bucket. The ferry dock on the other end of the island was the only place where he could unload the vehicles, but they got it done.

I hopped in the familiar little truck, rolling the window down to let the air in. The air seeped in from the cracked window, crisp and smelling like damp dirt.

We headed over to the property to look at what we were working with. Some of the cabins needed a little work, but they would do. Part of the old barn had lost a portion of the roof and would need repair... I began listing all the 'must dos' and the 'nice to haves' in a systematic order. Everything from high-top placement, and farmland, to wind and solar farms, to grazing land, a clinic, and what we hoped to be a school. Hopes and dreams were all laid out neatly, the urge to make new stronger than the urge to make war. The small farmhouse near the water where Cici and I had spent many summers was still standing. Hutch pulled up the drive. The covered porch was still in great condition, the screen door hanging by a single hinge at an odd angle, but easy to fix. I ducked past it, finding the front door just beyond. The door opened with a labored squeal, followed by the creaking of the uneven floorboards of the small dark entry.

Far from the grandeur of the Winter Estate, the farmhouse was snug and comfortable. The entry had very few secrets: A living room was situated to the left, kitchen with eat-in dining to the right, two bedrooms at the top of the stairs, and a small makeshift study to the rear.

Hutch stood at the doorway watching me pull the dust cloths off the furniture, exposing the outdated sofa and chairs beneath. I stopped at a small piece in the corner by the best window in the house, slowly peeling the cloth away, letting the sentimentality rush through me. Cici's drawing table was small, but perfect for the room. This would serve as the office for all intents and purposes. I was desperate for it to bring me the same ease and strength as her desk in the library had. I placed my palms flat against it, just like I'd done at Winter, pleading for it to bring me the same comfort. But the wood was cold and foreign, leaving me disappointed.

Hutch's presence was warm behind me. He stepped close enough for his breath to move my hair, disheveled and wispy from the night spent on the ship. His fingers from his mobile arm wrapped around my shoulder, gently squeezing, almost holding me up.

I wanted to sleep for a month, I wanted to cry for a year: My son had left me, and my husband had tried to kill me, and I had lost the only place I'd ever called home. *Oh, my sweet baby boy, it hurts so bad.*

I could feel the tears sneak out, but no sobs followed; I didn't have the energy to sob anymore. Or maybe I just didn't have any tears left to cry.

Hutch's massive hand slowly coaxed me to face him. I couldn't help holding my breath as I landed against him.

"Will you guys kiss already?" Zavier's voice made me jump, and I pushed Hutch away. "Oh geez, you guys are nerds. Hutch, my man, you have no game. Maybe someday we can have 'the talk'." We laughed as he flopped himself down in the armchair, releasing a cloud of dust around him.

***

The Canadian admiral was very tall and handsome, silver and regal in his uniform. This was the first time I had ever had an admiral for tea. We sat in the small living room next to the fire. We were still working out the logistics of electricity for the lodge community, and we had not gotten accustomed to the cool, damp climate of the island yet. The admiral didn't seem phased by the chill. I took a moment to digest everything he had just offloaded. The realization that I was now a military commander negotiating with our allies was still so foreign.

Canada was willing to offer aid to help secure their border, as they figured we would have better luck raising an army of leftovers in the United States than Canada would in making a play for colonization. By playing the role of leader, I had a better chance at gaining support. It made sense. Canada had held back the FN in the northern half of Washington and Idaho for almost a year, offering support to Montana, who had really held its own since the beginning—also, the winter had provided them an advantage, since no one wanted to take over Montana in the winter. Canada would like to return that control back to us and let us clean up our own mess—and of course, keep the borders clear, similar to what we had done with the co-ops. They were also providing trade opportunities for essentials. Hutch was working with their team on logistics.

I watched the steam rise from his cup as he brought it up to his lips. He was a local out of Victoria and he knew this coast like no one else did. He had arranged for the other leaders of the Northwest Territory to come together for a summit at Fort Worden, near Port Townsend, next week. Fort Worden now fell under my jurisdiction.

The admiral shared the grave news that San Francisco—including Woodside and Stanford—had been brutally 'reestablished' as FN territory. Most had been destroyed by their backup forces that came in from Fallon, and anyone not part of the FN was killed. The fires raged on for days. I could feel the guilt build between my ears, compounding the pressure in my head. *I let him live.*

We discussed the chain of command, and who was who, and all the other basic relevant information, and the information swirled by me in a hazy fog, a surreal dream filled with horrific imagery and the smell of Earl Grey tea. I bounced my feet close to the fire, the lizard tongue–like flame tips sizzling up the chimney, orange and red dancers. The ash bed was glowing between the white and black charcoal.

Orcas Island was now the makeshift capital for whatever we were calling ourselves, and I was its commander in chief.

Representatives for Bremerton had arrived yesterday and would be my escorts to Fort Worden. They would also join our mini fleet in defending the bays on both sides of the lodge.

I had passed off community management to Liz, who was now the acting general or mayor or whatever the title should have been. I was at a loss for military or positional formalities.

Without much formal accord, he nodded and excused himself. The whole situation seemed so bizarre: As we prepared for a full assault that would ultimately leave many dead, we sat and chatted over tea. As we bargained for trade and land rights, we warmed our toes before an open fire, the ways of queens and presidents for generations, I guess.

Sonia

The smell of spring warmed the air, a sneak peek of the fruitfulness to come. Winter's end had brought tragedy and new beginnings. But the island offered the fresh start I thought many of us needed, a safe harbor in which to heal.

The small paved road to the lower field separated the crop from the livestock. It was a nice flat walk. Being as big as a house these days, I appreciated an easy path. Eli insisted I stop walking all the way up to the inn, even though Mama T set aside biscuits and jam for Sonia every morning. Now Zavier ran to fetch them for me, still warm. The thought inspired a rumble in my stomach and dampness in the corners of my mouth, which glistened in the sunlight.

A sharp, steady pain took my breath away, and I paused mid-stride and held still a second. It felt like the steady pains I had been having for the last few weeks. *We are not ready for you to come yet, little miss, so you are going to have to wait. Eli is just now back to researching how to bring you into this world. We still got some time.*

The cows quietly grazed on the soft, supple spring grass. A few farmers were readying the adjacent field for planting. I let the April sunbathe me in its light. The last few months had been shrouded in gray, gloomy skies, so a little vitamin D was welcome. My feet ached from the swollen cankles I had developed recently. I hadn't been able to wear real shoes, so I was back to my fuzzy slippers.

In the afternoon, I planned to make it up to our high tunnels, which were situated in the upper field. I ran my fingers through the indoor vegetation, cleaning, grooming, and pruning—solitude at its finest. The hum of the energy farms in the upper field gave just the right level of white noise in the tunnels.

The end of the road took me closer to the shore, and the small path led me to the rocky beach. My favorite rock was higher than the rest and was perfect for resting. I waddled my way onto its smooth surface and placed my hand on the rock, just as another sharp pain reared its ugly head. *Not yet, sweet pea.* I stroked my bulging belly, calming her. I giggled as I patted her little upside-down butt.

The defensive fleet was flanked by simple fishing boats, an interesting juxtaposition between solider and fisherman. Our time here had provided the best seafood possible: Scales, shells, and wiggle tails, I loved it all.

The soft lapping of the tiny waves landing in the pebbly bed was rhythmic, the ocean breathing in and out. I could feel the tenseness in my shoulders lift as I closed my eyes and breathed with it. The tension moved from my shoulders into my lower back, tightening with a relentless grip. I shifted to make myself more comfortable. Sleeping flat at night has proved to be a challenge, leaving me with back spasms throughout the day, which Eli assured me were completely normal and a motherhood badge of honor. I couldn't wait until I could reach all the way to my toes again to stretch it forward.

I dangled my legs off the rock, sliding my feet to the stones below and letting the rest of me follow. I planted my feet square to the ground, stretched, reached to the sky, and brought my arms back down.

The boats bobbed in the water like little buoys all in a row. The seagulls cried and cawed, waiting for the fisherman to pull their nets so they could scavenge whatever dropped through.

The sides of my stomach contracted, hard as a rock, followed by a shockingly strong pain. I leaned against the rock, taking in the coolness of the stone against my forearms. I slowly shifted, rocking my hips back and forth until it passed, letting the motion and my breath do the work. I cushioned my forehead in the cradle of my arms, even when the pain passed. I took my time. It was a comfortable position here against the rock at the edge of the sea. Just as I moved to raise myself, though, another pain overtook me, bringing me back down to my rocking position. *Not yet, baby girl.*

With every attempt to leave the rock, the contractions brought me back, tearing into me, across my core, and crippling my back. I focused out to the sea, the blue sea where the waves crashed to the ragged shore. I couldn't cry out, I couldn't scream. It was just me and Sonia and the blue ocean.

The contractions were steady, and I couldn't help but to hold on to the rock, tears welling in my eyes. *Don't die without me this time, Sonia. We are in this together.*

I clenched my teeth against my arm with every substantial wave. My belly was so tight it stole my breath. I squeezed my legs together, not wanting Sonia to come into this world only to leave it without me. The pressure was so heavy, forcing me to bear down. With all my strength I tried to resist it. *No, no, no!*

I tried once more to make it away from the shore, only to reach the grassy edge a few feet away, trying to clamber and crawl up the path, resting on my hands and knees. The ocean wouldn't let me go.

The grassy edge came with cool, soft dirt, and the feel of the soil to my cheeks, the damp, earthy smell, brought me back to Sonia. *I can't lose you twice.*

The intensity was so great I clutched the grassy edge with both hands, digging deep, letting a small, excoriating cry seep out. I brought my knees to my chest as I crouched for relief.

I moved against a tree to try to pull myself up from the ground, climbing hand over hand to transition upright. A flood of water swept from me, soaking my pants and flushing me with panic. I could feel the urge to bear down, but holding tight to the tree, I fought it, fought every second. My body didn't even acknowledge what my mind wanted.

I reached past the elastic waistband of my favorite stretchy pants to feel the wetness, to prove it was not blood. My body was wide open, the firm surface of her head against my two fingers, the tufts of her hair easy to distinguish.

The tears streamed from my face, knowing this was the moment when we would say hello and good-bye, knowing I was not ready. I screamed silently as the agony brought my hands back to the tree. I knew now there was nothing I could do to stop her from coming into my arms. *We will do this together.* I shed my pants, leaving me in Kavik's oversized T-shirt and sweatshirt. Eternity, now she took her time, me and the tree. With each push she moved a fraction of an inch. I held my squatting position like a champion, my legs quivering.

Her head passed slightly, and everything was on fire. I squeezed and pushed. Seconds, minutes, hours, years.

I planted my feet firmly, gripping the rough bark with both hands and folding into the contraction. I counted softly to three and retched out a gurgled growl.

Her sweet little crown broke free. The next one brought her smile. I reached to add pressure and slow her down. And then I gave her everything I had, feeling instant relief when her shoulders passed. Reaching around her with two hands, I guided her into my awaiting arms. I rested on my knees, bringing her up to my chest. I gently turned her upside down to work out any fluid she had in her lungs. She squirmed slightly, wriggling about. I used my pants to wipe out her mouth and rub her little body to wake her up. And then she cried, like every baby cried. And I cried, too.

Sonia and I stumbled back to the rock, a few feet past the edge. Simon & Garfunkel made a come back with "April Come She Will". I gently hummed to her as I laid my sweatshirt out on the rock and wrapped her up in it, using the drawstring to tie off the cord. A second wave of contractions came and the afterbirth passed, leaving me weak and cold. I ground the cord in half with a flat rock. We found a grassy spot to rest a few steps away.

Sonia's little eyes flickered open, as she whimpered and rooted. *If these are to be our final moments, let you spend them in my arms, enveloped in my love for you.* I brought her to me. She was warm and pinking up. She was vigorous and thriving. I opened the sweatshirt and covered us both as she started rooting again. I lifted my shirt and brought her to me, skin to skin, and without hesitation she latched on, firmly pulling and suckling. I watched her as her mouth formed a tight seal around my swollen breast. She was perfect and amazing, beautiful.

We sat and enjoyed what was left of the spring sun, resting a few minutes, and then I let her latch again. I wanted to hold on to this moment as long as I could, as long as she was mine. We would stay on the shore as long as we could.

The air from off the water turned cool as the sun set, making my already-chilled half-naked body shiver. I collected Sonia and found the way back up the path to the road between the fields. I passed the farmers and the cows, and moved on to the lodge house, where Zavier was sitting reading on the porch. He sprang up, running to me, alerting Cate. My T-shirt was filthy, my pants lost, my legs covered in blood, as I stood there in my fuzzy slippers. But my arms were full. I was bringing Sonia home.

***

Day 2: I didn't remember much about the first day after I came to the lodge house. Sonia and I slept most of it. Sonia woke to nurse, her little body confident and active. She watched me while she ate until she couldn't hold her eyes open. Her warm little body snuggled against me.

Eli checked on us every few hours, watching for symptoms of the virus or other ailments. Every time, he said she was perfect. He didn't have to tell me. I knew.

I thought about Kavik and Hutch, not due back for another couple of weeks. They had been working to secure more substantial trade routes and bring in some people from the mainland.

Day 7: Her first symptoms were subtle: a slight cough, not wanting to eat, lethargy. Then came the fever. She wouldn't stay awake. Then she stopped eating completely. Her tiny body was helpless against the virus as it started to ravage her. Eli came, connected her to fluids, and prayed. His soft Southern voice hummed a slow, drawling melody, loving and sincere. The candlelight cast his magnified silhouette against the wall, and orange-yellow flickers danced around him as he held her precious little body, cradling her, waiting for the inevitable to take her.

With her back in my arms, I showered her with love, whispering to her in my real voice, letting her hear me.

Cate and Zavier took turns holding vigil. Zavier's crocodile tears fell with the devastation of a million heartbreaks. His broken voice repeated "You are my Sunshine" between fettered sobs. He had come to think of Sonia as a little sister or a niece—as he talked to my belly, he'd said he had 'grand plans' for her. He had lost so much, and watching him grieve broke little pieces from my heart. I loved him like my own, like a special nephew. A secret, selfish desire was for Hutch to marry Cate so no one could ever dispute Zavier as my nephew.

On Day 8, I clung to her limp and lifeless body, watching her faint breath barely lifting her tiny chest. I held my hand across her torso, hoping to feel her heartbeat against my palm, the drumbeat weak and fading. *Take me with you...we can sleep forever together.* I slipped away into a restless sleep, her tiny body in my arms. Cate pretended to read quietly at the bedside, but one hand held mine, both tucked under the swaddled bundle. Cate's strong face was damp with unacknowledged tears.

Day 9: It happened with very little fanfare, quietly in the dark. I was half asleep and unaware. I dreamed her tiny soul was floating above me, her sweet face watching from across the blue tent. My arms were outstretched, reaching for her, but she was too far away to pull her back. The desperation and panic were unwavering as she disappeared into nothing. I left the blue tent with empty arms, searching for my knitting bag.

My own cries woke me, tiny silent screams, pulsing between sobs. My heart raced, bringing me closer to consciousness.

Cate's face hovered over me. Her crying was obvious, overt tears. Her whole body shook. I reached out to console my poor Cate, and she clutched my arm, covered her mouth with the other hand, holding back all the pain and loss she had endured.

I moved to look around the room, and it was only us. I lifted my body in alarm and felt a tug pulling at me. The weight of her body was still cradled in my arms. I was too scared to look down and see her tiny face frozen in time. I closed my eyes and reached for Cate to ground me and give me strength to lift my precious Sonia away. *I am not ready to say good-bye.* I shook and shuddered, and Cate was still quivering. It was only then I realized that Cate's tears weren't tears of loss, but something else entirely.

She squeezed my hand, willing me to open my eyes to her, telling me it was all me. I slowly shifted my eyes down to the person I had created, to her little face, only to meet her eyes staring back at me. Big, soft, brown blinking eyes looking for food.

My gasp was audible, so loud it made both Sonia and Cate jump. I reached and grabbed for both of them, pulling them into me. I brought Sonia to my lips, kissing her and sobbing. Cate folded at the bedside, crying deeply, tears of relief shedding free. *There is hope.*

Epilogue (Preview book 2, *Destin's War*)

Cami, June 2026

After the uprising in California, Tom's army was pushed out past Oakland. Though it didn't matter much, the FN support was not far back. They came in like the angry hand of God, crushing everything with one swift swoop. The Air Force decimated any resistance before they even knew what hit them. Asher said that most of Cate's people had retreated behind a Canadian curtain, and from what I heard around the camp, they were all somewhere up in Washington. My kids were safe.

We had been in Fallon, about an hour outside Reno, for about five months. They moved the headquarters here as they gained more control across the states, many of which were now in FN control. The United States–held territory was shrinking by the day. Their control came with brutal authority, many times putting the territories in the hands of vicious militants and extremists who used horrific tactics to gain subservience, and what I could only equate to slavery.

Tom had become a cold figure who stomped through the camp, his temper easily triggered. The sound of gunshots from his office was common, followed by another failure dragged from his presence, leaving a trail of blood behind. At this rate, I was not sure he would have anyone left under his command.

Asher followed behind him like a lapdog, his childish features gone behind a new, brutish expression to match his father's. I was pretty sure he was the one who pulled the trigger in Tom's office, a gesture to prove his worth to Tom. By now he had lost any and all kindness, and he made sure I knew I was nothing to him but property. He would not make the same mistake his father had made in loving his mother. To Asher, she was a lying, cheating adulteress who had tried to kill his beloved father.

I was tolerated and allowed to be where Asher went, for the most part. I had made a few friends, as loosely as I could claim the term. They were other 'property' of the command. Sissy was young and beautiful, her milky-white porcelain skin crowned with long, flowing blond hair. She kept one of the senior leaders company. She had been captured somewhere close to Kansas. He was kind to her, bringing her sweets, and unlike the others, she was treated like gold. He also told her everything, and she loved to gossip. Liam, in his early twenties, was thin and taller. He had an unmatched wit and was super funny, but his leader treated him horribly. His laughter and smiles were usually framed by purple, swollen bruises, his movements stiff and sore. And Deb—she was a lot older, with a slight accent. She managed the domestic affairs: laundry, meals, housing for the leaders. She always reminded us we were children and we needed to stay out of trouble. She was like me, listening to the others, but she offered little in return.

The people here were not all the same as the crew from Alameda. Many had special skills, had been pilots and scientists. And not all were military. Many had bought into the FN rhetoric: 'We are building a new America'—others I was sure were creatively persuaded, and everyone else just kept their mouth shut.

***

We stayed in Tom's house, the largest on the base. It had a desert stucco façade and was sparsely furnished. Everything was simple and plain and missing anything that remotely felt like home. Asher and I shared a room. I wished we didn't, but I was glad I didn't sleep in a room by myself.

I avoided being there as much as possible. As soon as Tom was gone and Asher was asleep, I made my way to the recreation center, where most of the non-personnel people went. I helped Deb during the day, too, and sometimes helped with the few children who were still around. Anything to get me away from them.

I avoided being alone with Tom, but sometimes I couldn't help it. When he was home, he spent most of his time in his office, Asher by his side, typing through the night. When Asher climbed in bed early in the mornings, Tom, sleepless, went to the airfield for the day. But I would rather them both be gone.

It was just a matter of time before they killed me.

Asher stumbled in sometime around 5 AM, drunk from lack of sleep. For three days straight they had been in the office, neither of them leaving the house. Deb had come and dropped off food and helped clean up a bit the day before.

Like usual, I pretended to be asleep. Asher fumbled around, groping at me like an uncoordinated sea creature, trying to stir me awake. When I didn't move, he fell asleep. A deep sigh of relief washed over me. I hated the feel of him on me, kissing me. However, it was always quick and painless, unlike the guys who got me at the old folks' home where Cate had saved me and the kids.

I shifted in my pseudo sleep to test if he would wake, but he was out cold. I took that as my cue to sneak out. I grabbed the clothes I had left out on the dresser and eased my way out the door.

Before the virus had taken everyone, I used to sneak out of my parents' house in much the same way. I had tiptoed down the hall, past their room, and out the front door. A group of kids ran around all night. Out under the stars I was kissed for the first time, and it was magical. The next day, my parents and brother got sick, and within a couple of days my family was gone.

The house was still dark and silent. I rounded the corner from the stairs into the kitchen and looked back to make sure no one was following me, but the hall was clear. I turned, startled to see that Tom was sitting at the kitchen island with a cup of coffee. I froze, caught, his eyes burning into me. I clutched my clothes across my chest, covering the small tank and pair of Asher's boxer shorts I wore each night.

He did not drop his gaze, and like a deer in the headlight, I was stuck, my feet planted with lead blocks holding them down. My heart was pounding, and I trembled. He averted his eyes as he took a drink of his coffee, and I took that as a sign to move. I slowly crept through the kitchen toward the bathroom where I usually changed my clothes. I didn't look at him; I was too scared to.

In one quick motion, he reached me and flung me down, holding me against the island. He had my throat, and my pulse was beating against his hands. Through his anger, I could see a slight smirk. He enjoyed hurting people.

"Where the fuck are you going? Sneaking around...scheming." His voice was a wild growl.

I struggled to breathe and responded, "I help Deb..." His grip tightened; the question must have been rhetorical. I wriggled to try to make space to breathe. His whole body was pressed against me.

"You are a liar—like her, just like her!" I assumed he meant Cate.

"Please...what do you want from me?" I forced the words out, pleading. He lightened up, only to slap me openhanded across the face. I could taste the blood from my swollen lip.

"Shut up..." he said through gritted teeth.

I dropped my clothes and reached for my face in shock, then moved my hands up to try to push him away. He slammed me back down, pressing even harder against me, spreading my legs with his, and sliding me across the island by my throat. I turned my head, knowing what came next. The thin boxers made it easy to feel what he wanted from me. He didn't move or take action, though, just held me still, his breathing coursed with anger, but his mind somewhere else.

He reached his hand down between his body and mine, took his time feeling the space. Then he pressed his hand against me with his hips and closed his eyes.

"Go back upstairs, and don't leave this house until Asher is awake." He flung me to my feet. "And know that I will kill you if you say a single word..."

The next time he laid his hands on me, it was a little more aggressive. I was cleaning the house, and not knowing he was home asleep upstairs, I must have made too much noise. Tom came up behind me and pushed me over the wooden coffee table, breaking it into pieces. He picked me up and pressed me up against the wall.

"I told you I didn't even want to know you are here!" I didn't know why he was mad. Asher came down.

"Asher, take your girl upstairs—and teach her how to keep quiet!" That was the first day when Asher also put his hands on me in anger.

Asher grabbed my arm and dragged me upstairs. He was the same size as his father, so it was easy for him to throw me around. He shoved me up against the dresser, knocking over the lamp, which crashed to the ground, breaking into a million pieces. I bounced off the furniture, falling to the ground, but his large hand pulled me back up to where my face met his hand. The hit dropped me back to my knees.

"What the hell, Cami! This is how you repay him for taking care of you, for letting you live in his house? For not leaving you at a solider camp?" His expression was the same as his father's. The boy from Winter was gone, swallowed whole by the evil vortex.

"Now, show me you want to be here." His voice softened as he unzipped his pants. His belt at my eye level. He reached out to pull me close, stroking my hair. Not exactly how I imagined I would celebrate my sweet sixteen.

The rest of June and July were much the same. They took turns reminding me who I needed to appreciate more. I spent less and less time at the recreation center, too scared to leave for too long and what I would come back to.

***

On August 1, the house was quiet. I left the doors open to let the breeze pass through. The desert heat was pretty hardcore. No one was home, so to keep cool I put on a tank top and a pair of shorts. Deb brought over some fresh lemonade and dinner for me to put together when Asher and Tom got home from the airbase. I started to prep the food, and the sunshine streamed into the kitchen was nice. The lemonade was the perfect combination of sweet and sour, and the refreshing juice wet my mouth, quenching my thirst.

The slam of the front door startled me. I peered from the kitchen into the living room to see Tom at the front door, his expression one of pure fury. I stepped back deeper into the kitchen and began to pour him some lemonade. My hands were shaking so hard the lemonade splashed and spilled over the edge.

He charged like an uncontrolled bull across the room toward me. Dropping the pitcher, I ran, dashing around the kitchen, desperate to get away, shrieking and crying. He grabbed my dark ponytail, pulling me backward. My hands reached out and yanked the drawers open. The utensils spilled to the ground in a clatter. His large arms reached around under my own arms, pulling me free, yanking and lifting me off the ground. My bare legs jerked and kicked about.

"You planning to run? I hear you are quite the talker at the rec center. Yes, your friend sold you out. You going to take down the FN? What—do you think you are some sort of rebel like Cat? You going to join the resistance, too?" His voice was full of accusations.

"I don't know what you are talking about." I was honestly confused what he was talking about—I didn't have any plans, and if I did, I for sure the hell would not tell them.

"You wouldn't last a day in the desert. Maybe we should test that theory? But you *will* learn a lesson first, you piece of trash. Cat should have let you rot where she found you." He tossed me against the dining chairs, and I fell between them, crashing to the ground. I scrambled to get under the table, pulling on the furniture legs, looking to hide. He grabbed my ankles, dragging me out of the space. He ripped me up by my tank top, tearing it in half, exposing my body. I pulled the top shut with one hand. He spun me to face him, landing a fist to my cheek. I flailed my arms as I tried to fend off his advances. He pushed me into the island, laying me out next to the frying pan of uncooked veggies from Deb.

I slapped and fought against him. He reached for my wrists, forced them over my head. My wrists were so small in his hands he could fit both in one. His other hand reached for the kitchen knife, brought it up to my throat.

"Go ahead, 'overthrow' me." I felt the cool metal against my throat and him hard against my body. My chest was bare, my shorts thin.

He slid the knife across my throat, scraping the metal against my skin, deep enough to draw blood. His mood moved to something even darker. Without fail, he took advantage, just like he had taught his son to do, just like they all did. He dropped the knife to the side, forced my face to look away, instructed me to not look at him, then peeled his pants open, closed his eyes, and pretended I was someone else.

I felt the damp tears stream their way from the corners of my eyes to the counter between the veggies and meat. Every time I cried out, he lunged at me deeper, with more force. This was what all mothers warned their daughters about. "Mama," I sobbed out as if she could free me from beyond the grave. His hand moved over my mouth, muffling my childish whimpers. When he was done, he freed my arms, leaving me beaten and bare.

"Cover yourself up, for Christ's sake. You fucking deserve it, dressing like that. Fucking slut." I didn't know why or how, but my hand found the frying pan and the knife on either side of me, and I swung and slashed wildly. It was my turn to be angry.

Before he could get his pants closed, the cold metal frying pan met the side of his head. I watched the veggies fall to the ground in a tossed medley, the brightly colored collage speckling the kitchen floor. He reached for the pan, unaware of the knife coming across from the opposite side at his cheek, leaving a gaping gash.

Everything after that was a blurred mess, my body tossed around through furniture, against walls, on floors, over counters, against shattered glass. He punished me over and over, until nothing was left standing in the house, until nothing was left in me. He called out Cat's name as he raged into me, my body limp and sloppy, broken. He would rest and get a second wind, pummel me, use me, until he couldn't rage anymore. He finally carried me out the door, dropping my almost-dead body sprawled naked on the front lawn, tossed out for the vultures, the words 'traitor slut' carved on my chest.

Asher stepped over me as he went into the house. He couldn't have cared less.

I watched the sun set and woke to the sunrise. Neighbors walked past me without so much as a look, like I was a piece of discarded paper. It was just another day in the suburbs—nothing to see here, move along.

Soon the night fell again, and two men came, dragged me across the lawn, and threw me in the back of a truck. The truck rumbled into the desert under the dark night sky, speckled with stars. The grit of the sand between me and the truck bed ground into my wounds like sandpaper. My mouth was dry and cracked, and I dreamed of the lemonade. The dried blood across my skin felt tight as my skin shifted with the movement of the truck. The slow, steady squeak of the brakes signaled the end of my journey.

The two men hopped out, dropped the tailgate, slid me down from the bed, and let me fall haphazardly to the rough surface below.

The red taillights morphed into the eyes of a demon retreating far beyond where my eyes could see, letting the desert claim me.

It wasn't long before I was dragged deep into the desert by the ankles, taking all of Tom's secrets with me.

Liz's Playlist

- A Great Big World and Christina Aguilera (2013). Say Something. United States.
- Bob Dylan & Johnny Cash (1969). You are my Sunshine. Nashville, TN, United State.
- Coldplay (2005). Fix You.
- Disturbed (2015). The Sound of Silence. Las Vegas, Nevada, United States .
- Lynyrd Skynyrd (1973). Free Bird. Doraville, GA, United States.
- Simon & Garfunkel (1965). April Come She Will.
- Simon & Garfunkel (1965). The Sounds of Silence. New York City, New York, United States.
- The Byrds (1965). Turn! Turn! Turn!. Hollywood, California, United States.
- The Who (1973). Now I'm a Farmer.

Acknowledgments

To all the people who played a pivotal role during my journey, you forever have a place in my heart. Thank you for being a part of my team, whether you spent long nights reading through the manuscript, giving me advice, or cheering me on every step of the way.

To my husband, who was able to sleep through many late nights while I was pounding out chapter after chapter and entertaining our boys while I locked myself away on weekends, I am grateful for your understanding and support. Are you ready for book number two?

To my sister, who was with me every step of the way, dreaming about what came next, and listening endlessly as I poured out every thought, every idea, every twist and turn, and for loving every character as much I do, I love you more than Popsicles. And thank you to Joe and my fellas for not being jealous that she loved me first.

To my boys, you fueled every deep emotional mom moment within this book. You are without a doubt, my inspiration. And to MJ, you always took the time and initiative to ask how the book was going, and always offered encouragement and support. You are wise beyond your years and extraordinarily special. And to Mo, for sharing my headphone and watching me type just to be with me.

To my cheerleaders; my girls whom I have known for a lifetime, my work family, and all my friends and extended family, without you I would not know what it means to be part of a connected community or understand the power it holds.

To Cindy Coloma, you were the most amazing coach. You held me steady, demystifying the scary and explaining the confusing. And to Christy Phillippe, the newest member of my team, thank you for taking all my obscure questions (no matter how late the email), for your dedicated work polishing the manuscript, and for your critical feedback.

All of you inspired characters and a community worth fighting for. The sincerest thank-you.

And finally, I dedicate this book to you, Mom—I started this book late at night at your bedside, and you drove me to finish it so you could know how it ended. My heart aches that you won't be here with me to see it in print. I will

M. LaVon

miss hearing how proud you are and you asking me what comes next. Thank you for being the most curious person and inspiring me to want to know more, thank you for showing me what a strong female character looks like, thank you for convincing me to finally write a book, and thank you for being my biggest fan. You made me start this journey, so here it is. I did it, Mom.

Made in the USA
Monee, IL
21 February 2020